THE SECOND CHANCE RANCHER

Daisy blinked at him. "You don't want to be a rancher?"

"I do, but on my own terms." He looked around the barn. "I want to create my own place. Something I've built for myself."

"I get that." Daisy nodded. "Being the youngest in my family, I've always wanted to go my own way."

He propped one arm against the wall over her head and looked down at her. "May I kiss you?"

Daisy warily considered him. "I'm not sure."

"Was the last time that bad?"

"No, on the contrary, it was—"

He risked a kiss, and with a groan, she surrendered and kissed him back. It was as fantastic as last time, perhaps even more so now that she knew the taste of him. She wrapped her arms around his neck and just held on as he fitted her against him . . .

Published by Kensington Publishing Corporation

THE
SECOND CHANCE
RANCHER

KATE
PEARCE

ZEBRA BOOKS
KENSINGTON PUBLISHING CORP.
www.kensingtonbooks.com

ZEBRA BOOKS are published by

Kensington Publishing Corp.
119 West 40th Street
New York, NY 10018

All Kensington titles, imprints, and distributed lines are available at special quantity discounts for bulk purchases for sales promotion, premiums, fund-raising, educational, or institutional use.

Special book excerpts or customized printings can also be created to fit specific needs. For details, write or phone the office of the Kensington Sales Manager: Attn.: Sales Department. Kensington Publishing Corp., 119 West 40th Street, New York, NY 10018. Phone: 1-800-221-2647.

Zebra and the Z logo Reg. U.S. Pat. & TM Off.

First Printing: June 2019
ISBN-13: 978-1-4201-4823-7
ISBN-10: 1-4201-4823-0

ISBN-13: 978-1-4201-4826-8 (eBook)
ISBN-10: 1-4201-4826-5 (eBook)

10 9 8 7 6 5 4 3 2 1

Printed in the United States of America

ACKNOWLEDGMENTS

Lots of people to thank for making this book happen! Thanks to Dermot for information about venture capitalists. To Meg for all things ranch-related, to Sela for USAF, and to Jenny Hall Smith for the florist's point of view. I'd also like to thank Crystal Jordan, Sian Kaley, K B Alan, and Jerri Drennen for reading through the great comma and period fiasco when I definitely needed new contact lenses.

And we can't forget the Cook family's Chunky the chicken. Taken too soon by a fox, and no longer of this world, but now forever immortalized in print . . .

Chapter One

Morgantown
Morgan Valley, California

Jackson Lymond paused on the corner opposite the Red Dragon Bar and considered his options. The bar wouldn't open for another half hour, which gave him plenty of time to check the post office for any mail for the ranch, and find something to dazzle Nancy, the bartender, with.

He'd last seen her at the Morgan Ranch Christmas party two months earlier, and she'd told him she barely remembered him from school. He knew that couldn't be true because he'd been the school quarterback, valedictorian, *and* head of the newspaper and debate team. Everyone had known him whether they wanted to or not. And he wasn't being conceited. It was just the truth.

He hadn't spent much time in Morgantown since he'd won a coveted place at the United States Air Force Academy and set off on his military career. After twelve years he was back, helping his brother Cauy resurrect their family ranch. Morgantown was looking pretty prosperous, which was a nice surprise.

He considered going into Yvonne's café and surprising

Nancy with a box full of pastries, but as she was best buds with the owner, he suspected she could get as many sweet treats as she liked. His gaze turned to the small shop on the opposite side of the street wedged in between the dentist and the sheriff's office.

"Flowers," Jackson murmured. "Everyone loves flowers."

He crossed the street and walked up to the open door, where a diminutive figure with long brown hair was placing buckets filled with flowers and plants on the sidewalk outside the shop.

Jackson paused and tried not to admire her rather cute ass, which was difficult as she was bending down right in front of him. He gently cleared his throat. She straightened like she'd been shot and turned on him, one hand pressed to her ample bosom.

"Don't *do* that!"

"Sorry, I didn't mean to startle you."

He smiled down into her beautiful hazel eyes and tried to decide whether they were more green or brown. "Is the shop open yet?"

She considered him, her head tilted to one side like a bird about to take flight. "Yes. I'm late this morning, but it will be as soon as I get organized."

"Can I help you with that?" Jackson asked.

"Sure." She looked him up and down. "You look fit enough to carry heavy things."

Jackson resisted the urge to flex his muscles.

"I wouldn't want you putting your back out and suing me." She went into the shop, her voice floating out behind her, and he followed like a lamb. The strong smell of greenery, perfume, and cleaning fluids hit him squarely in the face, and he immediately sneezed.

"Don't tell me you're allergic to flowers."

Jackson grinned at her. "Not usually." He held out his hand. "I'm Jackson Lymond, by the way."

"Hi." She shook his hand. "I know. Do you want to carry that bucket of carnations out to the front while I make sure the cash register is up and running?"

"Sure." Jackson did what she asked, and then returned to the shop. There were two parts to it. A small space with a wide counter covered in wrapping paper, tissue, spools of ribbon, and wire. There was a larger room behind, which he assumed was where she kept the majority of her flowers and did all the fancy stuff.

"You do the flowers for Morgan Ranch, don't you?"

"Yes." She gave him a bright smile. "Now, what can I help you with today?"

Wow, she talked about as much as his brother Cauy . . .

"Well, it's like this," Jackson confided. "I wanted to give Nancy some flowers."

"Nancy from the bar, Nancy?" She blinked at him like she'd fallen into some alternate universe.

"Yeah, that one. What do you think she'd like?" Jackson asked encouragingly.

"That's a really good question." She worried her lower lip. "I don't think I have any Venus flytraps or deadly nightshade, but she might appreciate a cactus."

"You're kidding, right?"

"No." She held his gaze, her brow furrowed. "Why would I do that?"

"You do know which Nancy I'm talking about?" Jackson persisted. "The one who works at the bar and changes her hair color every other day?"

"Of course I know her. We were in school together."

"Then how about some nice roses or something?" Jackson suggested.

"For *Nancy*? I suppose you could go that way, but I

can't guarantee how she'll react." She hesitated. "If you're trying to persuade her to go out with you again, it probably won't work anyway."

"Who said anything about going out with her?" Jackson protested. "I was just trying to do something nice and thoughtful."

"Oh!" She blushed. "I'm sorry, you must think I'm really rude, but you aren't the first guy who's rushed in here wanting to buy flowers for Nancy."

"To persuade her to go out with them again?"

"Exactly." She nodded. "If you just want to be *nice*, maybe I could make you a spring bouquet?"

"That sounds great," Jackson said.

"How much do you want to spend?" She looked expectantly up at him.

"Why does it matter?"

"Because I'll pick the flowers depending on your budget."

"Let's go with twenty bucks." Jackson nodded. "I've never done this in person before. I usually just go online, pick a picture, and pay for it."

"I know. You've bought flowers from me that way."

"That's right! For the Morgans at Thanksgiving." He smiled at her. "Thanks for that. They looked awesome."

"You're welcome." She came around the counter and studied the buckets of flowers. "Nancy likes bright colors, so how about we start with daffodils, freesias, and sunflowers, and take it from there?"

Daisy picked out a selection of flowers, held them in one hand, and showed them to Jackson Lymond. He remembered Nancy from school, but he obviously didn't remember her or else he wouldn't have bothered to introduce himself, and he would've known her name. Daisy didn't let it worry her too much. He'd been two years ahead of her in school. She'd been much quieter then, trying to blend in and pretend she didn't have five older brothers who would've killed any boy who'd so much as looked at her.

"They look good." Jackson admired the flowers. "Now what?"

"Now we add some greenery." She chose various bits and pieces and took the whole lot back to the counter, laying everything down. She picked up a couple of the flowers, added a spray of green, and turned the whole thing around in her hand, adding from the pile as she went until she had completed the spiral bouquet.

"Wow, you make that look easy," Jackson said.

"Practice makes perfect." Daisy grabbed a rubber band and secured the stems before leveling them off with her scissors. "What color paper and ribbon do you want?"

"What color is Nancy's hair today?" Jackson asked.

Daisy smiled at him. "Orange, I think."

"Then let's go with that."

He grinned back at her. It dawned on her that he was the most ridiculously handsome man she'd ever met in real life. He positively glowed with good health and charisma, and he had just come out of the Air Force. If he'd worn his uniform, she might have swooned.

"Thanks so much for all your help. I owe you one."

Daisy considered that as she added the ribbon, shredding the ends and curling it in a vast bundle of bouncing spirals that reminded her of Nancy's current hairstyle. Owed her what? A kiss? A hug? The thought of him doing either of those things shouldn't even occur to her when he was off chasing another woman, but it was fun to dream . . .

She laid the bouquet carefully on the counter and rang

up the charges. Jackson handed over twenty-five dollars in cash.

"Keep the change."

"Thanks." Daisy handed him his receipt. "Just remember, I don't give rebates if she turns you down."

"No worries." He chuckled and picked up the flowers, stowing his wallet in the back of his jeans. "This is all on me."

"Then good luck."

"Thanks, Daisy." He nodded. "Have a good one."

He walked out into the sunlight, leaving Daisy open-mouthed behind the counter. So he'd known who she was all along . . .

Jackson went into the Red Dragon and walked right up to the bar, where Nancy was stacking bottles. As promised, her hair was orange and tied up in two high pigtails like an anime character.

"Hey you, what's up?" Jackson held out the flowers. "Daisy said you'd probably prefer a cactus, but I went with a spring theme."

Nancy looked down at the flowers and then back up at him. "Daisy was right, but they are very pretty." She took the bouquet and sniffed dubiously. "Thanks. Now, what can I get you to drink?"

Jackson settled onto one of the barstools. He'd hoped she would be a bit more excited to see him, but he wasn't too worried.

"You should put those in water." Jackson pointed at the flowers.

"Really?" She picked them up. "I'll be right back."

While she was gone, Jackson looked around the empty bar. At this time of day, in full sunlight, the place looked like it needed a makeover. In the evening, when it was full of locals watching sports or playing pool, it felt like home.

Nancy came back with another crate of beer and filled up one of the refrigerators. She'd added the curly ribbon from the bouquet to her pigtails. "Bella says she'll look after the flowers until I can take them home tonight."

"I could help you with that," Jackson offered.

"No, you couldn't." Nancy walked around the bar and stood directly in front of him, hands planted on her hips. He opened his mouth to argue, and she held up a finger. "You're obviously a nice guy, Jackson, but I'm not going to go out with you, so don't even ask."

"Why not?" Jackson had never been the sort to give up easily on his objectives. He was a great believer in plain speaking, which sometimes got him into trouble.

"Because you know too many people in this town I care about, and I don't want things to get messy."

"*Messy*?" Jackson asked.

"You know what I mean." She sighed. "I'm not ready for a long-term relationship, and that's what you're going to want because you're that kind of guy."

"How do you know?" Jackson persisted. "Maybe I want a one-night thing."

Nancy's lips twitched. "Jackson, don't be silly. You're way too conventional and uptight to walk away from a woman after one night."

He stared at her and then exhaled. "You're right."

"I know I am. And I also know that after that one night you *think* you want, you'd want more because I'm awesome, so let's not go there, okay?" She grinned at him. "Let's just be friends."

"Are you sure?" He smiled back at her. "I mean, *look* at me."

She let her gaze travel over him from head to toe. "Yes,

you are pretty spectacular, but no, I still don't want you. I always preferred your brother Cauy anyway."

"Ouch." He winced. "Got it."

"Good man." She went back behind the bar. "Now, what would you like to drink? This one is on me."

Jackson had lunch and a couple of beers at the bar and then wandered back along Main Street to where he'd parked his truck. The door to Daisy's flower shop was open, so he ducked his head in to find Daisy up a ladder banging a nail into the old timbers. Not wishing to scare her again, he leaned back against the wall and just appreciated the soft roundness of her figure.

When she climbed down and spotted him, she blushed and almost swallowed the two spare nails she held between her lips. She spat them out and hurriedly wiped her mouth.

"Hey! How did it go?"

"Well, I'm still alive." Jackson waited as she collapsed the ladder and propped it up against the wall. "She loved the flowers, but she still turned me down."

"It's probably for the best," Daisy said comfortingly.

"I suppose so." Jackson sighed. "She said we had too many friends in common and that things would get complicated."

"Oh well." Daisy picked up the ladder. "I'm sure you'll find someone else."

He held the inner door open for her, and waited until she returned from the interior of the shop.

"I just had a thought," Jackson said.

Daisy looked at him inquiringly, again reminding him of a cute bird. "Do you need more flowers?"

"Nope. I was wondering if *you'd* like to come out with me sometime?" He regarded her expectantly.

"Wow. Smooth." To his surprise, she marched over to the door and held it open. "Bye, Jackson."

"What did I say?" He followed her over, pausing at the door to look down at her. "I really would like to go out with you—in fact, the more I think about the idea, the better I like it."

In response, she shoved gently at his chest until he was out on the sidewalk and shut the door in his face, making the bell jangle like crazy.

Jackson stared at the door for quite a while before he backed up and headed for his truck.

He was still pondering exactly what had happened when he arrived home and found his older brother Cauy drinking coffee in the kitchen. Since Jackson had come back, the two brothers had made enormous strides in cleaning up the ranch buildings and pastureland. At some point they'd have to make a start on the house itself, because nothing had changed for thirty years.

He dumped the pile of mail on the table and helped himself to coffee.

"How was your day?" his brother inquired as he sorted through the mail. "Did you finally get it on with Nancy?"

"She turned me down flat." Jackson took a seat and added cream to his coffee. "I even took her flowers."

Cauy snorted. "Can't say I'm surprised. She's way out of your league."

"Thanks, bro." Jackson hesitated. "Do you know Daisy at the flower shop?"

"Yeah, of course I do. She's up at Morgan Ranch all the time when I go to see Rachel. Did you get the flowers from her?"

"She knows Nancy, and she definitely gave me the bene-fit of her advice," Jackson said. "When I popped back into the shop to tell her how it had gone, she shut the door in my face."

"Daisy did?" Cauy looked up from the letter he was reading. "Daisy *Miller*? What the heck did you say to her?"

"Why would you assume it was my fault?" Jackson demanded.

"Because you have a big mouth, and you usually put your foot in it. What exactly did you say to Daisy?"

"Well, while we were chatting, it occurred to me that she would make a far better girlfriend than Nancy, and that I was, in fact, quite attracted to her."

Cauy stared at him. "Go on."

"So, I asked her out." When his brother just continued to stare at him, Jackson shifted on his seat. "*What*?"

"Wow." Cauy sat back and shook his head. "You really are dumb, aren't you?"

"In what way?"

"You ask Daisy to help you pick flowers for another woman and then, when that fell through, you immediately asked her *out*?"

"What's wrong with that?" Jackson frowned.

"Dude, how would you feel if some woman made you her backup plan? Like she'd only chosen you because her favorite hadn't come through?"

Jackson thought about it. "Oh. You think I should've waited a day or two?"

"Yeah, genius." Cauy flicked a letter at him. "And buddy, if I can work that out, you're really in trouble."

"Hey, sis!"

Daisy jumped about a mile in the air and hastily scrambled to shut down her laptop before Adam, her oldest brother, came striding into her workroom.

"Hey!" She swiveled in her seat and smiled at him. She'd forgotten he had the spare key to the back door. "What brings you into town?"

"You." He leaned against her workbench and regarded her. "You're never home these days. We're concerned."

"Only because you're worried you won't get fed," Daisy quipped, even though all her brothers could look after themselves perfectly well. "I had a lot of planning to do for the next wedding up at the ranch. I was checking in with my suppliers."

"You could do that at home," Adam pointed out. "Thanks to the Morgans, we have the best Internet you can get in the valley, and you have a designated office space."

"I know, but sometimes I need to check on my stock, and calculate how much I can actually fit into my cold space, and . . ." Daisy waved her arms around. All the reasons she was giving Adam were perfectly true, but she still felt like she was making stuff up. That's what having a guilty conscience did for you . . .

"And you like your own space and privacy." He finished the sentence for her. His keen gray gaze fixed on her face. "I get it. Having five brothers breathing down your neck all the time must drive you crazy sometimes."

"I know you love me, but sometimes all that concern *does* get to me," Daisy admitted. "I've been back home for three years now and I'm *fine*."

"You sure about that?" Adam asked. As the oldest of six kids, he took his responsibilities seriously and was both bossy and way too well-informed. "You're not sleeping too good either. I see your light on at all hours of the night."

Daisy tried not to squirm in her seat. She often got up at night to complete her assignments, or talk to people in her team who traveled all over the world. But she couldn't tell Adam that because he and the rest of the family thought she'd broken off all contact with her previous life in Silicon Valley.

Adam straightened up. "Are you *sure* there isn't anything you'd like to tell me?"

"Nope!" Daisy slid off her seat. That was the problem with having an honest face: you couldn't lie about anything. "You're right. I should be getting home. I'll just lock up and follow you back."

Adam looked as if he wanted to say more but instead backed off and opened the door.

"Okay. I'll wait until I see you get in your truck and then I'll leave."

Daisy repressed a sigh. She'd lived in a big city for years, but her brothers still treated her like a delicate flower. She knew they meant well. When she'd returned home suffering from burnout, she'd spent about a month bursting into tears every time someone tried to speak to her. Eventually, her concerned family had persuaded her to seek help, and supported her until she felt more like herself.

Daisy picked up her keys, made sure the alarm was set, and headed out the door. She wasn't a good liar, and sometimes keeping her double identity secret from her family was a real strain. But she couldn't give it up yet. She'd walked away once and been lured back. This time, whatever happened, she would have to live with the consequences and see the project through to the end.

She slammed the door shut and locked it. She only had one life and was determined to do as much as she could with her talents in the time allowed to her. And if that meant deceiving her brothers and everyone else in Morgan Valley for just a little while longer, she would suck it up and deal with it.

Chapter Two

"Hey."

Daisy turned around to see Jackson blocking the light and propping up the doorframe of her shop. He had one hand in the pocket of his well-fitting jeans and in the other hand held a pink box. She'd managed to avoid all the pointed questions about why she was never home at dinner last night and had been feeling pretty good about everything until now.

She gave Jackson her most professional smile. "Hi again. How can I help you?"

"I came to apologize."

"For what exactly?"

He shrugged. "Putting my foot in my mouth?"

Daisy pretended to look puzzled. "When did you do that?"

He straightened up and advanced toward her. In his cowboy boots he was about a foot taller than she was. "I shouldn't have asked you out five minutes after I asked Nancy out."

"Correct." Daisy held his stare even though it put a crick in her neck. "*And*?"

"I'd still like to go out with you," Jackson added.

"Well, that's very nice and all, but I don't date." She fiddled with the ribbon spool on the counter and then put it back in its proper place.

"Why not?"

"I don't have time."

He frowned. "You run a flower shop, which is shut on Sundays and has regular opening hours that presumably you set. How can you never have any free time?"

Daisy was beginning to realize Jackson was as persistent as a dog searching out a bone.

"Maybe I was trying to be polite and I just don't want to go out with you."

He blinked at her. "Ah."

"I'm so glad we've straightened that out." Daisy had to wonder how long it was since two women had turned down the gorgeous Jackson Lymond in one week. "Anything else I can help you with?"

He came farther into the shop and carefully placed the pink box on the counter like an offering to a goddess.

"Yvonne said these were your favorite."

"You're trying to bribe me with pastries now, are you?" Daisy tried not to inhale the sweet scent of strawberry emanating from the box.

"Is it working?"

His smile was so hot, she couldn't help but stare at his mouth. "No."

He sighed. "Okay, it was worth a shot." He tipped his hat to her. "Thanks for hearing me out and have a great day."

He scooped up the pink box and went out, closing the door behind him, leaving Daisy staring openmouthed at the now empty space. Wow, he really was literal. She didn't want his cake? He'd take it away.

For a second, Daisy contemplated chasing after Jackson and wrestling him for the strawberry tarts but reluctantly concluded she'd probably look demented, and he'd probably win. Despite herself, she started to smile at the ridiculousness of their conversation, and its conclusion. Who would've thought having Jackson back in Morgantown would've made her days so exciting? She had to admire his ability to take a negative response right on the nose and not complain about it.

She wasn't so sure about his ability to take back his sweet gift, though . . .

Grabbing her tablet, she checked her schedule for the day. She had a wedding consultation up at Morgan Ranch late in the afternoon and two bouquets to make for local birthdays. That should keep her busy until lunchtime, when she would go along to Yvonne's and buy her *own* darn strawberry tart.

"Where are you going with that box?" Rachel Morgan called out to Jackson.

Rachel, who was engaged to his brother Cauy, was still sitting where Jackson had left her outside Yvonne's, drinking her coffee.

"Daisy said she didn't want to go out with me."

Rachel pointed at the seat opposite her, and Jackson sat down. "Okay, but why do you still have the tarts?"

Jackson frowned at her. "Daisy thought I was attempting to bribe her, so I removed the source of contention."

"*You took her tarts away?*" Rachel breathed out hard. "You really did that and you're still alive?" She shook her head. "Dude, no wonder you don't have a girlfriend."

"I've had plenty of girlfriends, thanks," Jackson retorted.

"Yes, but that was when you were in uniform. Now you look like every other cowboy in town and you're going to have to up your game." Rachel sipped her coffee and nodded at the box. "Can *we* eat them?"

Jackson cradled the box protectively against his chest. "No."

"Big meanie." Rachel grinned at him. "I'm telling Cauy when we get back."

"He'll laugh his ass off," Jackson predicted gloomily.

"Yeah, he will." Rachel's smile faded. "It's good to see him laugh."

"Can't argue with that, but I wish I wasn't the one providing all the amusement right now." Jackson stood up. "Can you hang here for a bit longer?"

"Where are you going now?" Rachel asked plaintively as he hightailed it down the street.

He approached Daisy's shop with all the caution of a man on a mission in enemy territory. The door was propped open and there was no sign of her in the interior. He darted in through the door, replaced the box on the counter, scribbled a note on the lid, and left as fast as he could.

The more he saw of Daisy Miller, the more he wanted to get to know her. She didn't take any shit, and he appreciated that. Hopefully, when she saw the returned cakes, she'd get in contact with him and they could laugh about it, and move forward.

Daisy parked outside the sprawling ranch house her family had called home for four generations, walked through the mudroom, and then into the kitchen. Her brother, Kaiden, was a carpenter, and he'd designed and built the country kitchen to replace the old one about three years ago. It was a beautiful open space and smelled like heaven at the moment because someone was cooking.

"Hey!" Adam called out to her. He was stirring a huge pot of chili on the six-burner range. "You're home early and you've brought cake! What happened? Did the flower shop burn down?"

"God forbid. Great-Aunt Florrie would come back and haunt me if I destroyed her legacy." Daisy hoisted herself up on one of the high stools and put the box on the countertop in front of her. "I had to go up to Morgan Ranch to consult on a wedding, so I thought I might as well come home after I was done."

"Good thinking." Adam tasted the chili and whistled. "Do you want a beer?"

"No, thanks."

Adam went over to the refrigerator and took out a gallon of iced tea. "This?"

"Sure." He found a glass, added ice and the tea, and brought it over to her. "Thanks."

He inspected the box. "This looks too small to feed everyone. Were you hoping to sneak it in and eat everything by yourself?"

"Yes, I was." Daisy hesitated. "Actually, someone gave them to me as a thank-you for doing some flowers."

"Nice." Adam opened the box. "Strawberry tarts, your favorite, and definitely not enough for everyone. Do you want me to hide them at the back of the refrigerator for you?"

"Well, you can certainly try, but Ben has a nose like a bloodhound."

He picked up the box and then stopped and squinted at the writing on the lid—writing Daisy had totally forgotten about until that moment.

"'Sorry I messed up again. Enjoy your tarts, Jackson,'" Adam read out the scribbled message. "'Kiss, kiss.'"

Daisy tensed as Adam slowly looked up at her. "Weird way to say thanks, and who's Jackson?"

She attempted a nonchalant shrug. "Jackson Lymond's back in town."

"The Air Force guy, right?" Adam said slowly.

"I believe so."

"What was he apologizing for?"

Daisy gave her brother the full-on stare. "None of your business."

Adam returned it. "I'm just—"

"Being nosy. Stop it."

"If he's bothering you, I'd like to know." Adam put the box in the refrigerator and came right back to her.

"He isn't bothering me," Daisy repeated patiently. "He got some flowers for Nancy at the bar, and she turned him down for a date—which I'd already told him she would, so this was his lame way of saying I'd been right all along."

"So why didn't he say that?" Adam asked. "An apology indicates you had an argument."

"We did—over Nancy."

Sometimes Daisy wished her oldest brother wasn't quite so thorough and pedantic about everything. It was incredibly hard to shake him off a trail. The timer bleeped, and Adam turned back to the stove, leaving Daisy alone for a few precious seconds to get her story straight.

"Hey."

Ben and Kaiden appeared, drawn by the scent of cooking chili, and Daisy leaped down off her perch to help them set the table.

"Where's Dad?" Daisy asked.

Ben grimaced. "There was something up with the tractor and, as Evan isn't around, Dad decided to fix it himself."

"God, no." Daisy breathed. "Last time he did that, he almost burned the barn down. Should we stage an intervention?"

"Nah." Kaiden, who was the most laid-back member of the family, shook his head. "He'll work it out."

"I hope so." Daisy put out the faded plastic water glasses they'd used since before her mother left, and brought the pitcher of iced tea over from the counter. "There's beer in the fridge if you want it to cool down the chili."

"If Adam's making it, that's a great idea," Ben agreed. He strolled over to the refrigerator and stuck his head inside. "Hey, isn't that one of Yvonne's boxes?"

Daisy stiffened as Ben produced the pink box of doom. Adam, who was bringing the chili over to the table, glanced at Daisy.

"Jackson Lymond bought them for Daisy."

"Thanks for nothing, bro," Daisy muttered.

After giving her oldest brother a death glare, Daisy turned to her other two brothers, who were now laser-focused on her.

"Jackson Lymond the air force dude?" Ben asked slowly. "Cauy's brother?"

"Yes." Daisy faced them down. Having five brothers, she knew there was no room for weakness. "What about him?"

"Why is he giving you things?"

She shrugged. "Because I helped him choose some flowers for Nancy."

Kaiden chuckled. "Poor dude."

"Exactly." Daisy turned to the most reasonable of her brothers. "He didn't believe me when I said flowers wouldn't work, and he bought me the cakes when I was proved right. End of story."

Kaiden shared a look with his two brothers. "You sure Jackson isn't the reason why you've been spending so much time in town the last few weeks?"

Daisy opened her mouth to refute that suggestion when everything became dazzlingly clear . . .

"So what if I have?" she demanded. "He's a really nice guy."

Jackson went into the health clinic to pick up a prescription Cauy had been waiting for, and came out into the parking lot behind the building. He figured it was too soon to call on Daisy, to see how she'd responded to the return of her tarts the day before. He had nothing else he needed to do in town except visit the lumberyard.

"Hey."

He looked up to see a vaguely familiar face coming straight for him.

"Hi." He squinted into the sun. "Are you one of the Millers?"

"Yeah. I'm Adam. The oldest."

Jackson held out his hand and it was firmly shaken. "Nice to see you again, Adam. I've spoken to Daisy, but this is the first time I've seen any of you guys around town."

"We tend to keep to ourselves. Daisy said she'd been seeing a lot of you."

There was an ominous note in Adam's voice that made Jackson stand at attention. "She's certainly been great at picking out flowers for me."

"Yeah, she's good at her job." Adam Miller paused. "Would you like to come to dinner tonight?"

"At your place?" Jackson asked dubiously.

"Yes."

"Is Daisy okay with that?"

"Why wouldn't she be?" Adam raised an intimidating eyebrow. "She said you'd been getting along real fine."

"Okay, then I'd love to come." Jackson nodded. "What time do you want me?"

"Six thirty? Do you need directions?"

"Nope, I'm good," Jackson said. "We're practically neighbors."

Adam tipped his hat and walked away, leaving Jackson staring after him. All the Millers were on the large side, but Adam was probably the biggest of the bunch. No one had messed with any of them in school, not even BB Morgan.

Maybe this was Daisy's weird way of changing her mind and asking him out? Whatever it was, he was more than willing to go along with it, and he loved a challenge. He'd faced down foreign adversaries in war zones. The Miller brothers didn't scare him.

"Can someone get the door?" Kaiden yelled from the kitchen as Daisy came down the stairs.

She'd managed to shut the shop on time and had arrived home to find Kaiden and Adam cooking up a storm in the kitchen. Adam had told her to relax and get changed. For once, she'd taken him at his word, had a long shower, washed her hair, and changed into her favorite pj pants and T-shirt.

"The front door?" Daisy yelled back.

"Yeah! Can't you hear the knocking?"

As she went to open it, Daisy wondered who on earth was at the front door. Regular folk all used the back entrance by the mudroom. But if Kaiden or Adam were expecting guests, it might explain all the cooking . . .

She opened the door and found herself face-to-face with Jackson, who was smiling at her from behind a bottle of wine and a big cake box.

"Hey!"

She almost shut the door in his face, and would've done so except Adam came up behind her.

"Hey, Jackson. You made it. Come on in."

Daisy looked up at her brother as he welcomed Jackson over the threshold. What on earth was going on? No one had mentioned Jackson was coming over, so why not? The penny dropped as Adam winked at her. Dear Lord, she'd suggested Jackson might be boyfriend material, and now her brothers were all over him like a rash . . .

She tagged along behind Jackson as Adam took him through to the kitchen to meet Kaiden and Ben, and put the wine and dessert in the refrigerator. Jackson didn't seem unnerved by being surrounded by Millers, which proved he was either adorably overconfident or totally unaware of the significance of being asked to dinner by the brothers. If she'd known what Adam had planned, she would've called Jackson and told him to run for the hills.

But it *was* her fault he was here, so she'd have to stick around and help him out.

"That's the Lymond boy, is it?" Her father spoke from behind her, making her jump. "He looks quite normal— unlike his pa, who had a miserable temper and a face to match."

Daisy put her hand on her father's plaid-covered arm. "*Please* don't tell him that, okay?"

"Like I would do that to a man my little girl is sweet on." He pinched her cheek like she was five. "At least this one has a real job, honey, not like that other loser you brought home."

"That 'loser' is now the head of a multimillion-dollar IT company, Dad."

"Well, that just goes to show you had a lucky escape." Her father chuckled. He was a man who believed in speaking his mind, and he had very few filters. Her second boyfriend, Art, had spent one night at the ranch and then fled back to Stanford, never to return or date Daisy again.

Daisy hurried to intercept Jackson before he met anyone else. She grabbed hold of his arm and marched him toward the mudroom.

"You can leave your coat and stuff out here, Jackson."

"Great." He met her gaze. "Thanks for inviting me up here."

"Oh that!" Daisy smiled. "That was all Adam's idea. Don't let me forget to thank him later."

He took off his jacket. "I have to say, it was a bit of a surprise."

"To me as well," Daisy murmured. "I had no idea you were coming until I opened the front door."

"To be honest, I thought you'd probably be glad to see the back of me for a few days after I messed everything up. I'm really glad you've given me a second chance," Jackson said.

"Thank Adam." Daisy led him back into the big kitchen dining area, where someone had even lit candles on the table and put out real napkins rather than from the roll of paper towels. "What's the occasion, Adam?"

He turned from his inspection of the oven and gave her one of his rare smiles. "Nothing's too good for my little sister."

The back door slammed, and Daisy just knew without looking that Danny and Evan, the brothers closest in age to her, had also arrived to watch the show. Usually on a Friday night they went down to the Red Dragon, played pool, and ate there before coming home to sleep it off. Adam had obviously decided to call in all his reinforcements to make sure Jackson Lymond got the grilling of his life, and Jackson was totally unaware of what awaited him.

Daisy mentally girded her loins. It was going to be an interesting night . . .

Being around all six of the Miller men at once made Jackson feel like he'd stumbled into the locker room of a college football team. There was enough testosterone in the air to make him dizzy, but he was used to dealing with USAF fighter pilots, so he didn't let it faze him too much. They were all being remarkably pleasant to him, which was slightly alarming. He guessed if he was meeting his sister Amy's potential boyfriend for the first time, he might be acting the same.

After seeing Daisy's horrified expression when she'd opened the door, Jackson was rapidly coming to the conclusion she really hadn't known about the invitation— which begged the question of why he'd been invited in the first place. At some point, he intended to get Daisy to himself and ask her about that interesting little detail.

At the moment, she was sticking close to his side and determinedly deflecting all the questions her brothers were showering down on him, which he found quite touching. If he took a wild guess, he suspected the Millers had always made a big deal about Daisy dating anyone. He didn't remember her ever having a boyfriend at school.

"Would you like some of that wine you brought, Jackson?" Mr. Miller called out to him. "Like a drink, do you? Your father sure did."

Jackson smiled and set out to parry the initial salvo. "I'm not a big drinker, sir. I brought the wine for you guys."

"Like we look like wine drinkers," Kaiden murmured. "Have you seen how much beer there is in our refrigerator?"

"I'm more of a beer drinker myself." Jackson turned to Kaiden, who seemed to be the most approachable of the brothers and was closest to Jackson in age. "But seeing as I'm driving, I probably won't have a drink at all."

"Come and sit here, Jackson." Ben Miller, who had reddish hair, patted the seat beside him. "Kaiden and Adam will bring the food over."

"Thanks." Jackson made a quick calculation that they had seated him as far away from Daisy as possible, and realized he couldn't do a thing about it. "It's a real pleasure to be here tonight. Thanks again for the invite."

The food at least wasn't some kind of challenge. Being men who worked outside, the Millers tended to eat big meals packed with protein and carbs, just like he and Cauy did. There were baked potatoes, cheese, broccoli, and some kind of salad, and those were just the sides to the biggest pile of different cuts of steak Jackson had ever seen outside a restaurant.

"You're not one of those fancy vegetarians now, are you?" Mr. Miller inquired.

"I work on a cattle ranch, sir," Jackson said as he speared himself a nice juicy steak. "I love beef in all its forms."

"Shame that Daisy's a vegetarian then," Kaiden mused as he passed the salad around. "Don't you feel conflicted when you're around her?"

Jackson took some salad and handed it off to Adam, who was on his other side. "That's something Daisy and I will have to come to terms with in our own time."

"I'm *not* a vegetarian," Daisy piped up from the end of

the table. "I just don't like beef, and you all take it like a mortal insult."

"Our beef is the best in the valley," Mr. Miller stated. "You're missing out."

Jackson took a baked potato and liberally anointed it with sour cream and butter. "This all looks great."

"Eat up." Adam thumped him so hard on the back, Jackson was glad he didn't wear dentures. "There's plenty more."

By the time Jackson was on his second steak, he was beginning to enjoy himself. He'd always relished a challenge, and fending off the Millers' intense interest was like balancing on a high wire over an alligator pit.

"So, you were in the air force?" Mr. Miller asked.

"Yes, sir."

"Pilot?"

"Not all the time. I mainly worked in strategic air intelligence at AFCENT in Qatar."

"What does that mean?"

Jackson shrugged. "Liaising with allied forces, coordinating air attacks, identifying specific targets for the planes in enemy territory, that kind of thing."

"Like the videos on YouTube?" Evan asked.

"Pretty much." Jackson started eating again, mainly to slow down the rate of questions.

"Why did you leave?" Adam asked.

"I'd served for ten years. When my dad got sick and died, I decided I should come home and help Cauy with the ranch."

That wasn't quite how the sequence of events had gone, but the Millers didn't need to know that.

"Your daddy certainly ran it into the ground." Mr. Miller sipped his beer. "I'm surprised you boys didn't decide to sell up to the Morgans."

"Cauy promised Dad he wouldn't do that," Jackson

explained. "We've established a good working relationship with the Morgans now. We're housing some of their horses until their new barn is built."

Mr. Miller snorted. "I can't believe Ruth Morgan's letting those city-slicker cowboys ruin a fine ranch."

"Are you talking about her grandsons, sir?" Jackson asked. "From what I can tell, if they hadn't come back, the place was doomed."

"There are better ways to save a ranch than turn it into a three-ring circus," Mr. Miller continued. "We've managed to keep going."

"Mainly because you have five sons who have been willing to stay here and stick at it," Daisy pointed out. "Poor Mrs. Morgan had nobody for quite a while, remember?"

"True," Mr. Miller acknowledged, and then turned back to Jackson. "If Cauy inherited the ranch from your father—which I find hard to believe because he never liked the boy—what are *your* plans? Are you going to spend your life as a hired hand?"

"I'm thinking I'd like to set up on my own at some point." Jackson conceded defeat and put down his silverware. "Preferably in Morgan Valley."

"Yeah?" Adam glanced down the table at Daisy. "Good to know." He got to his feet. "Let's clear this lot away and we can start on dessert."

Daisy volunteered herself and Jackson to do the washing up and firmly steered the rest of the Millers away by reminding them that the game they'd wanted to watch on TV was about to start.

She scraped a plate off into the pig bin and handed it to Jackson, who rinsed it and stuck it in the dishwasher.

He was still smiling, which, considering the interrogation he'd gone through at the dinner table, was quite remarkable. Her family had questioned his views on sports, the environment, religion, and politics and nothing had shaken the man.

"So how come Adam invited me to dinner without mentioning it to you?" Jackson asked casually. He'd rolled up the sleeves of his blue shirt to help with the washing up.

Daisy cast a furtive glance around and then turned back to her companion.

"It might have been something I said."

"About me?"

"Kind of." She fidgeted with a spoon until Jackson took it from her, washed it, and placed it neatly on the rack. "I don't want to talk about it here. Can I meet you at Yvonne's for lunch tomorrow or something? I'm buying."

He regarded her steadily for a long moment and then smiled. "After what I've just been through for you tonight, Daisy Miller, I should damn well hope you're buying."

Chapter Three

Daisy found a seat in the back corner of Yvonne's and settled in to wait for Jackson to arrive. After he'd left the ranch the previous night, she hadn't heard a peep of criticism from her brothers or father. Having been brought up in Morgantown just like the Millers, Jackson was very much like them, and had answered all their questions with aplomb and without backing down.

She'd expected them to annihilate him, ensuring that any further ideas he had of becoming her boyfriend would disappear altogether, but it hadn't worked out like that at all . . . The fact that she'd obtained some kind of grudging family approval for her imaginary relationship with Jackson had inspired Daisy with another idea. She fiddled nervously with the silverware as Lizzie came over to check if she wanted anything.

Just as she declined to order, Jackson came in through the door, and they both turned to look at him.

"He's cute," Lizzie breathed. "So darn cute."

"I suppose he is," Daisy conceded.

"Come on, *look* at him. Long legs, broad shoulders, no fat anywhere, a handsome face . . ." Lizzie sighed.

"If you like him so much, you should ask him out," Daisy suggested. "I hear he's looking for a girlfriend."

"He's not my type," Lizzie said. "I like the big, strong, quiet ones."

"I have a few of those at home," Daisy joked.

"Yeah, I know." Lizzie paused, then hissed, "He's coming this way!"

"That's because he's having lunch with me," Daisy explained.

"Ooh, you sly minx." Lizzie winked at her. "Then I'll get out of your hair."

Jackson came over, tipped his hat to Lizzie, who looked all flustered, and took the seat opposite Daisy. He wore his usual jeans, a thick working shirt and a Stetson, and looked like every cowgirl or cowboy's dream.

"Hey, Jackson, thanks so much for coming." Daisy smiled at him.

"I'm not sure how much I can actually eat." He patted his flat stomach. "I'm still digesting last night's dinner."

"Seeing as I'm paying, you can order as much as you like and take it home in a to-go box for Cauy."

"That's a great idea. Neither of us likes cooking much." Jackson nodded. "Now what's going on?"

"Shall we order first?" Daisy raised her eyebrows. Jackson was way too direct for her sometimes. "I'm starving."

Daisy looked her usual pretty self, her long brown hair in a single braid over her shoulder, a pink T-shirt advertising her shop with a flowery cardigan wrap thing over it. In fact, she looked as if butter wouldn't melt in her mouth, but he was rapidly deciding that was a front.

They both ordered the same thing and sat back to await

the food while Lizzie got them their drinks. Cauy and Rachel had waited up to check in on him when he'd gotten home last night. He'd regaled them with a quick rundown of his evening, which had left them in stiches. Neither of them had inquired about how he *really* felt about Daisy, which had been something of a relief until he'd realized they were too busy to worry about *his* love life when they could get on with their own.

"So what exactly is going on, Daisy?" Jackson decided to get the conversation back on track.

She regarded him over her glass of iced tea. "It's like this. My brothers are always on about me getting a boyfriend, and then when I *get* one, they're all over him and scare him away."

Jackson scrambled to catch up with her sudden flow of words. "Okay."

"I *happened* to mention to Adam that I'd seen you a few times in town. He assumed I was interested in you and went ahead and invited you to dinner to check you out." She sat back. "That's it."

She kept her eyes on her silverware as she fiddled around with it.

"So every time you talk to a guy and your brother finds out, he invites them to *dinner*?" Jackson asked cautiously. "That sounds . . . odd."

"Why?"

"Because I know your brothers, and while they might be a bit intimidating, none of them have ever struck me as crazy."

"That's because you're not their sister." Daisy folded her arms over her chest and finally met his gaze.

He stared right back, and eventually, she looked away.

"So you're sure you didn't say that you liked me or anything?"

"Well, as to that . . ." She sighed and put down her water glass with a thump. "I can't do this."

"Do what?"

"Lie convincingly."

"Good." Jackson held her gaze. "Keep talking."

"I need an alibi," Daisy blurted out. "So I was thinking I could get you to go out with me."

"I *want* to go out with you," Jackson reminded her. "What's *your* take?"

"My brothers are getting suspicious about the amount of time I spend at the shop. When your name came up the other day, I pretended to be interested in you so they'd think *that* was why I was staying late in town."

"Ah. That explains the dinner invitation." Jackson nodded.

"Yes, and I'm really sorry you had to go through that baptism of fire." She shuddered.

"It was a fun evening."

Daisy looked dubiously at him. "You certainly impressed everyone."

"I did my best," Jackson said modestly.

"So, seeing that they almost approve of you—which is, by the way, unheard of—I thought I could go out with you while I got on with what I *really* need to do."

"Which is?" Jackson inquired.

"Nothing you need to worry about," Daisy hastened to reassure him. "But I can't *pretend* to like you. That wouldn't be fair."

"No, it wouldn't." Jackson paused to consider her words and attempted to make sense of them. "So you wanted me to be your fake boyfriend?"

"Exactly." She beamed at him. "But I guess you'd work that out pretty fast, and I don't want you to feel used or anything."

Jackson suppressed a smile at her earnest expression.

"How long will you need this alibi for?"

"At least the next six months." She blew out a frustrated breath. "It's really hard leading a double life with a face like mine."

"I can imagine." Jackson sipped his iced tea. "Is what you're doing on the side illegal?"

"No, of course not." Daisy looked shocked. "It's *perfectly* legitimate. It's just I promised my family I wouldn't get involved with it anymore, and I have."

"Online gambling?" Jackson inquired.

"No. It's a fully paid and valid job."

"Drug dealing?"

"Nope."

"Stripping?"

"*No.*" She shook her head. "As if I had the body for that anyway."

Jackson didn't reply as he happily imagined just that in his head.

"Why can't you just tell your family?"

She sighed. "I don't want to hurt them and I don't want them worrying about me when there's no need. We're so close to completing this phase of the project that I just need a few more months before I can tell them and hand it over to someone else."

She reached for his hand. "I know it sounds kooky, but can you at least *consider* helping me out here?"

Their food arrived, and Jackson tucked in as he considered her plea. He did want to go out with her, that was a given, and she needed his help. He liked being useful, and he was starting to enjoy the idea of leading a double life with Daisy.

"So this fake relationship of ours," Jackson said, "what would it entail?"

"The usual things." Daisy shrugged. "Taking me out, hanging out with me, calling me on the phone, texting me."

"Kissing you?"

"Wow, you are direct, aren't you?" She worried at her lower lip. "Kissing in public has to be a yes, or else we would look fake."

"With tongue or without it?"

Daisy gave him an exasperated look. "*Really*, Jackson?"

"I'm just trying to make sure we're both on the same page here. I wouldn't want to assume anything," Jackson pointed out. "Same goes with physical contact. Can I hug you, hold your hand, and get to second base?"

"How about we negotiate the finer details as they come up?" Daisy suggested.

"Fine by me." Jackson held up his hands.

"Fine for you to be my fake boyfriend?" Daisy asked hopefully.

"Yes, but I have a couple of conditions of my own." Jackson put down his fork.

"Okay, fire away," Daisy said.

"Even though we're pretending, I want you to give it your all."

She nodded. "Okay. I can do that. What else?"

"Maybe consider making it a real relationship at some point?" Jackson raised his eyebrows.

"That's a big ask." Daisy sat back and folded her arms over her chest. "You do realize that due to my work commitments, I won't actually *be* spending much time with you?"

"I'm aware of that." Jackson nodded. "While we get to know each other, I'd like you to keep an open mind."

"About having a serious relationship with you?"

"Yeah."

"I can't do that," Daisy said. "I'm not . . . ready for that level of commitment."

Jackson stared at her, but the conviction in her eyes didn't falter. Okay, so he'd been pushing her a bit, but he was more than happy to back off. He'd take what he'd been offered and work with that. It wasn't the first time in his life he'd had to take a roundabout way to get to what he really wanted.

"Okay, then." He stuck out his hand. "I'm in."

"That's awesome!" Daisy squeaked and leaped to her feet.

Jackson barely had time to stand himself before she hugged him, went up on tiptoe, and gave him a kiss right on his lips.

He wrapped an arm around her waist and kissed her back before releasing her.

"One more thing," she said. "We don't tell anyone this isn't real."

"Not even my brother?"

"No." She held his gaze. "If we're going to do this right, it's going to have to remain between the two of us."

"But you're a terrible liar, and I blurt shit out all the time," Jackson reminded her.

"Then we're going to have to become the most convincing pair of fake lovers in the history of the universe," Daisy said and returned to her seat.

"Great." Jackson sat as well. He'd always been the kind of man who made up his mind fast, and his job in Qatar had only intensified that trait. He rarely regretted his decisions, and being with Daisy just felt right. If it blew up in his face, then so be it. He'd dealt with far worse. "So when would you like to have our first date?"

* * *

Daisy sent a text to Adam as she closed up the flower shop for the day.

Will be hanging out with Jackson at the Red Dragon for a while this evening. Don't expect me back for dinner. x

He texted back immediately.

Okay. Behave yourself. x

She and Jackson had decided that the quickest and best way to announce they were a couple was to spend an hour in Morgantown's one and only bar and diner. Everyone in town went there. Once they were spotted together, gossip would spread, and soon everyone in the valley would know.

She had a conference call at nine. Three hours in the bar would give her and Jackson plenty of time to eat, socialize, and hopefully spread the word. Going into the back of the flower shop, she checked her laptop to make sure she had the time right for the meeting, answered a couple of queries about flowers, and shut it down.

She'd asked Jackson to meet her at the bar at six. After brushing her hair and applying some lipstick, she locked up the shop and walked along the street to the corner where the bar stood. It wasn't much to look at, but inside, the welcome was always genuine and the company was great.

A waft of beer and spicy food engulfed her as she opened the door and saw Jackson sitting at the bar chatting with Nancy. He turned as she approached and gave her a huge smile, which was so sexy, she almost melted on the spot.

"There you are, Daisy. I was just telling Nancy about how we met."

Jackson held out a barstool for her and boosted her onto it.

"Like how exactly?" Daisy felt like an actor flubbing her very first line.

"Like him asking you for advice about flowers for me, and then realizing he liked you more than me all along," Nancy helpfully informed her.

Daisy gazed at Jackson with new respect. He'd kept close to their actual first meet, which made things much easier to remember.

"That's right. He wanted to give you roses," Daisy said.

"Dude, *no*." Nancy laughed, showing her pierced tongue. "Not unless you can get black roses. Can you?"

"They go pretty dark, but I don't think anyone has actually managed to produce a truly black one yet." Daisy fiddled with the coaster on the bar. "I can check if you like?"

"It's okay. I doubt I'll be needing a wedding bouquet anytime soon." Nancy handed Daisy a glass of cider. "Are you two going to eat here tonight?"

"Yeah, we are. We're just waiting on Cauy and Rachel," Jackson said.

"Then why don't you grab a booth before it gets too busy, and I'll send them through when they arrive?"

"Thanks, Nancy." Jackson grinned at her before turning to carefully lift Daisy down off the stool like she weighed nothing, which certainly wasn't the case. "See you in a bit."

He took Daisy's glass of cider off the bar, held her hand, and walked through to the diner part of the place, which was run by Bella Williams, the owner's mother.

"So far so good," Jackson said as he settled them in the

booth. "Nancy was really pleased you'd decided to go out with me."

"Only because it means you won't be bothering her," Daisy murmured as she slid in beside him.

"Possibly," Jackson conceded. He'd swapped out his thick work shirt for a light blue checked one with a white T-shirt underneath. If it was possible for a man to look even hotter, he'd somehow managed it. It suddenly occurred to Daisy that keeping her hands off Jackson might be more difficult than she'd anticipated. He wasn't quite as lean as some of the cowboys she'd grown up with, but he was definitely fit.

"While we've got a moment, are you okay to stick with the story I told Nancy?" Jackson asked as he checked out the menu. "It seemed easier to stay with the truth."

"Apart from the bit when I closed the door in your face?" Daisy said sweetly. "That was way funnier."

"I suppose from your side of the door it was." Jackson looked over his shoulder. "There's Cauy and Rachel. This is when things get serious. If we can convince *them* that we're going out together, the rest of it will be a cakewalk."

Jackson took a firm grip on Daisy's hand as they exited the bar. He'd enjoyed the meal with his brother and Rachel and was proud that neither he nor Daisy had put a foot wrong.

"It's no trouble, really."

"Are you sure?" Daisy looked up at him doubtfully. "I'm quite capable of walking back to the shop by myself, you know. Morgantown is very safe."

"You can never be too careful," Jackson said. "And I wanted to ask you how you think it went with Cauy."

"He seemed pretty skeptical," Daisy admitted.

"That's his normal worldview." Jackson looked both ways before he crossed the empty street. "I'll let you know if any awkward questions come up when I get back tonight."

"Okay." She punched in the code for the alarm and unlocked the door of the shop before turning to face him. "Good night, Jackson. Thanks for a lovely evening."

He braced one arm against the doorframe over her head. "Hold up."

"What?"

"The kissing thing?"

"Oh." She looked adorably confused.

"Do you want to give it a trial run?" Jackson suggested.

"I suppose we should."

She didn't sound very keen, but Jackson didn't allow himself to get distracted from his goal. He leaned down, angling his head to avoid clocking her one with his Stetson, and kissed her soft lips.

"Mmm," Daisy murmured. "*Nice.*"

"Yeah?" He kissed her again, changing the angle with each kiss until she moved with him and brought one of her hands up to his shoulder, holding him in place, which wasn't necessary because he sure as hell wasn't going anywhere. "More?"

"Mmm."

He nipped at her lower lip, and she let him inside her mouth, and then Jackson forgot everything else except the taste of her, and kissing her, and . . .

Daisy wrenched her mouth away from his, breathing hard. "Okay, I think we should stop now."

Jackson took a moment to process that when everything in him was yelling for him to continue, and reluctantly eased away from her.

"Got it."

Now she was staring longingly at his mouth. If she kept doing it, he was going to grab hold of her and kiss her until he could find somewhere horizontal where he could make love to her until they were both exhausted.

"Good night." Daisy whisked herself out of his arms and inside the door. A second later, he heard the lock click shut.

He took a couple of deep breaths and tried to ignore the suddenly uncomfortable fit of his jeans. Daisy had obviously not been as overwhelmed by his kiss as he was; otherwise she would have dragged him in by the hand and had her wicked way with him.

He'd kissed his fair share of women, but nothing had prepared him for that kiss with Daisy. He'd almost felt out of control and that wasn't acceptable. He was a planner, he took his time with things, and he wasn't the kind of guy who went off half-cocked.

With that reminder, he glanced down at his jeans, where his dick still didn't seem to have gotten the message that it wasn't getting any.

After another deep breath, Jackson turned away from the shop and went back to the parking lot behind the bar. Music drifted from the door and the roar of the people of Morgantown having a good time. He could go back in there and talk to Nancy, but he realized he didn't have the stomach for it. He squared his shoulders.

If Daisy had wanted to set the scene for their fake romance, mission accomplished. Anything else that had happened along the way was 100 percent on him.

Daisy slid down the door and just stayed there, holding her breath until she heard Jackson's cowboy boots clomping away. She pressed her fingers to her mouth and relived the most amazing kiss of her life. *Why* had Jackson done that to her? She didn't want to lust after him. It wasn't *fair* that he was so hot and kissed like a dream.

It was also a long time since she'd been kissed, so perhaps she was exaggerating somewhat. Encouraged by this more pragmatic point of view, she got off the floor, checked she'd locked the outer door, took off her shoes, and walked into her workroom. Her laptop sat where she'd left it. She typed in her password, found her headset, and settled in to catch up with the comments on the communal message board her team shared in the cloud.

She'd majored in systems design at college with a focus on machine learning and artificial intelligence and was currently working with a small team developing a completely new product for health care. The work was slow, painful, and on the cutting edge of what was scientifically possible, and she loved every minute of it.

Except when she hadn't.

The combination of living and working in a start-up in Silicon Valley 24-7 had screwed her up badly for a while, which was why she now owned a flower shop and worked remotely. It had taken her six years to crash and burn, and two more to recover from selling the company. She constantly strove for balance in her life, but every so often, the demands of the project tried to take over again. With the new company, she and the team had deliberately taken things way more slowly, which she appreciated. It was only now, when they were getting ready to test the market, that things had started to heat up again.

"Hey, you there, Daiz?"

A familiar voice came through her headset, and a pop up appeared on the corner of her screen, displaying her friend, Ian Chung, waving at her. She and her four partners had met in college and worked together ever since. They'd been through the debacle of their first company and were determined not to make the same mistakes with their new start-up.

"Yes, I'm here!" She waved back. "What's going on?"

Before Ian got into it, Daisy made sure to set an alarm. She had one and a half hours to get things done before she needed to get home and convince her brothers she'd spent a wonderful evening with Jackson. And she'd enjoyed her evening a lot—especially that kiss . . . Daisy resolutely set her thoughts back to work. She'd think about Jackson's extreme hotness as a reward for getting through the problems of the next hour or so.

Chapter Four

"Jackson?" Cauy yelled and banged on his door. "You up? Cattle need moving."

What cattle?

Jackson opened one eye and contemplated the clock on his bedside table. Did they have cows, or was Cauy just trolling him? It was six in the morning, and he'd spent half the night thrashing around fantasizing about Daisy Miller. His bed looked like he'd been in a fight, and his eyes weren't that keen on opening at all.

Cauy banged on the door again. "I've made some coffee and pancakes, so get a wiggle on."

Their mom used to say that to get them out the door to catch the bus into Bridgeport for high school. It was funny hearing Cauy saying the same thing. Jackson groaned and got up, rubbing a hand over his unshaven jaw. Since leaving the air force, his standards had definitely dropped. He went to use the bathroom and contemplated growing a beard. Would Daisy like that? A lot of women seemed to . . .

The kitchen door slammed shut, bringing Jackson back to the present. If he didn't put some clothes on, Cauy might end up having to do everything without his help, which wasn't fair.

When he finally stumbled into the kitchen, there was an envelope with his name on it propped up against his favorite coffee mug. He ignored the letter while he focused on the coffee. He rolled up several pancakes and stuffed them in his mouth followed by a glug of maple syrup directly from the glass bottle.

Grace, Cauy's dog, happily licked up the butter and syrup spilling out of the end of his pancake roll and looked up expectantly at him. Grace loved coming out and helping, but her enthusiasm didn't match her skill set. Cauy had reluctantly decided she needed to stay home and mind her puppies while they were gone.

Jackson washed his hands and splashed water in his face to dislodge the sticky sensation on his stubbled chin. Maybe a beard wasn't such a great idea after all. He went into the mudroom to put on his boots, thick coat, and Stetson. Cauy would already be in the barn mucking out their horses' stalls and making sure the Morgan Ranch stock were all present and correct when their ranch hands came to turn them out.

Whatever his private doubts about his ability to settle down and become a real rancher, Jackson loved this time of the morning, when everything was new, crisp, and fresh. He buttoned up his sheepskin jacket as he walked across to the barn and feedstore. Cauy was whistling, and that cheered Jackson up even more. After his brother was injured in an oil-rig explosion, Jackson had worried Cauy would never recover. Rebuilding Lymond Ranch and finding the love of his life in Rachel Morgan had transformed him.

Cauy called out to him. "Hey, bro, you look like shit. What did you and Daisy get up to last night?"

"What cattle?" Ignoring his brother's cheerful insults, Jackson had to ask.

Cauy looked at him as if he was crazy. "I told you last week. I took a few head off the Morgans they were about to send to market. We need to go fetch the cattle and put them on our land."

"Okay, good to know." Jackson picked up a shovel.

Cauy pointed. "Start on the other side of the barn. The Morgan Ranch guys are on their way."

"Got it."

Jackson mucked out the four stalls and led his newly acquired appaloosa horse, Rocket, out of the barn into the yard. He stopped, entranced by the scenery as the blue sky and the land rolled out before him and bumped against the foothills of the Sierras. His family had farmed the land for about a hundred years, and it was still his home wherever he chose to wander.

Still amazed that he'd survived his years in the military without a scratch and been *able* to come home, he fetched his saddle and bridle. Cauy had paused to chat with Luis, the lead guy from Morgan Ranch. Eventually, Cauy came over, and they set off together.

"Did you read your mail?" Cauy asked as he bent to unlatch the gate and relocked it as Jackson went past him.

"Didn't have time," Jackson admitted. "Was it important?"

"How should I know? I'm not into steaming open your letters and reading them, but I recognized the return address."

"You could just tell me," Jackson argued. "And save us both a lot of talking, which you hate doing anyway."

"Nah." Cauy gathered his reins. "We've just got to move part of the herd onto a new grazing area, so this shouldn't take too long."

"How will we know which cows are ours?" Jackson asked.

"Because Roy's marked them for us, dumbass."

Realizing his brother was now in shut-up-and-work mode, Jackson settled into the saddle, clicked to his horse, and loped after Cauy. A couple of hours moving cattle around would keep both his hands and his brain occupied. He wouldn't have to think about Daisy Miller at all.

"This Saturday?" Daisy silently groaned as Ian continued talking. "I've got a wedding up at Morgan Ranch."

"That's okay, we can do it later in the day," Ian said. "You'll be done by then, yeah? It's really important, Daiz. I wouldn't ask otherwise. It's a new venture capital guy, and you know we need the money for the A round."

"Did this guy approach us, or did one of you contact him?" Daisy asked.

"He came to us, which is good, right? And he's from a great VC company based in Sand Hill Road. We've got to start somewhere, Daiz."

"I suppose so," she sighed. "It's just scary."

"Don't worry, none of us are going to allow ourselves to get shafted again," Ian said. "We learned our lesson the first time. We'll keep as much control as we can this time, okay?"

"I wish we didn't have to get any outside money at all," Daisy groused.

"I hear you, but we've made such great progress since you came back onboard that we really need to expand from the prototype stage, and we've already burned through most of our seed money."

Daisy mentally calculated the timing. If she got some help, she might be able to make the call. She was already aware that the team was making a huge sacrifice in letting her work outside Silicon Valley, so she tried to be as available as she could within the limits she'd set for herself.

Limits that were slipping, and she needed to be aware of that . . .

"Okay, that's fine," Daisy capitulated.

"Great! This guy particularly wanted to hear from you, so that's awesome. I'll call you when the meeting is set up, okay?"

"Perfect." Daisy ended the call and stared blankly at the half-made centerpiece in front of her. Starting the whole process of expanding from a start-up to a fully staffed and financially viable company again was terrifying, but she believed in the product they were designing. If she wanted it to come to market, she'd have to conceal her doubts, cover all her bases, and make it happen.

She also had ten more centerpieces to complete, and not enough time to do them, so worrying about Ian's call and her other business would have to wait.

"Or I can multitask and worry in my head while I use my hands?"

Daisy was debating with an audience of one, but that wasn't unusual. Dell, her assistant, wasn't due in for another half an hour, seeing as he was attending classes at the community college. If he were available on Saturday, she'd get him to help her up at the ranch so she'd definitely be finished in time for the call.

She worked swiftly, separating out the various flowers and greenery, replicating the identical design for each table. She preferred a more natural approach to arrangements, but the bride and her mother had been very specific about uniformity, so she was going along with their request.

As she snipped and shaped the stems and leaves, she wondered what Jackson was up to, and then smiled to herself. He worked on a ranch. She knew *exactly* what he'd be doing—something involving horses, cattle, dirt, and the great outdoors. She'd never seen him on a horse. If he were anything like her and her brothers, who had learned to ride around the time they could walk, he'd probably look pretty spectacular.

She remembered his father, Mark, all too well. Her family hadn't liked him much because he'd refused to work with the other ranchers in the valley and then complained endlessly about discrimination whenever he'd gotten the opportunity. The Morgans, whose lands ran alongside the Lymonds, had also fallen out with Mark. Cauy had done a lot of fence mending, both literally and physically, when he'd come home and taken over.

Jackson had the same dark coloring as his father, but Cauy looked nothing like him. Local gossip insisted Mark had hated Cauy because he wasn't his real son, and recent developments seemed to point to that being true.

Her cell buzzed, and she looked down to see a message from Jackson.

Hey, do you want to come and have dinner at the ranch tonight?

Daisy considered the pros and cons. She'd get some time to study up on this new venture capitalist before the meeting without her brothers breathing down her neck, she'd be fed, and she'd get to ogle Jackson Lymond. As long as she didn't kiss him, what could possibly go wrong?

"Jackson, calm down. We've got this," Cauy repeated patiently. "It's Daisy Miller coming to dinner, not the queen."

"I know that, but I like to get things right." Jackson stirred the cheese sauce with one hand and checked the roasting vegetables in the oven. He wasn't a great cook, but he liked to try his hand at it occasionally. "I'm just about to stack the lasagna. If you hear her truck coming up the drive, let me know, okay?"

"Yes, chef." Cauy was shaking his head as he walked away. "I'm going to call Rachel. She's bringing dessert because Mrs. Morgan made pie."

"*Dessert*." Jackson winced. "I forgot all about that."

"Then it's a good thing Rachel didn't, eh?" Cauy was chuckling now. "I've set the table so you're good to go."

"Thanks, bro."

Jackson checked the recipe in one of his mother's old cookbooks he'd found on the shelf and put the lasagna together alternating roasted veg, tomatoes, cheese sauce, and sheets of lasagna with a final topping of grated cheddar and Parmesan. He covered the dish in foil and put it in the oven for just under an hour.

Even as he let out a relieved breath, a truck pulled up outside. He found a marker for the recipe and slammed the book shut. No need to look like an amateur when Daisy came in. He could always check up on the details later.

Cauy opened the kitchen door and ushered Daisy in. She wore jeans, cowboy boots, and a fluffy green sweater that reminded Jackson of a spring meadow.

"Here's your guest, Jackson." Cauy retraced his path. "I'm going to check on Rachel, okay?"

"Thanks, Cauy," Jackson replied. "Tell her to thank Mrs. Morgan for the pie."

"Hey." Daisy smiled at Jackson and held up a six-pack. "I brought beer, seeing as we all like it."

"Great!" Jackson smiled back. "I've just got to clean up in here and then we can eat."

"I'm starving," Daisy confessed. "It's been—" She broke off as Jackson advanced on her to take the beer. "Nice apron."

Jackson looked down at his front. "It's one my mom left behind."

"It's certainly . . . colorful, and I love all the purple ruffles." Daisy bit her lip. "The ribbons match your eyes, too."

"Thanks." Jackson appreciated the twinkle in *her* eyes. "I have matching oven gloves as well."

"Awesome." Daisy looked around the room. "Is there anything I can do to help?"

"Not really. Cauy's done most of it. The lasagna's in the oven. All I have to do is make a salad and we're good to go." He pointed over at the couch. "Why don't you grab a beer and make yourself at home?"

Daisy took her purse off her shoulder. "Would you mind if I checked my e-mails? I haven't had much of a chance to get to them today."

"Go ahead." Jackson nodded. "I'll get you that beer."

Daisy sat on the couch, did a quick check through her e-mails, and spotted one from Ian immediately. She read it through, noting the time, and looked up as Jackson approached with her beer.

"Are you free on Saturday?"

"What time?" Jackson sat on the arm of the couch, clinked bottles with her, and took a long swallow. He smelled like a really good Italian restaurant.

"Between four and nine?" Daisy asked. "I've got to do

something relating to my other job and I'll need some privacy."

"You can come up here if you're worried about your brothers," Jackson offered.

"That would actually work really well because I'll be at Morgan Ranch for the earlier part of the day." Daisy met Jackson's gaze. "I'm going to need at least an hour, maybe two, completely to myself."

Jackson regarded her curiously. "Are you one of those influencers?"

"Influencers of what?" Daisy wrinkled her nose at him.

"Like on social media, they blog, or vlog, have huge followings, and make bank."

"As if." Daisy laughed at the very idea. "I hate video-conferencing with a vengeance."

"How about instructional videos?" Jackson asked. "I bet there are people all over the world who'd be interested in learning new flower things."

"Stop fishing." Daisy poked him in the thigh with her index finger and instantly regretted it because he was all hard muscle there. "I'm not going to tell you what my second job is."

"It was worth a try." Jackson sighed and stood up. "I'll ask you again after you've had a couple of beers."

"Dude, I have five brothers." Daisy waved him away like the amateur he was. "I can definitely hold my drink."

The roasted vegetable lasagna was really good, and Jackson accepted Daisy's compliments with a modest shrug of his shoulders. She was rapidly coming to the conclusion that if she did want to go out with someone seriously, he would make a great boyfriend. His relationship with his older brother was also warm, and coming from a large family, Daisy appreciated that.

Rachel Morgan was always good company, and as she brought three kinds of pie, she was already high on Daisy's awesome person list. Jackson had managed to find both ice cream and whipped cream in the freezer, so the pies had gone down a treat. Grace and her puppies milled around the table, trying to look cute enough to beg scraps but, like the Millers, the Lymonds didn't feed them at the table, or at least tried to pretend they didn't.

"Would you like to walk over to the barn with me, Daisy?" Jackson put down his napkin and glanced across at her. "I've got to make sure everyone is tucked in for the night."

Daisy checked the time, surprised to see she'd been there for almost three hours and hadn't thought about work at all. This was how she'd meant her life to be after she'd returned home, and yet somehow, it had gotten way more complicated.

"Rachel and I will clean up, so take your time." Cauy winked extravagantly at his brother. "Unless you have to go, Daisy?"

Everyone looked at her, and Daisy hastily stood up. "I'd love to see the barn."

Jackson held the door open for her and they went out into the star-studded night. Being away from the city meant they got to see way more of the universe turning above them than most people ever would. It was a world away from Silicon Valley, and Daisy reminded herself to appreciate it.

"It just occurred to me that seeing a barn full of horses isn't exactly a new thing for you," Jackson said as he took her hand.

"True, but I haven't seen *this* barn, and they're all different," Daisy pointed out. "It looks like you've put on a new roof."

"Yeah, we just did that with the money generated from leasing half the barn to the Morgans."

Jackson paused to check that the chickens were safely inside their run and was just about to shut the gate when Daisy pointed toward the shadowy side of the barn.

"I think there's one over there."

"Of course there is." Jackson peered into the gloom. "I bet it's Chunky."

"Chunky the chicken?" Daisy suppressed a gurgle of laughter. "Really?"

"She's a big strong girl." Jackson crept toward the chicken. "Can you cut her off from the other side?"

Fortunately for them, Chunky wasn't the fastest of movers. Jackson soon had her tucked under his arm and restored her to the chicken coop.

They resumed their walk until they stood in the center of the barn between the rows of stalls and the drainage channels. Jackson picked up a piece of straw and dropped it back into one of the stalls.

"Dad left everything in a terrible state and dumped the whole problem on Cauy."

"Which *my* dad thought was odd because Mark never had a good word to say about his oldest son," Daisy commented.

Jackson turned to face her. "Cauy's not his son."

"Ah." Daisy nodded. "Right." She should've known Jackson would just throw out the pertinent details without her even asking. It was lucky she was used to working with a bunch of guy nerds who basically did the same thing.

"Mom was seventeen and pregnant when she married him." Jackson's smile was wry. "And Mark never let Mom or Cauy forget it."

Daisy went over to pet one of the horses who had stuck his nose out over the half-open stall door. "That's tough.

I can see why Cauy left when he was sixteen." Daisy scratched the horse's muzzle. "Why didn't Mark leave the place to you instead, then? You two got on fine, right?"

"When I wasn't having to step in between him, Cauy, or Mom, yeah." Jackson blew out a breath and came to stand beside her, his gaze focused on the horse. "Cauy offered me half the place—or even to give it to me, but I don't want it."

Daisy blinked at him. "You don't want to be a rancher?"

"I do, but on my own terms." He looked around the barn. "I want to create my own place. Something I've built for myself."

"I get that." Daisy nodded. "Being the youngest in my family, I've always wanted to go my own way."

He propped one arm against the wall over her head and looked down at her. "May I kiss you?"

Daisy warily considered him. "I'm not sure."

"Was the last time that bad?"

"No, on the contrary, it was—"

He risked a kiss and, with a groan, she surrendered and kissed him back. It was as fantastic as last time, perhaps even more so now that she knew the taste of him. She wrapped her arms around his neck and just held on as he fitted her against him, his hand planted firmly on her ass, the rigid length of his shaft between them.

Eventually, he drew back, panting. "That was . . . good."

"That was *amazing*!" Daisy agreed.

"So could you possibly consider the being-my-real-girlfriend thing again?" Jackson asked.

Daisy eased out of his arms and walked away a few steps. "I can't do that right now. It wouldn't be fair to you. I don't have time for a proper relationship."

He leaned back against the wall. "How about an improper one? Like just for sex?"

"I've never done that," Daisy said dubiously. "I don't think they work."

"Why don't they work?" Jackson asked.

"Because usually one of the people involved is genuinely okay with that scenario and the other isn't, but goes along with it hoping for more."

"Okay. I can see that." Jackson nodded.

"People get hurt." She held his gaze. "I can't . . . risk that again."

"Again? Did someone do it to you?"

"I just *said* I'd never had a sex-only relationship." She'd never even gotten close to it with Art, who was her only other boyfriend apart from Brody. Daisy continued talking, anxious to distract Jackson's attention from dissecting any of her exes. "You really must learn not to ask all the most embarrassing questions right out front."

"Why shouldn't I?" He shrugged. "I like to know how things stand."

"We're just pretending to go out so I can finish my project without my family knowing. That's what we agreed to," Daisy reminded him.

"So why *are* you kissing me back?"

The fact that Jackson had a valid point made Daisy continue down the barn, meeting and greeting the horses as she went.

Of course he kept talking as he walked behind her. "I mean, not that I *mind* you kissing me back, because it's awesome, but wasn't there something in our agreement about you considering *really* going out with me?"

Guilt and panic coalesced around her heart. Daisy stopped and swung around to face him.

"You're right. It was a stupid idea, so let's forget all about it." She walked past him back toward the house. "I'll get my stuff and I'll just go. Thanks for a lovely dinner."

"Daisy, that's not what I meant . . ."

He called after her, but she was too embarrassed to slow down. He was perfect boyfriend material, which was exactly why she couldn't risk getting too close to him, or allowing him to get too close to her. She'd allowed her family to run off her second boyfriend, but they approved of Jackson. What if she fell for him? What if it all blew up in her face again?

She barged into the kitchen, surprising Cauy and Rachel, who leaped apart like two guilty teenagers on the couch. Cauy attempted to smooth down his hair and rebutton his shirt as Daisy gathered up her stuff and averted her eyes from Rachel's giggles.

"Thanks for a lovely evening, I'm sorry I have to rush off," Daisy said.

"Are you okay?" Cauy frowned at her. "Did Jackson say something stupid? Do you need me to kick his ass?"

"He was the perfect gentleman," Daisy reassured him as she frantically searched for her car keys. "I just have to go—there's something I have to do at home."

She rushed out the door and straight to her truck. There was no sign of Jackson. If he had any sense, he'd wait until she'd gone before he emerged from the barn, but she hadn't ever noticed him having an urge to be discreet. She felt like an idiot, and that wasn't his fault.

She started up her truck, backed out of the drive, and turned around. She was halfway home before she remembered to take another breath. Now she had an event to organize on Saturday, a conference call with Ian and an unknown venture capitalist, and no one to back her up.

And it was all her own fault.

Chapter Five

Jackson parked his truck behind Daisy's at Morgan Ranch and headed for the guest center, where most of the wedding receptions and parties were held. From what he could tell, the latest wedding was in full swing, with a large white marquee beside the guest center covering a dance floor and seating for the guests, who were picking up their food inside and coming out to sit in the sun.

He paused to admire the flower arrangements on each table and to take note of the color theme just in case Daisy asked him about it, and then went in search of her. He bumped into Avery Hayes, Ry Morgan's fiancée, who was the event coordinator. She looked superefficient, with a tablet in one hand and an earpiece in one ear.

"Hey, Jackson! Are you lost?" Avery greeted him.

"Hey, Avery. I'm looking for Daisy Miller. I'm supposed to be picking her up at four."

"She's in the kitchen," Avery told him. "And I think she's about ready to go. Dell's staying to make sure everything hangs together, but I don't think there's much that can go wrong with the flowers at this point."

Jackson had no idea who Dell was, but he tipped his Stetson to Avery and made his way into the guest center and toward the kitchen. Inside was a hive of activity as Gustav the chef and his staff kept up with the demands of the buffet, which was still going strong.

At the back of the kitchen, Jackson spotted Daisy with a tall, youngish guy who looked vaguely familiar.

He went toward her, trying to look like he didn't have a care in the world. After she'd walked out on him the other night, he'd had a chance to think about what he wanted, and whether he should just give up on Daisy and move on. He really liked her, and he'd rushed her into making a decision she wasn't ready for. The thought of her needing his help today and him being petty and denying it hadn't sat well with him.

So he'd decided to take a chance and see what happened. If she turned him down flat, that was also okay.

Daisy's horrified expression when she saw him approach wasn't reassuring. He was fairly certain she glanced behind her as if searching for an escape route. He smiled encouragingly at her.

"Hey, do you still need me this afternoon? I'm ready and available to take you over to my place whenever you like. Cauy and Rachel have gone to Bridgeport, so we won't be interrupted for hours."

She glanced at her companion, who was regarding Jackson with deep interest.

"Have you met Dell Turner?" Daisy asked.

"Nope." Jackson shook the kid's hand. "Nice to meet you. Do you help Daisy out?"

"When I have some free time I do." Dell hesitated. "You're the dude who was in the air force, right?"

"Yeah."

"What was it like?"

"Awesome." Jackson gave his automatic reply. At Dell's

age, he'd thought of nothing else than being accepted into the USAF and becoming a fighter pilot.

"Did you fly planes?"

Jackson shrugged. "I could already fly when I went in. My dad got me lessons."

"Wow." Dell whistled. "I wish my mom could afford to do that for me."

"I was lucky. Because this valley can get cut off in the winter, a lot of the ranches around here have small planes and crop dusters, so I was able to learn quite cheaply and get a lot of practice hours in."

Daisy cleared her throat. "Um, Dell. Could you possibly do a walk-around and make sure everything floral is in the right place and still standing?"

"Sure. And I'll make sure Nolly hasn't escaped again." Dell nodded at Jackson. "Nice to meet you, dude."

Jackson waited until the teen sauntered off and then turned to Daisy. "Who's Nolly?"

Daisy smiled for the first time. "Chase's favorite horse. He's a bit of a performance artist who likes to get involved with the weddings. His specialty is eating flower arrangements and wedding cake."

"Oh, right." Jackson nodded after Dell. "Is he related to Nate Turner the sheriff?"

"Yes, he's his nephew," Daisy said. "He's a great kid."

Jackson leaned back against the countertop and studied her. She looked frazzled. He wanted to pick her up, take her in his arms, and tell her that everything was going to be all right—except she probably wouldn't like that.

"Why are you here, Jackson?" Daisy asked.

"Because you asked for my help." He held her gaze. "I know things didn't end well between us last week, and I totally respect your decision, but I didn't want to leave you without cover today."

"That's . . . really sweet of you."

"It's okay. You can tell me to go to hell if you like." He hesitated. "I'm not asking for anything in return, I swear it. You just look like you need a friend right now and I'm trying to be that person."

"You promise not to try anything?" Daisy asked.

He traced a cross over his heart. "On my brother's grave."

"You murdered Cauy?"

"I wish." Jackson grinned at her. "I was just kidding."

And he wouldn't try anything. If she didn't want him as a boyfriend, maybe they could just be friends who helped each other out occasionally. Everyone needed friends. Maybe when she'd finished her supersecret job, she'd be more amenable to taking him seriously without any strings attached. He'd always been a long-term planner, and he rarely let anything get him down for long.

"Let me help you out." Jackson coaxed, and she bit her lip.

"Are you sure?" Daisy still looked conflicted. "I feel like I'm taking advantage of you."

"I tried to pressure you into agreeing to something you weren't ready for," Jackson said firmly. "The only person who needs to worry about that is me."

"The thing is," Daisy met his gaze, "I could really do with your help."

"Then you've got it." He nodded and pointed at the stack of boxes on the worktop. "Do you want me to load this stuff into your truck? I'll drive you over to my place and drop you back here when you're done."

Daisy glanced over at Jackson as he drove her back to Lymond Ranch, admiring his strong profile and the curve of his lips. She still wasn't 100 percent convinced that he wouldn't, in typical Jackson style, start asking her questions she had no answers for. She also knew she shouldn't have agreed to let him help her, but the sincerity in his voice and in his eyes had convinced her to trust him.

"I really appreciate you helping me out," Daisy said.

"You're welcome." Jackson pulled up the truck, got out, and opened the gate that led up to the ranch house. He got back in, drove through, and then shut the gate behind him. "As I said, Cauy and Rachel are going to be out until at least ten tonight, so you shouldn't be disturbed."

"The meeting shouldn't take much longer than an hour," Daisy said. "I hate videoconferencing, but this is important."

"Why do you hate it?" Jackson inquired as he turned onto the graveled driveway leading up to the house.

"Because I hate seeing myself and hearing the sound of my voice," Daisy confessed. "It's like watching someone else and it freaks me out."

He glanced over at her. "You look and sound pretty good to me."

"Thanks, but with all due respect, you're not the guy I'm trying to impress today."

Jackson chuckled. "Now you've got me wondering what you're selling."

"Probably not what you're thinking," Daisy retorted. "I've got to appear rational, intelligent, *invested*, and enthusiastic all at the same time."

"Wow." Jackson shook his head. "I'm not sure I could manage that myself."

"You're like that all the time." Daisy poked him in the side. "I look way too sweet to be left in charge of anything."

His smile widened, but he didn't say anything, which somehow made her feel a lot less stressed.

"I *look* like someone's twelve-year-old sister," Daisy added.

"Not twelve," Jackson corrected her. "Because that makes me feel like a perv. How old are you actually?"

"Twenty-eight."

"Okay, so you look eighteen." He turned off the engine. "Maybe that's what you're doing—managing a worldwide cosmetics empire, and your face is your best-selling point."

He got out of the truck and came around to Daisy's door.

"Have you ever considered writing fiction?" she asked as he lifted her out of the truck. "Because that's some imagination you've got going there."

"I'm tenacious. I like to know stuff." He set her on her feet and immediately let go of her like a perfect gentleman.

"I noticed," Daisy murmured as she followed him into the ranch house. "And I'll have to be careful."

"What was that?" Jackson turned to look at her.

"Nothing," she called out. "Just talking to myself."

After Jackson made her some coffee and she changed into something a little more formal than her flower shop T-shirt, Daisy was ready for the call. Jackson set her up in the farm office and then went off with Grace and her puppies to do some chores in the barn, leaving her in complete possession of the house. She brushed her hair, put on the minimum amount of makeup necessary so she didn't look like a ghost, and sat down in front of her laptop, making sure the camera and microphone were operational.

The call was going to be between her, Ian, and the VC guy. The other three on their team were too techy to make much sense, hated company, and generally only emerged at night. Ian was right: Getting funding for their A round was important, and even if this guy didn't work out, it was a chance for them to perfect their pitch before they went wide.

Daisy let out a calming breath and tried to forget how royally their merry band had been screwed over by their investors on the first go-around. Someone, somewhere, was making a very nice living out of their work, and it definitely wasn't them.

A screen popped up on her laptop and Ian's face appeared swiftly, followed by a second screen.

"Hey, Daisy, this is Ron Kopek."

Daisy smiled at the middle-aged guy, but he didn't smile back. He had eyes like a shark.

"Good afternoon, Ms. Miller."

"Please call me Daisy." She wasn't that keen on him already but tried to be positive. "What would you like to know about our company, and how did you hear about us?"

Mr. Kopek started talking, and Daisy immediately forgot about his looks and concentrated on what he was asking her. After a couple of questions, when it became clear he really knew his stuff and wasn't wasting their time, Daisy started to relax.

"Yes, that's correct." Daisy nodded. "The question we're working on is how to get crucial medical data in front of the right person in real time and improve survival rates. We're convinced that by developing a product using AI to crunch all this big data *and* allow the machine to learn as it goes will significantly improve treatment of casualties for our military."

"That sounds fantastic." Mr. Kopek finally smiled at her. "Tell me more."

* * *

Jackson kept away from the house for well over the hour Daisy had requested. It wasn't difficult. Living on a ranch meant there were endless jobs to be done and never enough hands to do them. He'd spent a while reapplying paint to the backside of the new feedstore that faced the wind coming down off the Sierras. He also kept an eye on Grace and her puppies as they played in the sunshine.

Eventually, when the light started to fade, he washed out his brush, put the paint away, and went back into the house, tripping over the puppies as they crowded around him to be fed. It was quiet inside, and the office door was closed. He paused to listen but couldn't hear a thing. He made his way through to his bedroom to strip off his clothes and took a quick shower.

With a towel wrapped around his waist, he went into the kitchen and spent a couple of minutes fiddling around with the new coffee machine Cauy had purchased before he could work out how to brew a whole pot rather than a piddling little mug.

A slight snore came from the couch behind him and he wandered over, mug in hand, to find Daisy curled up asleep on the couch in the most uncomfortable position imaginable. He considered her for a moment and then sat on the edge of the couch and gently shook her shoulder.

"Daisy, if you sleep like that, you're going to end up with a crick in your neck."

She muttered something, which sounded like an impolite way of telling him to leave her alone, and he fought a smile.

"Daisy . . ."

This time she literally growled at him, and he stood up. "Don't say I didn't warn you."

She rolled over onto her back and stared unblinkingly up at him.

"Why are you naked?"

"I just took a shower." He rolled his eyes at her. "I'm not about to have my wicked way with you or anything."

"Oh," she sighed. He suspected she wasn't quite awake because she sounded disappointed. "You have great abs and lats."

"Thanks." Jackson sucked in his gut. "Just no peeping up my towel, okay? I don't want you regretting what you gave up."

She gave a little choke of laughter that went straight to his lower regions and made him check how secure his towel was.

"If you want a nap before dinner, why don't you get into my bed?" Jackson suggested.

"Nice try," Daisy said.

He shrugged. "I'm going to be out here catching up on the baseball game, so I can promise you peace and quiet. It's only five thirty, and you said you don't have to be back home until nine."

She struggled to sit up and regarded him. Her hair was all over the place. She'd obviously forgotten she'd put on mascara and rubbed her eyes, leaving her looking like a cute panda. "I really am tired."

"Then finish your nap. I'll wake you in an hour and we can have something to eat." Jackson turned away. "Just let me go put on some clothes, and then my bedroom is all yours."

As soon as Jackson left, Daisy sat up. She really needed to pee, and that would have to happen before she made any other decisions. She used the bathroom, washed her hands, dealt with her hair and raccoon eyes, and made her way to Jackson's bedroom, which was next door.

He was just stepping into his boxers, so she caught a great view of his muscled ass as he bent forward.

"Hey," Daisy called out, making him jump. "What's that tattoo?"

He turned to face her, hands on his hips. "What tattoo?"

"The one on your ass."

"Oh that." He actually blushed, which Daisy enjoyed immensely. "It's nothing."

She wandered toward him, but he held his ground until she hooked one finger in his boxers. "Let me see."

He looked down at her finger. "You're going to pull them down?"

"Maybe."

His smile was shockingly hot and intimate. "If you do that, don't be surprised if you get to see a lot more than just a stupid tattoo."

Of course now she had to look at the impressive bulge filling out the front of his boxers and getting larger every second. She wanted to lick her lips.

"Daisy . . . not fair." His voice softened, even as his body hardened. She reminded herself he was not one of her brothers, that she was standing way too close to him, and that she practically had her hand down his boxers.

"Sorry." She stepped back, accidentally snapping the elastic, which made him wince. "That was rude of me."

He let out a long, slow breath. "No problem." He took a T-shirt out of a drawer and put it on, covering up those amazing abs. "I'll get out of your way."

He picked up his jeans, took one harassed look down at his erection, and slung the jeans over his shoulder. "I'll call you about six thirty, okay?"

Daisy contemplated his neatly made bed and the overall tidiness of his space. She imagined having been in the military, he'd had to learn to keep his stuff in good order.

The walls were painted white and there were no pictures, photos, or posters on them. On top of the chest of drawers there was a photo of Jackson in uniform, which made him look even hotter, if that were possible, a picture of his family, including Cauy, his mom, and a very young Amy, and that was it.

She stripped off her jeans and got into Jackson's bed, struggling to get between the tightly fitted, starched sheets. Talk about military corners and sheets you could bounce a dime off . . . you could probably bounce a dime off Jackson's ass, too.

She lay on her back and stared up at the ceiling, all thoughts of sleep far away as her mind insisted on running through a frame-by-frame rerun of Jackson Lymond's spectacular body. By the time she'd considered every detail, her hand had settled between her legs, and she was imagining what would've happened if she'd followed her instincts, stripped him bare, and encouraged him to have his evil way with her.

But he was right. She wasn't being fair. She couldn't heavy breathe all over him one minute and then tell him to back off the next. She sighed, all thoughts of sleeping now escaping her. How long was it since she'd actually had a living, breathing man in her bed? She'd tried a couple of drunken hookups with old friends, but none of them had made her feel any better. Perhaps once you'd found and lost the love of your life, you couldn't recapture that feeling.

But she was only twenty-eight. Was that it? Was she *done*? And she missed it. Missed having a man inside her, kissing her, loving her . . .

Daisy sat up, put her jeans back on, and went into the kitchen, where Jackson was feeding the dogs. He turned to her, a can of dog food in his hand.

"I thought you were sleeping."

"I was thinking too hard." She'd also been fantasizing about his amazing body, but she wasn't going to mention that. "I wanted to ask you something."

"Okay." He threw the can in the recycle bin. "Shoot."

Of course now that she was facing him, Daisy didn't know where to start. He washed his hands and gestured for her to sit opposite him at the kitchen table.

"Seriously. Just tell me what's going on."

"I was just thinking about being twenty-eight and never having sex again in my life," Daisy confessed.

He blinked at her. "Okay."

"That seemed kind of . . . unfair," Daisy added.

"I agree." Jackson nodded vigorously. "That would be terrible."

"But I've always believed that sex comes after you fall in love with someone." She worried at her lip. "But as I've decided never to do that again, does that mean I have to accept I can never have sex again either?"

"For some people I guess it would." Jackson, at least, appeared to be taking her ridiculous questions seriously. "I suppose it depends on whether you have the ability to separate the sex thing from the love thing—if you know what I mean."

"Exactly," Daisy said. "And you'd have to be very clear with the person you chose to have sex with that they wouldn't be getting the love part."

Jackson sat back in his chair and regarded her. "Are we talking specifics here, or are you just expressing an opinion?"

"I'm not sure," Daisy confessed. "I feel like I'm being very biased."

"There are plenty of places you can find hookup sex with no consequences online, Daisy," Jackson said gently. "If you truly just want an anonymous body."

"Yes, I know that." She made herself meet his gaze and found nothing but understanding there. "So what would you do if you were me?"

He was silent for so long, she thought he wasn't going to answer her, and then he stirred. "I suppose I'd look for a friend who was willing to go along with the just-for-fun, no-strings-attached sex thing."

"Is that something you would be willing to go along with?" Daisy held her breath and immediately began blathering again. "I know I said it wasn't fair if one person wanted different things than the other, but if we were both on the same page from the get-go?"

She looked so hopeful, he almost gave in immediately. He'd already said he'd be amenable to just having sex. To give himself some time, he locked his hands together and stretched them over his head.

"I'd have to think about that, Daisy. I'm an all-or-nothing kind of guy. When I was younger, I had sex with women just because they loved my uniform, so I can't say I haven't been there, but I'm not particularly proud of my behavior." He met her gaze. "*Can* I think about it?"

"Of course." Daisy nodded. "And I won't be at all offended if you turn me down. We can go back to just being friends, and maybe I can look elsewhere."

The thought of her looking elsewhere for sex didn't sit well with him at all. But the thought of just having sex and nothing else wasn't great either. He rose from the table and went back to the refrigerator.

"We'd better get something to eat or your family are going to think I never feed you." He peered inside the refrigerator. "We've got half a chicken pie or some noodles in sauce. What do you fancy?"

When she didn't answer, he looked back at the table where she was still sitting. "Daisy?"

"You hate me, don't you?" she whispered.

"Nope," Jackson reassured her. "I appreciate your honesty."

"But I keep messing you around."

"Yeah, you do. Some might say it's good for me, as I'm normally the person who expects everything to function in a perfectly straight line. Maybe I need this."

She didn't look any happier, and he abandoned the quest for food and came back over to her.

"Don't look so worried."

"I'm worried about what you think. Apart from two stupid drunken nights at college, this isn't like me at all."

"Maybe you thought of it because we have chemistry," Jackson suggested.

"We *do*, don't we?" Daisy agreed.

"Maybe I'm the first man to stir your loins?"

"Ew." She wrinkled her nose at him. "That's hardly romantic."

"But you don't want me to be romantic, do you?" He held her gaze. "When I kiss you, it's awesome."

"Yes, it is." She stared right into his eyes as he bent his head and kissed her lightly on the lips.

"See?" She nodded, and he drew back. "Now, what do you want to eat?"

Chapter Six

"What gives with you and Jackson Lymond?" Nancy asked.

Daisy was sitting in Yvonne's apartment above the coffee shop after enjoying an excellent dinner with her friends. The plan was to watch a romantic movie, have a good cry, drink some wine, and be sort of ready for Monday morning.

"What about him?" Daisy stalled for time.

"Are you two going out?" Yvonne asked. "Because if you are, good for you, Daisy. He's supernice and hot as hell."

"You're practically a married woman; should you even be noticing such things?" Daisy asked.

"I'm getting married; I'm not going blind." Yvonne winked at her. "No one compares to Rio, but Jackson is hard to miss."

"So are you going out with him?" Nancy asked again. She was much better at staying on topic than Yvonne.

"I'm not sure," Daisy said, making both her friends stare at her.

"What do you mean, you're not sure?" Nancy asked.

"Jackson doesn't strike me as the kind of guy who needs encouragement, and he seemed really into you when I spoke to him last."

Daisy tucked her feet underneath her on the couch and tried to think of an explanation that would fool Nancy, a woman she'd known since kindergarten, without divulging details of her secret job.

"I think Jackson wants a committed, long-term relationship, and I'm not sure I'm into that right now."

Both women stared at her like she was speaking a foreign language.

"Why not?" Nancy was the first to recover. "He's a good guy, and I bet he wouldn't dick around on you."

Daisy tried again. "I'm not into commitment."

It was Yvonne's turn to look at her funny. "You . . . aren't?"

"Maybe I'm more like Nancy than you think," Daisy insisted.

"Oh, I'm into commitment," Nancy said. "I'm committed to having the best time ever, and never settling down with one man."

"See?" Daisy pointed at Nancy. "Maybe that's how I am, too."

Both of her friends shook their heads.

"Nope, sorry," Nancy said. "Your idea of a wild night out is a couple of beers at the Red Dragon."

"And what's wrong with that?" Daisy grabbed a cushion and held it against her stomach.

"There's nothing wrong with that," Yvonne agreed, "but you aren't exactly chasing men down, are you?"

"Hey, I don't chase them down," Nancy interjected. "They come to me."

"You're a special case. We're talking about Daisy."

Yvonne waved a hand at her. "In fact, I've never seen you out with anyone the entire time I've lived in Morgantown."

"I've only been back three years," Daisy protested.

"But did you date after college, while you were in Silicon Valley?" Nancy asked.

"Of course I did," Daisy defended herself. "Once or twice. And what does this have to do with Jackson Lymond anyway?"

Nancy and Yvonne exchanged a glance. "We're just trying to work out why you won't go out with a nice man like Jackson."

"Because I don't have to?" Daisy grumbled.

"True, and if you don't like him, Yvonne and I will shut up immediately," Nancy said promptly. "But seeing as the gossip mill has you being seen with him at least three times, and that he had dinner up at your place, it sounds like maybe you *do* like him just a little bit?"

"Hang on. Jackson had dinner at the *Millers*?" Yvonne pressed a hand to her heart. "*Mon Dieu*. With your brothers and your dad, and you're not *married* to him yet?"

Daisy sighed. "I made the mistake of mentioning Jackson to Adam. He assumed I was interested in him and invited Jackson to dinner."

"And did Jackson go?"

"Of course he did." Daisy glared at her cackling friends.

"And he survived to tell the tale?" Nancy grinned. "The man's obviously into you big-time."

"I don't have time to get involved with anyone right now," Daisy repeated.

"How about you ask Jackson to keep it light?" Yvonne asked. "Would you go for that?"

"That's kind of what we're doing."

"So you *are* going out with him?" Nancy collapsed

back on the couch. "Wow, that took way too much time to get back to where we started."

Daisy looked down at the cushion she was holding. "The thing is . . . I asked Jackson if he'd consider being my friend and having sex with me, but not be in a serious relationship."

This time the silence went on even longer before Nancy managed to close her mouth.

"You asked Jackson Lymond to be your *hookup*?" Nancy said. "*Ballsy* move, babe."

"That sounds horrible," Daisy said. "I *meant* that it would be nice to have sex with someone occasionally who I *liked*." She scowled at her friends. "Why are you both looking at me like that?"

"Because that's a very un-Daisyish thing to do," Yvonne finally said.

"It's quite simple. I don't want a serious relationship, but I do want sex. I'm twenty-eight and I have needs just like everyone else."

"Of course you do," Yvonne hurried to reassure her. "So what did Jackson say?"

"He asked for time to think it over," Daisy said. "Which I thought was very nice of him."

"Definitely." Nancy tried to keep her face straight. "*Very* noble of him. Free sex and no strings attached; what man would want that?"

Daisy threw the pillow at her and Nancy threw it back.

"Shall we get on and watch the movie?" Yvonne asked. "We all have to get up for work in the morning and it's already getting late."

"Rachel, can I ask you something?" Jackson inquired as he came into the kitchen. She'd stayed the night with Cauy after getting back late from Bridgeport.

"Sure! What's up?" Rachel put down her phone, and motioned for Jackson to join her at the table. "Is everything okay?"

"Where's Cauy?"

"He's out talking to Santiago about the hay ration or something. Why, do you want him to be here when we talk?"

"God, no." Jackson shuddered. "This is embarrassing enough as it is." He sat down. "Firstly, anything I say is in the strictest confidence. That means you don't even get to tell Cauy, okay?"

Rachel made a face, but nodded anyway. "So what can I help you with?"

Jackson decided he'd just lay it out there. He'd never been a great dissembler.

"Hypothetically, what would you do if a woman you liked and wanted to have a committed relationship with said she'd prefer to be your friend, but with sexual benefits?"

Rachel blinked at him. "Daisy Miller said that to *you*?"

"How do you know it's Daisy?" Jackson asked. "I said *hypothetically*."

Rachel rolled her eyes, but at least she didn't get up and walk away. "Hypothetically, I suppose it would depend on how I felt about that. Would it be enough to satisfy me? Or would I come to resent that restriction as time went on, and feel like I wasn't important enough to that person to be trusted with their complete, one-hundred-percent love." She paused for breath. "I obviously have a strong opinion about this."

"I can tell," Jackson agreed. "Go on."

"It's what I said. If you're okay with the friends-with-benefits kind of thing, and you *both* are, that's fine."

"Do you think it's possible for the other person to change their mind and want more?" Jackson asked.

"It's possible, but I wouldn't go into a relationship

assuming it will change to the way you want it to. You'd have to decide you were okay with things remaining the same, or even that one day one of you might find someone they *did* want to give that one-hundred-percent commitment to." Rachel paused. "Did you ask Cauy about this?"

"Like I'm going to ask my big brother for advice about my sex life," Jackson grumbled.

"Got it." Rachel chuckled. "That would be weird, like me asking Chase or BB." She reached over and patted Jackson's hand. "It's up to you, really. If you're planning on living here, you've got to think about seeing Daisy, or that hypothetical person, around all the time if things go wrong."

"Good point." Jackson nodded and rose to his feet. "That was helpful. Thanks, Rachel."

"I'm not sure how, but you're welcome." Rachel grinned up at him. "Let me know if I can solve any of your other problems, okay? I'm not planning on going anywhere."

Jackson was still smiling as he stepped out into the yard and walked down to the white fence that enclosed the pasture. The horses were out grazing at the lush grass without a care in the world. Jackson braced one booted foot on the bottom rung of the gate and stared out over the fields. He wanted Daisy Miller, that was a given, but could he abide by her terms?

If the military had taught him anything, it was to have a backup plan for your backup plan. He'd learned to swallow his disappointment and make the best of things before, and not being with Daisy, never touching her, or laughing with her, wasn't an outcome he wanted. Life was too short to wait for things that might never happen.

At one time, the idea of ever giving up his military career would have been impossible for him to imagine. It was what he'd always dreamed of, and he'd gone into the service expecting to be a lifer. But things didn't always work out, and now he was a man without a purpose or a real plan. Meeting Daisy had given him some much-needed direction, and he'd jumped at the chance to become her fake boyfriend.

Which left him in the acceptance part of the deal. He'd take what he'd been offered, and go with it.

Daisy opened the back door to her shop and let Jackson inside. She'd just closed for lunch, so it was perfect timing.

"Hi! What's up? I just shut the shop for an hour, and—"

He leaned in and kissed her so passionately, she moaned his name and had her arms around his neck in less than a second. He continued to kiss her, his hands roaming over her back and hips, pressing her firmly against the hardness encased in his jeans. Oh God, he felt so good . . .

"Okay." He drew back a scant inch. "I'm in."

"In what?" Daisy croaked.

"You, hopefully."

The smile he gave her was so hot, her knees trembled. "What, *now*?"

"Why not?" He walked her back toward the wall, lifted her up, and held her pinned against the hardest parts of him. She wondered whether it was actually possible to faint from sheer lust. "You've got a skirt on, I can work with that."

He shifted slightly, releasing his right hand, and gathered up her skirt in his fist. "Hang on to this."

"What if someone comes in?" Daisy bleated.

He reached across her and locked the back door. "Not happening."

"What about protection?"

"In my back pocket. Get it out for me."

Daisy curved her hand over possibly the most beautiful ass she had ever had the privilege to touch, and delved into his back pocket, making him groan and grind himself against her.

"Yeah. Let's start with you first."

He set her down, which was slightly disappointing, but immediately slid onto his knees, which made her pulse race. He kissed her fingers and then pressed them into her skirt, making her draw it away from her legs.

"Let me see you."

Secretly thrilled by the commanding note in his voice, Daisy gathered her long skirt and brought it up to her waist. She only had a moment to wonder what pair of panties she'd put on that morning before Jackson pressed his mouth to her mound, and she forgot everything else.

"May I?" He looked up at her, and she nodded.

He ran his thumbs along the lace edge of her panties until he reached her rounded hips and then back again, the edge of his fingers now beneath the lace, touching her bare skin, making her shiver uncontrollably. She'd showered that morning, right? And when had she last shaved her legs?

"Oh . . ." Daisy breathed out as his thumb settled over her bud, and suddenly nothing else mattered. "*Yes.*"

Jackson eased his finger lower, delighted and humbled to find that she was already wet for him. His dick throbbed, but he concentrated on the amazing taste of Daisy's skin, and the slick promise of her secrets as she opened to him like a flower. He added his mouth to his probing fingers and she came apart, knocking off his hat to grab his hair and hold him exactly where she wanted him, which was just fine by him as he sucked and licked her.

He speared two fingers inside her and she came again. He reached up and took the foil packet out of her unresisting hand, unzipped his jeans way too fast for safety, and covered his dick. He stood, picked her up, and in one swift motion eased her down over the hard column of his flesh, setting off another climax.

"Jeez . . ." Jackson growled against her mouth as he gathered himself and thrust upward until he was fully inside her and her feet were planted firmly on his ass. He pumped once, twice, and then his climax was wrenched out of him, leaving him blind with lust and satisfaction as she came all around him.

He braced his forehead against the wall and just held her, luxuriating in the rapid thump of her heart and her ragged breathing. When he regained some strength, he picked her up and walked her into her office, sitting her down on the high counter while he dispensed with the condom.

She stayed where he left her, her bosom literally heaving and her thighs still slightly apart, which did all kinds of things to his libido. He approached her again, and her eyes widened as she took in the excited state of his body.

"You can't possibly be ready for more *already*?"

"Daisy, that took less than five minutes," Jackson said. "I can do better than that. *You* can do better than that."

He moved between her spread thighs. "And there were important pieces of you I missed the first time around." He cupped her breasts, his thumbs finding her already hard nipples. "Like these."

She leaned into his hands, her fingers coming to rest on the back of his neck as he gently bit her through the cotton of her shirt and bra. While he kissed her, he worked the buttons free on her blouse and offered up a silent prayer when he realized her bra was a front loader.

And then he forgot everything but the heat and weight of her breasts, and his need to kiss and fondle them while his other hand cupped her mound. She moaned his name, and he was suddenly as hard as a rock. He eased back, and she frowned.

"What's up now?"

"Condom," he explained. "In my other pocket. I always like to be prepared for all eventualities."

"Were you a Boy Scout?" Daisy inquired.

"Eagle Scout." Jackson covered his way-too-excited dick.

"Of course," she murmured. "You have to be the best at everything, don't you?"

"I certainly try to be, ma'am." He slowly eased inside her. "Let me know how I'm doing with that."

This time they both lasted a bit longer. Daisy didn't have to worry about whether Jackson could bear her weight, and the table was at the perfect height for him. She came so many times, she started to wonder if she should be holding back, but Jackson soon put a stop to that. He was bossy as hell, and she didn't mind it one bit.

She closed her eyes and let the last climax ripple through her as he came as well, his breathing harsh against her throat as he leaned forward. She ruffled his hair, scraping her nails over his scalp, and he shuddered.

He eased out of her, dispensed with the protection, used the small bathroom, and came back to her. His jeans were now zipped, his Stetson back in place. She blinked as he lifted her down and kissed the top of her head.

"That was awesome."

"Yes, it was," Daisy said as her brain decided to function again and she realized he was heading back toward the door. "Wait. Are you *going* somewhere?"

He turned to stare at her, his brow furrowed. "I thought I'd get out of your way. You've still got half an hour to get lunch."

"Did it occur to you that I might want to have lunch *with* you?"

He rubbed a hand over his stubbled chin. "To be honest, Daisy, seeing as I've never had this kind of relationship before, I wasn't sure what the criteria were. Do I just have sex and walk away? Do we chat? What about foreplay? What about—"

"Stop talking right now." Daisy pointed her finger in his face. "I'm going to use the bathroom, and when I come out, I expect you to still be here, do you understand?"

Jackson took one look at her, raised his hands, and backed up to sit at her workbench. "Yes, ma'am."

Daisy washed and went back to collect Jackson, who was sitting meekly where she'd told him to.

"Come on. I'm taking you to lunch."

She unlocked the back door and went out into a blue sky and bright sunshine. Traffic was already building up, and they had to wait quite a while to get across the street to Yvonne's.

Daisy found a small table at the back of the shop and sat down with Jackson, who hadn't said a word since she'd told him to shut it in the shop. She raised an eyebrow at him.

"You can talk now."

"I wasn't sure," he replied with his usual engaging smile. "As I said—"

"You're not sure how to manage this new relationship

with me." After telling him it was okay to talk, Daisy immediately interrupted him. "I think we should just try to be honest with each other. If I want you to hang around, I'll tell you, and you can do the same with me."

"Sounds doable." He nodded. "Would you be willing to come over to my place and spend the night sometimes, or is this strictly a workday thing?"

"Spend the night?" Daisy blew out a breath. "I'm not sure I'm ready for that yet. If my brothers didn't know where I was, they might freak out and come looking for me."

"Knowing your brothers, they might freak out and come looking for me anyway," Jackson said. "I'd like to see you naked in my bed."

Daisy glanced furtively around to see if anyone had overheard Jackson, and saw that Lizzie, who was taking an order from a nearby table, was laughing her socks off. Daisy didn't think it was because of the hilarity of the order she was taking either.

"Can you keep it down, Jackson?" Daisy whispered. "I'm sure no one wants to hear about our potential sex life."

"I'm okay about it." Lizzie appeared beside them. "I hear all kinds of stuff in here." She winked at Daisy. "I promise I won't tell a soul, especially one of your brothers."

Jackson shuddered. "Yeah, thanks. I'd rather cling to life for a few more years."

"What can I get you?" Lizzie inquired. "We've got some *great* specials today."

Jackson eyed Daisy as she ate her salad with obvious enjoyment. His body was still humming and he just wanted to take her home, strip her naked, and start all over again.

Although what Cauy would make of being abandoned with a herd of cows in a distant field didn't bear thinking about.

But he had to pace himself. Daisy wanted things kept light and easy, and as neither of those things came naturally to him, he'd have to follow her lead. He was a long-term planner and a plotter, and this uncertainty was probably good for him.

"Was it okay?" He started speaking before considering the warning he'd just given himself. "The sex, I mean."

"For goodness' sake." Daisy put down her fork. "Do you want a *score*?"

"Why? Did you have one in mind?" Jackson asked.

"No, strangely enough, I was enjoying myself too much to think about such things." She lowered her voice. "Did you not notice how many times I *came*?"

"You were pretty impressive," Jackson admitted. "I almost lost it a few times there."

She looked so pleased with herself, he wanted to lean over and kiss her soft lips. Then he'd be back to asking her to spend the afternoon in bed with him, raising the wrath of not only Cauy but the Millers and possibly those wanting to purchase flowers from the shop.

"I would like to spend some more time with you, though," Daisy said.

"In bed?"

She rolled her eyes at him. "You're being way more specific about this than I anticipated. Yes, in bed, and maybe elsewhere, like on the couch, or watching a movie, or eating food?"

"Like a real date?" Jackson asked dubiously.

"Exactly." She picked up her fork again. "How about Friday? You can pick me up from the flower shop and take me to dinner at the Red Dragon."

"And then can I take you home and ravish you?"
She smiled at him. "Yes."
Jackson sat back.
Mission accomplished.
"Awesome."

Chapter Seven

"Jackson, did you read that letter I left out for you the other day?" Cauy asked as he poured himself more coffee.

It wasn't yet six in the morning and the sky outside was a forbidding gray. They'd gotten up early to go help one of the other ranchers in the valley brand their cattle. As they had decided to ride over, it would take a while to get there, hence the early start.

"Which letter?" Jackson yawned so hard his jaw cracked.

"The one from the coin guy—you know, the person who was supposed to be finding out how much all those old coins Dad saved up were worth?"

Jackson frowned. "I don't know what happened to it. I left it on the table. Did you throw it away?"

"Don't blame me." Cauy spread his arms wide. "I didn't touch it."

"Doesn't this coin guy have e-mail or anything?" Jackson grumbled. "Can I call him?"

"He doesn't do 'the Internet,' but you can definitely go ahead and leave him a phone message. It only took him three months to get back to me the first time I called."

"How *old* is this guy?" Jackson demanded.

"He sounded about ninety, but I could be wrong," Cauy

said. "January Morgan put me in touch with him through her contacts in the historical society. Mr. Perkins used to live around here. I guess Dad consulted with him occasionally when he was buying stuff."

They'd found the hoard of coins in an old filing cabinet taken from the abandoned silver mine, half on their land and half on the Morgan side. The mine was slated to be filled in after some dude ranch guests had gotten inside and almost trapped Cauy and Rachel Morgan in there forever.

"Then I'll have to look for that letter," Jackson muttered. "What the hell did I do with it? I bet the coins aren't worth much, but I'd love to know why Dad was keeping them."

"I wish I'd opened the damned thing when I had the chance instead of being all honest and leaving it for you." Cauy finished his coffee and got to his feet. "No time to worry about it now. We've got to get going. Cattle won't brand themselves."

Daisy checked her laptop and reviewed her worksheet. She had another wedding coming up in two weeks at Morgan Ranch. Today she had a consultation up there with the bride-to-be and her mother.

A message popped up from Ian on her cell.

Have you got a sec?

Daisy typed a thumbs-up, and her cell phone rang. "What's up, Ian?"

"Can you come out here Friday and Saturday the week after next?" he asked. He kept talking as if aware she was going to refuse. "We've got a couple of other VCs who heard about our product and want to get in early and meet us."

"Can't you guys handle it?" Daisy asked.

"You know what the gang are like. They're amazing at what they do, but none of them can put it into words."

"Maybe it's time they learned." Daisy eyed the paper calendar on her desk and flipped through the pages. "At some point, I'm not going to be around to articulate every thought those geniuses have."

"I hear you." Ian paused. "So can you come?"

"Hold on." Daisy checked out her plans for the weekend Ian was talking about. "Nope. I can't do that weekend, but I can do the following Wednesday through Saturday. Will that work?"

"I'll find out. If they're that keen to meet with us, I can't see why it would be a problem. Thanks, Daisy. Love you."

Daisy ended the call and scribbled a cryptic note to herself in her calendar. She could drive into the Bay Area, or get on a plane from the small local airport. She preferred to drive, but sometimes the passes over the mountains were still blocked by snow even this late in the year.

She stuck her pen behind her ear and stared at her laptop screen. She'd also need an excuse for leaving Morgan Valley, which meant she'd have to conjure up a flower show event or a class or something to stop her family from worrying about her. Daisy sighed. Sometimes she hated all the deception, but the thought of telling them what was going on when the start-up was at such a precarious point, and everyone was depending on her to get them through, was too difficult. She couldn't let her team down. All of them had lost money on their first business venture, and they'd all put seed money down for the new one without hesitation simply because she'd been so passionate about the cause.

Their new product would save people's lives. If she had to explain why it was so important, she'd have to tell her family a whole lot of personal stuff she'd kept hidden from everyone.

Daisy turned her calendar back to the current week and shut down her laptop. Keeping secrets was hard and getting worse every day. She put on her jacket, found her purse, and put her laptop in it. An afternoon spent with a bride-to-be would calm her nerves. Then she had a date with Jackson, which certainly wouldn't calm her nerves but might make her forget her problems for quite a while longer.

"Hey, Cauy, Jackson," Adam Miller greeted the brothers as they tied up their horses at the fence. "Nice to see you out here helping your neighbors."

Cauy nodded at Adam. "Shep asked me to come and I was happy to do so."

Jackson admired Cauy's calm expression. The fact that Cauy was nervous as hell because he was standing on the very ground his real father had grown up on didn't show on his face at all. He also wasn't rushing off toward the ranch house to see if his "grandparents" were there. Jackson wasn't sure he would've shown such restraint, which was probably why Cauy had only let him tag along after a stern talking-to.

Last year, Cauy had finally found out that his real father was a seventeen-year-old guy named Benjamin Gardin, who'd been walking out with their mother, Anita. He'd died when a tractor trailer had rolled over on top of him. leaving Anita pregnant and alone.

It also explained a lot about how Mark, Jackson's father, had treated his eldest son, driving him to leave the ranch at sixteen and not return for almost twenty years. Jackson unzipped his jacket and followed his brother and Adam toward the barn, where the smell of coffee overlaid the more regular smells of horseshit and straw.

The elderly woman dispensing the coffee looked up with a smile as they approached, and then clutched at her heart, almost dropping the pot.

"Oh my stars!" She was staring right at Cauy, who looked calmly back at her. "Shep! Look who's here!"

She put down the pot, came around the table, and drew Jackson's laconic brother into a fierce hug. "Why didn't anyone tell me how much you looked like my Ben? Shep! Where *are* you? Our grandson is here!"

"I'm right behind you, Marjory. Now why don't you put the boy down and let him get his bearings?" Shep advanced on the brothers, and even Jackson could see the likeness between his brother and the older man. "Thanks for coming, Cauy. We appreciate it."

Marjory reluctantly released Cauy, but hung on to his sleeve. "Now, when we're done with the branding, you come and visit with me in the house, do you hear me?"

"Yes, ma'am." Cauy smiled at her. "I'd love to do that."

Marjory went back to pouring out the coffee, and Shep disappeared into the barn. Jackson touched Cauy's shoulder.

"You okay?"

"Sure." Cauy's smile was resigned. "Who wouldn't want to provide Morgan Valley with the best gossip ever?"

Jackson looked around the circle of cowboys and recognized faces from every ranch in the valley. Seeing as Marjory hadn't even attempted to lower her voice, he was pretty sure everyone in the vicinity who hadn't already worked it out had heard her declare Cauy was her grandson. By tomorrow, the news would be all over town.

"At least you got it all over with in one hit," Jackson said encouragingly. "Now everyone knows."

"Yeah." Cauy sipped his coffee. "Gee. Thanks."

It took Jackson a few minutes to work out that there were three Miller brothers present at the branding: Adam, Danny, and Evan. Kaiden worked as a carpenter and helped out part-time on the ranch, and Ben ran the Miller place with his dad and Adam, which meant he was busy all the time.

It was a long time since Jackson had branded anything, and rather than make a complete fool of himself, he'd decided to volunteer for cutting the calves from the herd and running down escapees, tasks well within his ability and unlikely to cause any serious holdups or harm.

He and Cauy barely had any cattle yet, so going to all the other ranches and polishing up on their skill set was really helpful. When Shep divided them up into teams, Jackson ended up with the Millers, who showed him how skillful they were at every task put in front of them. He had to bet Daisy knew her way around a horse and all the jobs related to running a good ranch.

"Hey! Jackson!" Evan Miller shouted at him. "Yo!"

One of the calves was making a run for it, so he wheeled his horse around to cut her off. Rocket was as fast as his name, and Jackson was secretly proud of how fast he reacted. None of the Millers looked very impressed as they swiftly dealt with the calf and sent it bawling back to its momma. He had no doubt Daisy would be getting a report on her boyfriend's skill set from her brothers, and he doubted he'd make more than a C average.

The eye-watering smell of hamburger and burned hair drifted toward him, and he moved upwind of it, one eye on the pens that contained the calves, the other on their mothers, who didn't appreciate being separated from their babies. Most people thought cows were docile creatures, but that wasn't always the case.

Shep Gardin came up alongside Jackson and stopped his horse.

"Good to meet you, Jackson, and thanks for helping out today. I'm sorry I didn't get a chance to speak to you before we set out. I was too intent on heading Marjory off at the pass."

Jackson grinned. "Cauy's looking forward to speaking to her later, so we're all good."

Shep made a harrumphing sound, his gaze drawn toward Cauy, who was currently on the tagging part of the operation. "He's a good boy."

"Yeah, he is." Jackson nodded. "You can be proud of him."

"I'm just glad he wants to be associated with us," Shep said. "Mark wouldn't allow Anita to speak or contact us after Cauy was born. It was one of his conditions for agreeing to marry her."

Jackson winced at yet another example of his father's unpleasant nature. Sometimes he wondered if he'd end up like Mark—alone and unloved. His father had gotten what he wanted when he married Anita, but like everything else in his life, it hadn't given him the satisfaction or happiness he expected. His grudge against the world had just gotten bigger.

"My dad sure made some bad choices in his life," Jackson agreed. "Cauy got away from him when he was sixteen, which was the best decision he ever made."

He'd been guiltily relieved when Cauy left, because it meant he only had to worry about protecting his mother and sister. But Cauy's absence had turned Mark's attention back to his wife and other children, and things hadn't gotten much better. At some points, he'd even envied his brother's freedom . . .

Shep nodded. "I can't believe Mark left him the ranch, though."

"Yeah, Cauy was pretty shocked."

Shep eyed him closely. "Did you expect it to come to you?"

"To be honest, I was far too busy with my military career to care what was going on around here," Jackson said. "When Mom divorced Dad, I came and helped her move to her condo in Florida, spoke briefly to my dad, who was too furious to make much sense, and that was it for quite a few years."

"Don't you want to be a rancher?" Shep asked.

"Yeah, I do." Jackson smiled at the older man. "It's kind of in my blood."

Shep smiled back. "Good man. Since my only son died, I've been hanging on here, hoping someone in the family would take an interest in the place, but no luck so far. It would be a shame for all this tradition to die. Mark did one thing right by getting you two boys to come back and save his place." Shep nodded and clicked to his horse. "We'll be getting some grub in an hour, so stick around."

Jackson settled back into the saddle. Rocket appeared to be taking a nap but would quickly respond if Jackson needed him.

Did he mind that Mark hadn't left the place to him? Everyone kept telling him he should, and yet he hadn't really thought about it until Cauy presented him with his father's will and he'd discovered he'd been left nothing at all. That had been a shock. Cauy already had plenty of money from his days in the oil business and was embarrassed to be left the ranch, considering how Mark had felt about him. He'd even offered it to Jackson, who had immediately repudiated the suggestion.

But had it hurt? He'd always considered himself the favorite son, and to end up with nothing . . .

A piercing whistle to his right alerted him to another escapee, and he eagerly went after the calf, more than willing to escape his uncomfortable thoughts. He'd never been the kind of guy who whined about anything, and he wasn't about to start now.

"Saw your boyfriend up at the Gardin Ranch yesterday," Adam remarked to Daisy as he held the door of Yvonne's open for her.

"Doing what?"

"It's branding season." Adam looked like he couldn't quite believe she didn't know that. "Remember? When we all help one another out?"

"Ugh."

Adam's slow smile lightened his face. "No one would ever guess you grew up on a ranch, sis, I'll give you that." He found them a table. "He did okay."

"That's high praise from you."

"We let him do the easy parts." Adam shrugged. "He's a good team player."

"Impressive," Daisy teased her big brother.

"You could do a lot worse." Adam perused the menu, glancing up as Lizzie came into view. "Hey."

"Er, hi!" Lizzie fidgeted with her notepad and didn't look directly at Adam. "What can I get you guys?"

"I'll have the double fish sandwich," Adam said. "What about you, Daisy?"

"Just a pecan and cranberry salad." Daisy sighed. "I'm going out with Jackson this evening, so I don't want to eat too much."

Lizzie waggled her eyebrows at Daisy behind Adam's

back. "Good thought. Focus your calories where you need them."

Adam turned to look at Lizzie, who immediately composed her features. "Anything else I can get you guys?"

"Just water, please," Daisy said, and Adam agreed. "Thanks."

She waited until Lizzie went back to the counter. "What is it with you and Lizzie? You have this really weird vibe between you."

"I have no idea what you're talking about," Adam replied. "We get along fine now."

"Now?" Daisy pounced on the word. "What happened before?"

"How about we file that under 'none of your business'?" Adam returned his attention to the menu.

"You went to school together, didn't you?" Daisy ignored his unsubtle warning. Sometimes brothers needed to be put in their place. "Did you go out with her?"

"Nope. I only went out with Louisa." His smile disappeared, and a world of hurt flashed in his eyes. "You know that."

She reached across the table and took his hand. "I'm sorry. That was really insensitive of me."

"It's okay." He squeezed her fingers. "If anyone needs lightening up around here, we all know it's me."

Despite their parents' objections, he and Louisa had married right out of high school. He'd lost his wife to cancer three years later, and he hadn't been the same since. He'd changed from the happiest, most-open guy ever into a much quieter, self-contained man who rarely smiled and kept a rigid hold on his emotions even around his family.

"Lizzie was at school with us, and she was best friends with Louisa," Adam continued talking. "Sometimes I think that makes it a bit awkward for us."

Daisy wondered why, when it had been fourteen years since Louisa had died. Had they resented each other, the best friend and the husband? Had Louisa's death divided them in ways Daisy hadn't been aware of? Sometimes, she wished she had Jackson's gift of just asking all the questions without shame. She sensed Adam held on to things way too long, and she didn't know how to help him when she was that way herself.

"So where are you and Jackson going tonight?" Adam asked.

"Just to the Red Dragon, and then the new pizza place. Have you been there yet?"

"Nope. I make great pizza myself."

"Don't you even want to try it?" Daisy coaxed. "Evan said it's really good."

"Traitor." Adam smiled. "Bring me back a slice. If it's that good, I'll stop making my own dough and you can all suffer."

"Oh, don't do that," Daisy said. "What happens if the pizza place shuts down?"

He flipped his balled-up napkin at her and she pretended to dodge. It was so nice to see him smiling. Perhaps one day she'd broach the idea that he should go out on a date again. If she could dip her toe in the dating world, Adam could, too. He was a good man, and he deserved to be loved. But she wouldn't push her luck today; she'd already ruffled his feathers quite enough.

Jackson was at her back door promptly at six, which Daisy appreciated. She stood on tiptoe to kiss his newly shaven cheek and breathed in his aftershave.

"Mmm . . . you smell good."

He kissed her cheek and then recoiled "Ew. You smell like the stinky old water left in a vase of flowers."

Daisy burst out laughing. "You—" She held out her T-shirt. "I almost dropped one of those big metal vases on my foot and got soaked through."

"That explains it." Jackson's appreciative grin was hot enough to make her want to jump his bones. "Do you still want to get pizza, or do you want to come straight home with me and take a shower?"

"Pizza, please." Daisy liked the way she could just say it how it was. "We can get it to go so we don't have to stink up the whole shop. I don't think the Ranieri family would like that."

"Neither do I." Jackson waited as she shut down her laptop, got her bag, and locked up the shop. "Starting a new business is hard enough without having someone stinking of . . . weeds sitting in the shop."

"Very funny." Daisy poked him in the ribs and he dodged out of the way. "I have to get a slice for Adam to try. He's in a huff because he usually makes our pizza."

"Adam's in a huff?" Jackson asked. "I can't quite picture that somehow."

"You'd be surprised at what a sensitive guy he is about his cooking."

Daisy let Jackson take her hand as they walked up the street. It was nice being by his side, and her day felt so much brighter. They had to walk down to the far end of Main Street to reach the new pizza parlor, which had opened up in one of the shops on the side of the medical center. The smell of garlic, grilled cheese, and tomatoes was phenomenal.

When they reached the front of the line, Jackson looked at the choices. "Pesto and Parmesan okay?"

"Ew, no way. It's *disgusting*." Daisy mock-shuddered. "Let's go with anchovies and black olives."

Jackson made a retching sound. "God, *no*."

Gina Ranieri who was serving at the counter, gently cleared her throat. "We could do half and half."

Daisy and Jackson stared at her and then at each other.

"That sounds like a great idea," Daisy agreed. "You okay with that, Jackson?"

"Sure, as long as there's a clear demarcation zone down the middle."

Daisy rolled her eyes at Gina, who fought a smile.

"Thin or thick crust?"

Daisy said thin just as Jackson said thick. Gina sighed.

"I can go with a thick crust this time, but next time we have it my way," Daisy conceded. "And can you give me a slice of your cheese pizza to go, and some cheesy garlic bread?"

Gina tapped everything into the order and looked up. "I'm guessing this will be a large-size pizza?"

"Yes." They both nodded and grinned at each other.

"Finally, we agree on something," Jackson said as he handed over his credit card. "Do you want a drink here while we wait, or shall we go to the Red Dragon and come back for the pizza?"

"It'll be about half an hour, I'm afraid," Gina said apologetically. "It's Friday night, and we get quite busy."

"Not a problem." Daisy smiled at her. "Can you text me when it's ready?" She handed over her business card. "Thanks so much."

They left the pizza place, made their way to the Red Dragon, found a small table, and sat down.

"I'm buying," Daisy said, pulling out her wallet. "You bought the pizza."

"I'm okay with that," Jackson said. "I'll have a beer, please."

Daisy got their drinks and brought them to the table, where Jackson was checking his phone. She hoped he could deal with the smell of old flower water for a little while longer. He looked up as she offered him the bottle and declined the glass.

"Thanks." He put away his phone and gave her his complete attention, which was something she appreciated. "Cauy and Rachel are babysitting Maria Morgan tonight."

"She's a teenager so hardly a baby," Daisy said. "I bet she doesn't appreciate it."

"But that means they won't be back until midnight." He winked at her.

"So if you wanted to chase me through the house naked, we could do that?" Daisy tried to look innocent.

He choked on his beer. "I'd just like to *see* you naked first."

"And lying back against your sheets?" Daisy asked. "Writhing around in ecstasy?"

"Yeah, that." He slowly licked his lips, which did all kinds of things to her stomach and made her wish they hadn't ordered pizza.

"Maybe we could eat afterward." Daisy only realized she'd spoken out loud when Jackson blinked at her.

"You're reading my mind here." He took another swig of beer. "Pizza heats up great in the microwave, right?"

She nodded and almost jumped when he put his hand on her thigh under the table. Was it possible to spontaneously combust from lust? She desperately tried to think of something else to talk about.

"You know when you met Dell?"

Jackson took a moment to follow her new, completely random train of thought. "Dell Turner?"

"Yes. He asked you about being in the air force and whether you were a pilot."

His hand disappeared from her thigh. "What about it?"

"Well, you didn't say whether that's actually what you did, only that you learned to fly before you even went to the USAF."

Jackson sat back, one arm on the back of his chair. "What made you think of that right now?"

"I've got a really good memory." She shrugged. "And I just wondered."

"I tried out to be a fighter pilot. I didn't make it."

His flat tone made Daisy pay attention. "I suppose most people don't make it."

"I was convinced I would." His smile was wry. "It was the first time in my life when something in my control that I'd really wanted didn't work out for me. I couldn't believe it. I was so cocky, I thought I couldn't fail."

"It's rare to go through life without failing at something," Daisy said softly.

"I suppose you're right. I didn't take it well. For a while, I didn't know what I was going to do with myself and almost ended up getting thrown out. Then I was posted to logistics in Qatar and got immersed in that." He put down his beer. "Do you want another one?"

Daisy checked her phone. "Gina says the pizza will be ready in five minutes."

"So I guess that's a no." Jackson picked up the bottles. "I'll take these back to the bar and meet you out front."

Daisy grabbed her purse and took herself off to the bathroom. She'd certainly succeeded in ruining the mood. She almost hadn't recognized the always-smiling, always-relaxed Jackson Lymond when he'd started talking about not becoming a fighter pilot. She guessed that for someone who was supergoal-oriented that any perceived failure would bug the hell out of him. The fact that she wasn't dissimilar, and had gone back to redo and reclaim her place in Silicon Valley, resonated with her.

If he knew what she was up to, she could've sympathized with him, and shared why she'd gone back. He, of all people, would probably understand her drive to succeed. But she couldn't tell him because he was also the world's worst blabbermouth.

She met Jackson at the door, high-fived Nancy as she passed by with a tray of empty glasses, and then headed back to the pizza place. Jackson was unusually silent as they picked up their pizza and took it back to Daisy's truck. He'd been dropped in town by one of the ranch hands, so Daisy would drive back to his place and eventually on home.

He frowned as he settled in the passenger seat beside her. "Your steering wheel is set really high."

"I inherited this truck from Adam." Daisy wrinkled her nose at the wheel. "Are you saying it moves?"

"Yeah, you can usually adjust the height." He reached over, and Daisy smacked his hand.

"Don't touch anything, okay? I like it where it is."

"When you can barely see out the windshield?" Jackson asked.

"It's fine." She turned on the engine. "Stop fussing me."

She backed out of the spot and turned toward the exit of the parking lot.

"Your side mirror is way off as well, and there's a warning light on your dashboard about your oil level."

Daisy stopped the car and looked at him. "Would you like to walk home?"

"No, of course I wouldn't." He blinked at her. "What's up?"

"Then stop criticizing me!"

"I'm *not*. I'm just pointing out stuff going on in your truck."

She fixed him with her most intimidating stare. "I already have five brothers telling me what to do, Jackson. I don't need another one."

"I don't feel very brotherly toward you." He met her gaze, and she almost fainted with lust.

"Then if you ever want a chance to see me naked, stop talking right now!"

"Yes, ma'am." He sat back and looked out the window, allowing Daisy to successfully navigate them back to Lymond Ranch. He got out first.

"Let me get the alarm and let Grace and the puppies out."

"Okay, I'll just get my bag."

By the time she reached the kitchen door, Grace came flying out to greet her, followed by all five of her puppies. The smallest one peed on Daisy's boot, but she didn't take it personally.

Scooping up the offender, she went in and shut the door while the puppy wiggled and tried to lick her face.

"Are you going to keep them all?" Daisy asked as Jackson zoomed around, putting on various lights and setting the table for their pizza.

"The dogs?" Jackson found the napkins. "I don't know what Cauy's planning."

Daisy kissed the puppy on the head. "Let me know if you plan on sharing the love. This one seems to have taken a shine to me."

"That's Rollo."

"Like the chocolate?" Daisy put the dog down, wiped off her boot, and washed her hands.

"Nope, the Viking." Jackson pointed at the other dogs. "We also have Ragnar, Floki, Siggy, and Lagertha."

"Poor old Lagertha." Daisy smiled at the black-and-white-spotted puppy.

"Hey, she'll grow up to be a renowned warrior queen, so it's all good." Jackson pointed at the pizza. "Do you want to eat now or later?"

Daisy breathed in the siren call of the pizza. "If I eat it now, I'll probably fall asleep."

"Which isn't good." Jackson set down the pepper and came toward her. "Because I really would like to see you naked."

She allowed him to take her hand. "It's not worth all this excitement, you know. It's just a body."

"A lush, beautiful female body that makes me hard every time I think about you."

"Really?" Daisy halted at the door to his bedroom.

"Oh yeah." He leaned in and kissed her so thoroughly, she was almost panting with lust. "You just do it for me. I don't know why, but I'm not going to argue about it."

"Which makes a change," Daisy murmured against his lips. "Seeing as you like to argue about everything."

"I'm naturally inquisitive." He kissed her again. "I can't help it."

She gently pushed him away and went into the bedroom, which was in its usual immaculate state. Turning to face him, she pulled her T-shirt over her head and undid the zipper of her jeans to reveal her fancy matching underwear. He visibly swallowed, and she allowed herself a quiet moment of triumph.

"Do you want to help with the rest?"

He nodded and came toward her, his hands warm on her skin as he undid her bra and helped her step out of her jeans, panties, and socks. Being naked when he was still clothed did all kinds of interesting things to her heart rate.

"Lie down." She pointed at the bed.

"I'm still dressed," Jackson pointed out.

"I know."

He held her gaze for a second and then complied, easing one hand behind his head so he could still look up at her. She climbed onto the bed and straddled him, allowing the hard ridge of desire in his jeans to settle just where she needed it most. Bending down, she kissed him and enjoyed his groan as her breasts swung forward and grazed his shirt.

"Daisy . . ." He breathed her name like a prayer.

"Hmm?" She freed the top button of his shirt and then the next, to reveal the swirl of dark hair on his chest.

"I really like this."

"Good." She finished undoing his shirt and eased it free of his jeans, making him curse. She fingered the silver clasp on his belt and worked out how to release it, allowing the leather to slide through the loops of his jeans.

"Daisy?"

She paused to look up at him. "*What*?"

"May I touch you?"

"No, I have to concentrate." She frowned at him.

"On what?"

"You, you idiot." She leaned in and bit his nipple, making him start. "Now be quiet."

Jackson gripped the rail of the headboard with one hand as Daisy carefully eased the zipper of his jeans down. She gave a little satisfied growl, which made his dick leap to attention. The sight of her sitting naked on his lap, her long hair free and her breasts almost in his face was enough to drive a man wild.

She studied his straining boxers and smiled like a woman with a mission. He tensed as she ran a finger down over the curve of his cotton-covered shaft and then bent to kiss him.

"Please . . ." Jackson couldn't stay silent.

"Please what?" Daisy asked.

"Don't stop."

"If you didn't keep interrupting me," Daisy said, "I would be moving along much faster."

Jackson pressed his lips together as she shoved down his jeans and boxers and threw them onto the floor. Now he was as naked as she was.

She pushed on his right knee, and he obligingly spread his thighs wide enough for her to kneel between them.

"First things first," Daisy murmured and eased her hand under his buttock. "Oh! It's a flower!"

He shivered as she traced the raised and inked petals of his tattoo. Trust her to remember that right at this moment.

"It's a buttercup and a bee." She slowly looked up at him. "Why on *earth* . . . ?"

He shrugged. "I was drunk. My friends told me it was going to be an eagle. It took me days to work out why everyone was laughing at my ass."

She chuckled and kissed his knee. "Idiot."

"Yeah."

Her hair tickled his skin, making him shut the hell up as she slowly refocused her attention, zeroed in on her target, and took him in her mouth.

"Oh God . . ." Jackson breathed. "That's—"

Speech deserted him as she sucked him deep. He fought the need to curve his hand into her hair and hold her there for all eternity. After a while, he couldn't help but rock his hips into the rhythm she demanded as she used her tongue and teeth to take him to paradise.

"Daisy . . . I'm going to come if you keep that up," Jackson blurted out.

"Mmm." Her purr of satisfaction reverberated around his shaft, and he couldn't hold back any longer.

When she sat back, she licked her lips like a cat and smiled at him.

"Was that okay?"

He nodded, too shattered for words.

"Good. It's been such a long time since I've tried that, I was worried I'd forgotten how." She grinned. "It was really fun."

"Yeah?" Jackson finally regained his voice and reached for her. "Not half as much fun as this is going to be."

Daisy ate her third piece of pizza, finished her beer, and then burped discreetly behind her hand.

"Do you want my last piece?" she asked Jackson, who sat opposite her, looking attractively rumpled and bright-eyed after all the sex. She was fairly sure she looked the same, which was why she was happy to delay going home for quite a while longer. No need to draw attention to herself from her brothers.

He made a face. "Hell no."

"You sure?"

"Anchovies are the devil's spawn. Wrap it up and take it home with you." Jackson got up. "I'll find you something to put it in."

Daisy contemplated the remaining piece of pizza. Didn't sex use up lots of calories? Perhaps she could finish it before Adam spotted it when she finally got home. She could distract him with his own piece of pizza she'd brought him. The thought of moving anywhere right now wasn't high on her priorities list.

Jackson came back with a paper plate and a plastic bag and efficiently zipped the plated pizza inside the zip-lock bag.

"So how long has it been since you did that to a man exactly?"

Daisy gazed at him reproachfully. So much for enjoying the moment. She'd forgotten he remembered everything and had no qualms about discussing it.

"Why does it matter? I didn't bite anything off, did I?"

He shuddered and fixed her with his usual thoughtful stare. "I was trying to work it out. I don't remember you having a boyfriend in school, so it has to have been in the last twelve years. And as you haven't dated anyone in Morgan Valley for *three* years, that narrows it down to your last two years in high school, when I wasn't there, your time at college, and in employment."

Daisy folded her arms over her chest. "Very clever."

He raised an eyebrow. "So when was it? You went to college in California, correct?"

"Yes."

"Stanford, according to your brother."

Daisy wondered which one of her brothers she needed to strangle for giving away that piece of information.

"And your dad mentioned you bringing some tech guy back to the ranch for a weekend once." Jackson smiled. "He didn't like him much."

Daisy mentally added her father to her not-speaking-to list.

"So what?"

"Was it him?"

"Possibly." Daisy shrugged. "Why does it matter?"

"Did you date him for long? Your dad said he was some namby-pamby computer guy." He paused. "His words, not mine."

"I didn't date him for long, no." Daisy picked up the bagged pizza. "Can we talk about something else now?"

Jackson studied her for a long moment. "Sure."

"Good."

"You went to Stanford, and then into IT?"

"I *thought* we were changing the subject," Daisy objected as he put two and two together way too fast for her liking.

"We are." Jackson looked affronted. "We've moved on from your love life to your employment status."

Daisy slowly rose to her feet. "And now I'm leaving."

"Why? It's still early."

She put her hands on the table and leaned forward to glare at him. "Because you're being extremely annoying."

"I'm always annoying. You know that." He shrugged. "What in particular did I say?"

"If you don't know, I'll leave you to think about it," Daisy said sweetly. "Thanks for the pizza." She put on her jacket as he slowly rose from the table. "And the sex. It was great."

Grabbing her bag, she stuffed the pizza in the top and turned toward the door, petting Grace on her way out.

"Is it because you don't want me to know you worked in Silicon Valley?" Jackson said from behind her.

She froze by the door but didn't turn around.

"Night, Jackson."

In fact, she'd been so busy deflecting his interest in her love life, she'd left herself wide open to his conjectures about her alternate career. She dug in her pocket for her truck keys. It was better he guessed about her job than about the disaster of her love life, so perhaps she'd just have to admit it and hope he'd let it go.

"Right," Daisy muttered to herself as she got into the truck. "Jackson Lymond let something go. He's about as tenacious as bindweed."

Chapter Eight

So Daisy definitely worked in tech . . . Jackson made a pot of coffee and went to bang on Cauy's door to wake up his brother. She hadn't been pleased about him working it out, which made him guess her second job was somehow still connected to it. But why was she being so secretive? Tech jobs weren't exactly something to be ashamed of.

He poured himself some coffee and toasted two bagels while he microwaved some scrambled eggs. By the time Cauy emerged, he had everything on the table, ready to be eaten.

"Thanks, bro." Cauy sat down and yawned. "We've got a long day ahead of us."

"Doing what exactly?" Jackson asked. "You weren't very specific last night."

"We're helping the Morgans with their new barn."

"Oh, a barn raisin'!" Jackson slapped his thigh. "That's awesome."

"Don't get too excited." Cauy gave him a wry look. "We're not in Amish Country now. The barn's already in place; they just need help with the interior."

Jackson finished his bagel. "And when that's completed, the Morgans will take their horses back from us, correct?"

"Yeah." Cauy sighed. "Which means we'll lose that income string."

"It helped pay for the reconstruction of our barn, all the new fencing, and gave us free labor, so I think we're good," Jackson reminded his penny-pinching brother. "And it helped us get on better terms with our neighbors."

"I thought I did that by dating Rachel Morgan." Cauy offered one of his rare smiles. "Wait. Don't ever tell her I said that, even as a joke."

"You can count on me." Jackson sipped his coffee.

"Yeah, to drop me right in it."

Jackson winced. There was some truth in what his brother was saying.

"It's okay," Cauy answered Jackson's unspoken thought. "One of us has to be the talker in the family, and it's definitely not me."

Cauy got up to fetch more coffee and then returned to his seat. "There's a meeting in town tonight I'm planning on attending. I'd like you to come with me."

"To do the talking?" Jackson asked. "What's it about?"

"It's a regular community meeting between the town, the ranchers, the sheriff's office, and the county board. The idea is to keep everyone informed of what's going on and stop shit going down that no one anticipated."

"Sounds like a great idea," Jackson agreed. "So what's on the agenda tonight?"

"The expansion of the town." Cauy added cream to his coffee. "As you can imagine, it's a point of friction between the ranchers and the business owners."

"If I'm planning on living here, I should definitely show up," Jackson said.

"You still going ahead with that?" Cauy asked. "Maybe you could ask the Millers if there's a job going up at their ranch."

"Ha ha. Right, what with all those guys already running the place." Jackson shuddered. "And Daisy wouldn't like it either. She wants to get away from them, not live there for the rest of her life."

"She told you that?"

"Not in so many words, but she's very independent, and she likes her own space." Jackson considered his answer. "Not that she'd go too far away. She loves her family."

"So if you do stay, you'll need to be in Morgan Valley?"

"You think I want to leave?" Jackson met his brother's gaze.

Cauy shrugged. "I think you're bored here."

"You'd be wrong about that. I'm enjoying myself," Jackson replied. "It's interesting to come back and see all the changes and the things that stayed the same."

"It's backbreaking work," Cauy stated. "With little reward sometimes."

"And you think I'm not up to it?" Jackson wasn't smiling now. For some reason, Cauy's comments weren't sitting well with him. "Hell, you're the one they had to piece back together after the oil-rig explosion, and you seem to be doing okay."

Cauy raised his eyebrows. "There's no need to get all defensive. I'm asking a valid question."

"Then maybe you should shut up?" Jackson stood and dumped his plate and mug in the sink. "I'm going to check on the horses. I'll see you out there."

He grabbed his coat, boots, and hat from the mudroom and went on out into the cold brightness of the day. He wasn't sure why Cauy's questions bugged him so much, but he wasn't prepared to sit there and let his brother lecture him about the ranch or his place in the grand scheme of things.

His breath coalesced in the cold as he marched toward the barn.

"Hey."

He turned as Cauy appeared at the back door.

"What now? Are you going to tell me to leave?" Jackson asked. "This is your place, isn't it?"

Cauy just looked at him, one eyebrow raised. "You left your phone on the table." He held it up.

"Oh. Thanks." Now Jackson felt like a fool, but he couldn't take the words back.

Cauy cleared his throat. "Maybe you should rethink your decision to turn down half this ranch and stop being so passive-aggressive about it."

"Passive-aggressive?" Jackson scowled at his brother. "Where'd you get those big words from?"

"Rachel." Cauy didn't back down. "But they're right on the nose about you."

"Bullshit. I'm not passive about anything. I speak my mind," Jackson protested.

"Not when it's something close to your chest." Cauy didn't give an inch. "You don't talk about Dad, your military service, or what the hell you intend to do with the rest of your life."

"And you do?" Jackson couldn't seem to shut up. "You're like a clam."

"I talk to Rachel," Cauy said. "I try to talk to you."

Jackson looked out over the horizon, avoiding his brother's steady gaze. Why was he arguing again? What gremlin had gotten into his brain and made him sound like a dissatisfied, selfish brat?

"I'm sorry, Cauy." He forced himself to meet his brother's eyes. "You're right. I'm still not sure what I'm going to do, but that doesn't excuse me for getting all up in your face about it. It's my problem. Not yours."

It was Cauy's turn to look skyward. "Look, I don't need you to apologize. I want to *help* you, but if you can't be honest with yourself about what you want and share shit with me—even the bad stuff—I don't know what to do."

"When I work it out, you'll be the first to know," Jackson promised. "I'm really grateful you've let me stay here and sort myself out."

"I don't want your fricking gratitude. This is still your home."

"I know." Jackson offered his brother a placatory smile. "I'd better get on and see to the horses."

The sound of the door slamming behind his brother made him think that perhaps things hadn't gone as well as he'd hoped. Cauy might not talk much, but he wasn't stupid. Everything he'd said had been dead on, which made Jackson feel like a worm caught on a hook. For the first time in his life, he really wasn't sure of his direction, and it was killing him.

He went into the barn and checked in on Rocket before mucking out his stall and feeding him. Physical exercise was usually a great way to avoid thinking too much, but this time it wasn't working. Did he covet the ranch? Should he accept his brother's offer of part ownership of the place after all? He'd never gone back on a decision once he'd made it—had prided himself on that choice until now.

Cauy had the money to do anything he wanted to the ranch but preferred to take his time and get things right. Jackson would want a more direct approach and instinctively knew he and Cauy would clash over it. Having only recently reconnected with his brother, Jackson was reluctant to destroy that new bond. It would be better to start fresh and make his own decisions. But was he simply finding excuses not to follow through on his plans?

"What plans?" Jackson muttered to himself as he wheeled a barrow load of soiled straw around to the compost heap. "I'm not ready to own my own place yet."

He needed to stay put, learn as much as he could, and then move on. That had been his original strategy. What was so hard about that? Being at the ranch, with reawakened recollections of his father's petty cruelties and memories of his last months in the air force circling in his brain had made him doubt himself again.

And his on-again, off-again relationship with Daisy wasn't helping much either. The fact that he'd impulsively accepted her terms without thinking things through were yet another symptom of the uncertain state of his mind. He hated not having a purpose; he absolutely *hated* it.

He emptied the wheelbarrow and went back into the barn to start on the second stall, which housed Cauy's favorite horse. Maybe for the first time in his life, he had to accept that it was going to take time to sort things out, and that he'd just have to roll with it.

Cauy emerged from the house and Jackson stiffened, but his brother did nothing more threatening than hand over his forgotten phone and get to work. Cauy had never been one to belabor a point, and for once, Jackson was grateful. Whatever was going on, he was the only person who could solve it.

It appeared that half the valley had assembled at the Morgans' to help out with the new barn. Ruth Morgan, who had lived on the ranch for over sixty years, was in her element, welcoming all the ranchers and directing operations from the railed front porch of the Victorian ranch house.

Jackson noticed Adam Miller and his father in the line for coffee and made sure to acknowledge them. Daisy had left in a huff the night before, but that was becoming the norm. He hoped she'd be willing to see him when he went to town later that evening.

"Are you going to the meeting tonight?" Jackson asked Adam after they'd nodded cautiously to each other.

"What meeting?"

"The one about the expansion of the town," Jackson explained. "Cauy thinks it's important that the ranchers are well represented there."

"He's right." Mr. Miller entered the conversation. "We're some of the oldest residents of this valley and we often get forgotten." He slapped his son on the back. "I'm sending Adam and Kaiden to represent me because, apparently, I can get too loud and blunt."

"So can I," Jackson said with a wince. "But I'm going anyway."

"Good for you. Make sure you speak up." Mr. Miller gave Jackson an approving glance. "I'll tell Daisy she should pop in too."

Jackson suspected Daisy's perspective as a shop owner might differ from her father's but didn't mention it. He was in enough trouble for opening his big mouth for one day to create another ruckus.

"Are the Morgans coming?" Adam asked.

"As Chase is the chairperson, I guess so," Jackson said. "And I bet Ruth Morgan will want to be there as well."

"I bet she will." Mr. Miller smiled. "She'll make sure everyone gets to hear the ranchers' side of the story."

"I sure will." Ruth had appeared to replenish the coffee and smiled up at Adam and Jackson. "I know the history of this valley better than anyone, Jeff, and I'm not shy about sharing it."

Mr. Miller tipped his hat. "You sure do, Ruth. I'm counting on you to stop any more silliness coming into this valley."

"Silliness?" Ruth looked him square in the eye, and Jackson and Adam instinctively took a step back.

"One 'dude ranch' is enough, don't you think?" Mr. Miller said. "Don't want everyone getting into the entertainment business now, do we?"

Ruth Morgan drew herself up. "It's not for me to tell anyone else in this valley how to save their ranch now, is it Jeff? We all have to do the best we can to survive."

"No need to get your dander up now, Ruth." Mr. Miller held up a placatory hand. "I'm just saying . . ."

"I know exactly what you're saying, but seeing as you turned up to help me and mine today, I'll keep my thoughts to myself." Ruth fixed him with a steely glare. "Have a good day now, won't you?"

Jackson let out his breath as the diminutive Mrs. Morgan turned on her heel and went back into the house.

Adam shook his head. "Maybe not the wisest thing to say, Dad."

Mr. Miller snorted. "Somebody had to."

"She kept the ranch going all by herself for years before her grandkids came back. If she didn't believe in a family legacy, she wouldn't have done that, would she?"

"Funny way of showing it, letting complete strangers prance around the place pretending to be cowboys," his dad muttered.

"Those guests pay the bills, have some fun, and learn something important about the history of California," Jackson couldn't help butting in. "The ranch also does weddings, which seems a fine way of sharing the beauty of this place with people who would never get to experience it otherwise."

Mr. Miller stared at Jackson. "Who asked you?"

"No one, sir." Jackson met his gaze.

"And no one asked you either, Dad, so let it go, okay?" Adam patted his father's lean shoulder. "This isn't the time to be getting into it. We're here to help our neighbors."

Mr. Miller went off to speak to a group of older men, leaving Adam and Jackson facing each other. Adam grimaced.

"My dad has a big mouth."

"So do I."

"I noticed." Adam looked Jackson up and down. He rarely smiled, and his height and bulk made him appear quite intimidating. "I'm surprised Daisy puts up with you."

"Me too." Jackson kept talking. "Is she going to the meeting tonight?"

"I think so. She's involved in some businessperson's alliance in town, and they always show up. Didn't she mention it?"

"She might have, but I've probably forgotten," Jackson said hastily. "I'll check in with her later, to see if she wants to go with me and hang out afterward."

Adam tipped his hat. "You do that."

Jackson went to find Cauy, who was canoodling with Rachel Morgan and wasn't terribly pleased to see his brother. Roy, the Morgan Ranch foreman, who was as old as dirt, stood on the top step of the ranch house and called everyone to attention.

"Okay! Thanks to everyone who turned up; we owe you one. There's a list posted right outside the new barn. We're going to ask you to choose a team where you think you can be the most useful. If you can do everything, then pick a team that needs the most help."

Everybody laughed, and Roy continued.

"We'll be serving lunch at noon, so stick around, and thanks again."

It was hard to miss the new barn, towering over the original wooden structure built over a hundred years before by the first member of the Morgan family to settle in the valley. Jackson wasn't sure what he was going to help with, seeing as his skill set wasn't ranch-centric, but he was willing to do anything, which had to count for something.

"Hey." BB Morgan, a retired Marine and all-around badass, nodded to Jackson. "What's up?"

"Nothing much." Jackson fell into step beside the second-oldest Morgan brother. "I was just trying to work out where I could help."

BB looked him up and down. "Are you scared of heights?"

"Dude, I was in the air force," Jackson countered.

"A chair warrior; yeah, I know all about you guys." BB winked. "I need someone to help me with the interior lighting setup."

"I could do that."

"Great." BB slapped him on the back. "I'll just get my tool belt."

"Are you sure you're okay?" Cauy asked again as he glanced over at Jackson while they drove into town. They'd worked all day at the Morgans', only stopping for lunch and the occasional hit of coffee until the barn was functional.

"I'm good." Jackson blinked hard. "I just stared at too many lights today."

"And hit your head on a couple of beams," Cauy reminded him.

"Yeah, that too." Jackson rubbed his temple. "But I didn't electrocute myself or fall off the ladder, so I'm calling it a win."

He'd worked with BB and a qualified electrician, stringing up the wiring and lighting inside the huge barn. He'd enjoyed the challenge, but he had a terrible headache.

"Can you drop me off at Daisy's?" Jackson asked.

"You don't want to get something to eat first?" Cauy turned onto Main Street. "I was looking forward to a burger and fries at the Red Dragon."

"Can I check in with Daisy? She might want to join us, or she might tell me to take a hike and find her at the meeting."

"Are you two fighting again?" Cauy chuckled and shook his head.

"Not exactly." Jackson checked that he had his wallet and phone as they approached Daisy's shop. "We just have the occasional misunderstanding."

"Yeah, so I've noticed." Cauy stopped the truck right outside the flower shop. "Like every time you speak to each other. It's a family tradition. I'll park behind the bar. Text me if you're coming, okay?"

"Will do."

Jackson got out of the truck and waved his brother onward. He checked his cell, noticing it was almost five, and hurried to get in the shop before Daisy shut him out.

"Hey!" He smiled as he spotted her behind the counter. She wore a green version of her shop T-shirt, and her hair was up in a ponytail. Somehow, just the sight of her brightened his day. "How's it going?"

"Pretty good." Her gaze swept over him. "Did you fall off your horse and get dragged through a hedge backward?"

Jackson brushed at a patch of mud on his filthy jeans. "Nothing so exciting. I helped out at the Morgans' all day."

"Adam and Dad were there, too. Did you see them?" She came around the counter, the cash from the register in her hand.

"Yeah." Seeing as she didn't seem to object to his presence, he followed her through to the back of the shop and waited while she secured the cash in her safe. "Your dad's a good carpenter."

"He taught Kaiden everything he knows." Daisy straightened and looked at him again. "Are you okay?"

"I've got a headache," Jackson admitted. "Do you have any painkillers?"

"Yes, of course I do." She pointed at the stool near her raised workbench. "Sit down and I'll get you some water to take them with."

Jackson did as she suggested, noticing her laptop was still open. She definitely wasn't logged into her flower shop account, but to a chat room called TRAUMA. His headache was so bad, he couldn't even attempt to read the complex numerical messages scrolling rapidly down the screen.

Daisy came back with two pills in her hand and a mug of water. "Here you go."

"Thanks." While he took his medicine, she deftly shut down her laptop. "Is that for your other job?"

"It might be." She faced him.

"Looked technical."

"Do you really want to go there right now?" She raised an eyebrow.

"Nope." Jackson took off his hat and blew the dust from it. "I'm just glad you let me in the door."

She made a face. "I can't really see you tonight. I have to go to a meeting."

"It's okay. Cauy asked me to go as well."

"Why?"

"Because we're ranchers in Morgan Valley." He frowned at her. "Your brothers are going to be there, too."

"Which ones?"

"Don't you know?"

She shrugged. "I keep out of ranch business as much as I can."

"Why's that?" Jackson asked as he waited for the pills to work on his thumping head.

"Too many cooks already." She offered him a smile. "I love the ranch, but I wouldn't want the responsibility of running it."

"I think your dad said Adam and Kaiden were going."

"Makes sense. Adam manages every aspect of the ranch and Kaiden's job as a carpenter spans both the town and the ranch."

Jackson's cell buzzed. He took it out of his back pocket and checked the text from Cauy.

Are you coming? Am dying of starvation over here.

"Cauy wants to know if I'm joining him at the Red Dragon," Jackson said. "Do you want to come with me and get something to eat before the meeting?"

Daisy nibbled her lip, and Jackson remembered he hadn't kissed her yet.

"I was planning on eating the sandwich left over from my lunch, but hot food does sound better."

"Then come with me." Jackson caught her hand and gently brought her to stand within the circle of his arms. "I'll pay."

"Cool, I'll have steak, then."

He kissed her mouth. "You don't eat steak."

"I might if you're paying for it, with caviar on the side and a bucket of champagne."

"Caviar?" He breathed against her lips before delving

inside her mouth to get a real taste of her. "Don't think they have that at the bar."

"Then you'll have to owe me." Daisy nipped his lip, making him instantly hard.

"I'm happy to pay my debts after the meeting."

"Good." She eased out of his arms. "I'll just lock up."

Chapter Nine

Daisy found a seat in the same row as her brothers and a whole load of Morgans. Jackson and Cauy filed in behind her. The community hall was packed, but the atmosphere was friendly, with locals, ranchers, and business owners catching up with one another.

At the front of the room was a table facing the crowd occupied by Chase Morgan, who was of a similar age to Adam; Ted Baker, who ran the one and only gas station in town; and Mrs. Hayes, who operated the Historic Hayes Hotel, which had once been the town's saloon and brothel. Chase was staring down at his laptop, his fingers flying over the keyboard until an agenda flashed up on the whiteboard against the wall.

Jackson nudged Daisy and handed her a box of cookies. "Mrs. Morgan said to help ourselves."

Daisy took a white chocolate and cranberry cookie, Cauy declined, and Jackson took two chocolate chip before passing the tin back up the row.

BB Morgan leaned across Daisy to address Jackson. "Hey, Ruth wants to know how Amy and your mom are doing?"

"They're both great," Jackson said. "Amy's working at

a hospital close to where Mom lives now, so she sees her quite often."

"Cool." BB nodded and turned away to repeat the information up the line to his grandmother.

"What's Amy doing now?" Daisy asked as she chewed her cookie.

"She's a pediatric nurse."

"Wow. Good for her."

"Yeah, she's awesome," Jackson agreed. "Cauy and I are trying to get her to come out here for Christmas with Mom, but she's not sure she can get the time off."

Chase stood and cleared his throat. "Let's get started, shall we? There's a lot to get through tonight." He pointed behind him. "The agenda's here, and there'll be plenty of time afterward to hear everyone's opinion."

Daisy doubted that, unless they stayed until midnight. There were a lot of people with "opinions" in Morgantown.

"First up, did you all read the copy of the minutes of the last meeting I sent out?" Chase asked.

Everyone nodded. Daisy noticed a few guilty faces, or maybe that was just her own guilt calling to her for not bothering to read them.

"If you didn't get to it, there are printed copies at the end of each row if you want to pass them around." Chase waited as several people handed out papers. "We didn't have much to talk about last time, so it's a quick read." After a few minutes, he checked the time. "Anyone got any comments?"

No one spoke up, and Chase looked around the room. "So can we have a resolution to accept the minutes of the last meeting and a seconder?"

The ayes came thick and fast, and Chase moved on.

"Okay, now to item one. The county board has finally allowed us to push forward with the matter of closing Main Street to traffic by constructing a bypass around the historic center of the town. Unfortunately, it's got to go up to state level." Everyone groaned. "We'll be taking our case to Sacramento next month. If anyone wants to be involved with this issue, please come talk to me after the meeting."

A hand went up, and Chase paused. "Yes, Dev?"

"Did you complete the study about the effect on the town's businesses?" Dev Patel, who was an architect and the current president of the town business owners' organization, stood up.

"Yes, and I have a copy for you right here. Eliminating the traffic should have a positive effect on sales and the overall tourist experience, meaning people stay longer in town and spend more money."

Dev nodded. "We'd have to make sure there's good signage directing people into town, and great parking as well."

"Exactly, which is why I was hoping you'd be up for heading the Sacramento delegation." Chase grinned at him. "Come speak to me afterward, okay?"

Dev groaned. "I knew I shouldn't have stood up."

He sat down, and Chase moved on to the next item, while Daisy let Jackson hold her hand and rub his thumb over her knuckles. She'd enjoyed having dinner with him and Cauy at the bar and was feeling pleasantly tired and looking forward to her bed. Or maybe Jackson's bed. She couldn't decide.

"Okay, so on to the last item, which I suspect is the reason why a lot of you are here." Chase looked out over the crowd. "I didn't want to get too specific in my agenda, but this is a matter that affects all of us, so it needs to be discussed openly."

He paused to consult his notes.

"I'm not going to name names, but a couple of the ranches

here in the valley might soon be up for sale. Neither of these ranchers *want* to sell their land, but they both have valid reasons why they can no longer keep the land in the family."

Cauy and Jackson sat up straight, as did Adam and Kaiden.

"One of them has been approached by a housing developer," Chase continued.

"Damn . . ." Adam muttered.

"And here's the dilemma." Chase didn't look away. "We've all agreed we need new housing in Morgantown to attract people to work here, and to allow our legacy families to stick around, but no one wants a housing development in their own backyard."

Adam spoke up. "This development: Would it be close to the existing town?"

"Would it make a difference if it was?" Chase asked.

"Yeah, because if it's out in the middle of nowhere, they'd have to build new roads, lay pipes, provide power, and all that other infrastructure stuff, possibly right through other ranchers' land. If it's close to the current town border, it's more doable."

Another of the older local ranchers got to his feet. "The thing is, Adam, once they get a foothold in among the ranches, you invite a whole 'nother load of problems. My cousin used to farm in the East Bay near Dublin, and he had to sell off his ranch after both his neighbors sold to housing developers. Folk started complaining about the smell, about the cows coming into their yards, and the farming equipment making the roads dangerous for their kids . . . and then my cousin couldn't get enough insurance to cover his back, so he sold the whole thing to another developer. A hundred years of history gone under someone's new swimming pool."

There was a moment of silence and a lot of nodding heads.

"I hear you," Chase said. "But we also know that if we can't get hired hands out here or people to work in the hotel or the local businesses, we're on a downward path anyway."

Yvonne waved her hand. "Could we attract the kind of builder we want? Someone who'd be willing to work with us and make sure the development was small and not offensive in any way?"

"I don't know," Chase said. "I'll definitely look into it."

"And make sure any development is close to the infrastructure of the current town and not in the middle of the ranching community," Dev Patel said. "I think I might know some small developers, Chase. I'll get you a list."

Daisy stood to get Chase's attention. "Can we also talk about repurposing some of the vacant buildings in the town itself for housing purposes?"

"Absolutely." Chase looked over at his wife, January, who was walking back and forth with their grizzling baby, who appeared to be teething. "January was talking about that this morning. The historical society is okay if the exterior of any repurposed historic building is maintained." Chase nodded at Dev. "Which happens to be our local architect's specialty."

Dev groaned. "Lucky old me."

"So it comes down to money." Daisy looked back at Chase.

He nodded. "And what the county and state will allow us to do."

Everyone groaned again. Ranchers weren't big fans of government legislation and restrictions.

"I do have news of a couple of grants we've been offered,

which will help with the refurbishment costs and low-cost housing." Chase grinned at everyone.

"Yeah?" Roy spoke up. "Big ones?"

Daisy concealed a chuckle. Trust Roy to get to the point.

"Big enough." Chase checked his notes again. "One from the Howatch Foundation, and—"

"Who are those guys?" Ted Baker asked.

Yvonne waved a hand in the air again. "My fiancé Rio's father's charitable trust. Ruth talked him into it when he was in Morgantown last year."

"Awesome!" Ted high-fived Yvonne and smiled at Ruth Morgan.

"And the other is from Give Me a Leg Up." Chase carried on speaking. "We'll be concentrating our efforts on the refurbishing of local buildings for apartments in town, and on Morgan Ranch land, while the Howatch money will be used for a potentially bigger housing development."

"Could you use the Howatch money to buy the two ranches that are up for sale and keep the land safe from any development?" Adam asked.

"The Howatch grant isn't really for the purchase of land but for the development of a housing community. We can check back with the foundation and make sure of that," Chase said. "We need houses, Adam."

"But purchasing one of these ranches might offer us the opportunity to make that happen before a big home builder comes in and destroys the landscape," Adam argued.

Daisy glanced over at her brother. He was fiercely protective of the family ranch and the valley, and any change wouldn't sit well with him.

"I'm not disagreeing with you, Adam," Chase said. "I'm just not sure I can make that happen."

"Could the rancher concerned donate the land to the town?" Daisy asked.

"And live on what for the rest of his life?" Adam asked.

Daisy ignored her brother and continued speaking. "Or what about a land swap, or a guaranteed residence in town cost-free for life in exchange for a slice of the ranch?"

Chase typed away on his keyboard. "That's not a bad idea, Daisy. I'll check into the legal issues and let you know where we stand on that."

"What's the time frame on these sales, Chase?" Adam asked.

"Sooner rather than later, I suspect." Chase grimaced. "So we'd better have a plan in place as soon as possible."

Chase ended the meeting and was soon surrounded by a group of people while his grandma Ruth dispensed coffee, cookies, and goodwill to her neighbors.

Adam shifted restlessly in his seat. "I don't like any of this."

"I knew you were going to say that." Daisy patted his rigid shoulder.

"Why can't they leave this place alone?"

"'They'?" Daisy squeezed his arm. "You know we need hands for the ranch; you've been complaining about that for the last two years. Finding them housing would help us out, too."

"Yeah, I know that, but—"

Kaiden elbowed his big brother. "Any idea which ranches Chase is talking about? I was wondering whether one of them was Louisa's family's. Did they mention it to you, Adam?"

Daisy tensed as Adam's face went blank, but Kaiden kept talking.

"Louisa was their only child, right? Maybe they haven't been able to find anyone to pass the ranch down to."

"Excuse me." Adam abruptly got to his feet, pushed past Daisy and Jackson, and headed for the door.

"What did I say?" Kaiden asked.

"You mentioned Louisa, you big dope." Daisy glared at him.

"Daisy, she died years ago, I can barely remember her, and it's stupid the way no one speaks her name around Adam," Kaiden protested. "If we talked about her more, maybe Adam would get over her and start getting on with his life."

Despite his easygoing manner, Kaiden had all the frankness of their father. Daisy was just glad he hadn't said the words to Adam's face.

"He's got to come to terms with it in his own way, and in his own time," Daisy reminded her brother. "So let it be for the moment, will you?"

Kaiden shrugged. "Sure, seeing as he's probably gone haring off to ask the Cortez family if they're selling up and won't be coming back." He sighed. "Which means I'll have to hitch a lift home with you, sis."

Daisy glanced back at Jackson, who didn't look too happy with that idea.

"How about you take my truck and Jackson can bring me home?" Daisy suggested.

"Sure." Kaiden held out his hand for her keys. He was a good and careful driver, so Daisy wasn't worried about what he'd do to her truck. "I'll tell Dad you'll be back later."

He strode off whistling, leaving Daisy with Jackson, as Cauy had gone to talk to Ruth Morgan.

"I should have checked. Are you okay with taking me home?" Daisy asked him.

"Absolutely—except I came with Cauy."

Daisy gawped at him. "I didn't think."

He grinned at her. "It's not a problem. We'll just have to restrain ourselves until we get behind my locked bedroom door."

Not for the first time, Daisy appreciated his practical way of dealing with potential problems. "I can wait."

"Good." He took her hand and placed a kiss on her palm. "I'm not sure I can, but I'll do my best."

Daisy wriggled on her chair, aware she was blushing. "What do you think about all this?"

"Getting you into bed?"

"*No*, doofus, the ranch, and the housing, and all that stuff," Daisy said, eager to move the subject away from her very interested libido.

"I'm torn," he admitted. "I get that we need housing, but I also don't want to see the valley disappearing below a sea of houses. How about you?"

"I feel the same, but Adam wants to keep everything exactly as it is." Daisy sighed.

"Do you think Kaiden is right about the Cortez place?" Jackson asked. "Adam married their daughter, right?"

"Yes, when they were barely out of school. Louisa died three years later."

"That must have been tough on both of them. I can't even imagine . . ." Jackson's voice tailed off, and he shook his head. "I suppose if Louisa had survived, she and Adam might have continued to run the Cortez ranch or extended it into the Miller place."

"I suppose so, although the lands don't touch on any of our property lines. They're much closer to town."

"Could your father afford to buy the Cortez family out?"

"No." Daisy didn't even need to think about it. "We don't have that kind of money sitting around. We don't even know if it's the Cortez place that's up for sale anyway."

"It *is* near the town border," Jackson reminded her. "And they definitely don't have any sons to run it."

"Or daughters."

"True." He studied her. "If you were the only kid and you'd been left a ranch, would you keep it?"

"I don't know what I'd do," she confessed. "I'd do my best to save it, but I'm not sure if I'd want to run it all by myself."

"Ruth Morgan did."

"Well, she's amazing, and she had Roy beside her all the way," Daisy said. "I know you and Cauy decided to come back and save your ranch, but surely with two of you owning it that was easier?"

"Hardly." The twinkle in his eyes disappeared. "I don't own a thing. Dad left it to Cauy, remember?"

"Which makes no sense at all." Daisy watched him carefully. "That must have hurt."

"When it originally went down, I was still in the air force and wasn't considering leaving at that point, so I kind of accepted it." He shrugged. "I figured it was better if one of us took it on, and if Cauy was up for it—which wasn't a given—I would support him."

"And do you still feel that way?" Daisy asked.

"I'm not sure." His ragged smile made her catch her breath. "Since coming back to live here, I've remembered how much I love it, and how when Cauy left, I dreamed of carrying on the fine tradition of family ranching. It was stupid of me, seeing Cauy was the eldest."

"Ranchers don't always leave the ranch to their eldest son," Daisy pointed out. "In fact, I don't think my dad has even made a will yet, despite my nagging. He fondly imagines the six of us will just work it out ourselves, which might open up a whole 'nother can of worms."

"I suppose at least my father made a will." Jackson looked over to where Cauy was deep in conversation with Ruth Morgan. "Cauy offered to give me half of the place."

"And what did you say?"

"I refused."

"*Why*?" Daisy asked.

"Because it didn't sit right with me. I can't pay him back." His mouth set in a familiar hard line Daisy was coming to recognize. "If my dad had wanted me to have part ownership of the ranch, he would've written me into that will."

"But your brother is trying to do the right thing." Daisy persisted, even though she knew she was on dangerous ground.

"Yeah, I know. That still doesn't mean I have to go along with it."

Daisy sighed. "So you're going to be stubborn and reject the thing you want."

"I suppose I am."

"You know that's stupid, don't you?" Daisy met his gaze.

"Yeah." He smiled at her.

"Men," Daisy muttered. "You're as stubborn as my brothers."

"Like you're not?" Jackson poked her in the arm. "You're currently pretending to date me rather than admit to your family that you have a second job."

"That has nothing to do with being stubborn," Daisy argued. "It's to stop them being hurt or worrying about me." She poked him back. "And how come we're suddenly talking about me again?"

"Because you're easy to distract?" Jackson got to his feet and held out his hand. "Come on, let's go find Cauy so we can get back home."

Daisy allowed him to pull her upright and followed him across the still-crowded hall to where Ruth was dispensing coffee. If her current start-up received a new round of investment and the company went public, she might be in a position to buy up the whole of Morgan Valley. Unfortunately, that probably wasn't going to happen before the ranches were sold.

She stared at the back of Jackson's head. Why wouldn't he let his brother give him half the ranch? She was fairly certain Cauy, who loved his brother, had genuinely meant the offer. Was it simply hurt pride that stopped Jackson from accepting it? It must have stung, seeing as Cauy wasn't even Mark Lymond's natural son. If Mark had left it to Jackson, he would probably have been fine about letting Cauy work the ranch, so why not take part ownership?

Perhaps Jackson didn't really mean to stick around. The thought of that upset her more than she'd anticipated. Had he cheerfully gone along with her subterfuge knowing he'd be gone? And did that make it better or worse?

She touched his arm, and he turned and bent his head to listen to her.

"What's up?"

"You do want to stay in Morgan Valley, don't you?"

"Yeah. What made you think I didn't?"

"Well, not accepting half ownership of the family ranch might be considered a great big honking clue," Daisy said.

"I want my own place."

Daisy just about resisted rolling her eyes. He turned down half a ranch and now thought he could buy another one. "How do you plan on affording that?"

He grinned at her. "Find a rich partner?"

"Chase Morgan's already taken," Daisy retorted. "And don't look at me."

"Wait—you're not a tech billionaire in hiding?"

"Not quite." Daisy shoved him hard toward Cauy. "I thought we were going."

* * *

Jackson considered sitting in the back seat with Daisy on the way back to the ranch so he could cuddle her. She put a stop to his plans by climbing into the passenger seat next to Cauy and leaving him on his lonesome. She chatted away with Cauy about the implications of the meeting, speculating who the two ranchers who wanted to sell might be, and finding a lot to agree on. He was glad they got along because Cauy wasn't great at coming forward, and he took a while to warm up to people.

Cauy let Grace and the puppies out into the yard and put on the coffee before turning to Jackson. "I'm going to call Rachel, and then I'm going to watch a movie in my room with my headphones on."

"Got it." Jackson nodded to his brother. "I'll try not to disturb you when I take Daisy home."

"I'd prefer it if you didn't disturb me *before* she leaves," Cauy muttered as he picked up his coffee. Daisy had gone to the bathroom, so they were alone.

"*What*? I was planning on running through the house naked and swinging from the lights. Way to ruin my night, bro." Jackson grinned at his brother's revolted expression. "We'll keep it down, I promise."

"You do that." Cauy smiled as Daisy came into the kitchen. "Night, Daisy. See you in the morning, Jackson."

"Night, Cauy." She waited until he went through the door before she spoke again. "If you want to run around naked, go for it, but don't expect me to join in."

Jackson took her hand and drew her close. "You're as bad as Cauy."

"Then I'm in good company." She looked over at the counter. "Is that coffee?"

"Yeah. Do you want to bring some through with you?" Jackson asked.

"To where?"

"My bedroom." He raised his eyebrows and waggled them. "If that's okay with you of course."

"Don't you have to check the barn?"

"Dammit, yes." Jackson groaned. "And get the dogs and chickens in."

She set down the two mugs. "I'll help. It won't take long."

"Long enough for you to fall asleep on me," Jackson complained as he headed for the mudroom.

"If I drink the coffee, I'll be good for at least another three hours." She smacked him on the rear as he went out of the door, and he laughed.

They both put their coats and boots back on and trekked out to the barn. The Morgan Ranch horses were still there but would be leaving in the next week or so. Jackson would miss them. He had plans to coax Cauy into buying a few horses of their own.

He took Daisy's hand, smiling as he realized she'd brought her coffee with her. For a woman who asked him all the awkward questions he'd rather avoid, she was adorable.

"If you are in tech," Jackson asked carefully, "do you get paid well?"

"Are you trying to find out how rich I am?" Daisy teased.

"I might be." Jackson shrugged. "You know what I'm like."

"Nosy as hell."

"Yup, that's me." He waited to see what she'd say next.

"I suppose it's a valid question, seeing as you've worked out what I do." She hesitated. "But I don't earn a lot right now, and the flower shop barely breaks even, so I don't have a lot of spare cash hanging around." She put down her mug, leaned against the wall, and faced him. "The thing is . . . five years ago I was in a start-up that got bought out."

"And?" Jackson prompted her.

"Put it this way: We worked for years to produce our software, took too much outside funding, and ended up with almost nothing when the company finally went public."

"Like those Facebook guys?"

"A bit like that, but no one came along and decided to compensate us afterward." She sighed. "All that work gone, all those long hours, and making do, and stress. It almost destroyed me."

"Is that why you came home?"

She nodded. "I came back when my obligation to help the new company ended."

"You mean you had to keep on working there even when you'd got nothing out of it?" Jackson whistled. "That must have sucked."

"It did." She scuffed her boot against the cobbled floor. "It almost broke me."

He reached out and cupped her chin. "Then you made a good decision to come home, didn't you?"

She smiled up at him and rubbed her cheek against his palm. "It certainly improved my life for the better. Just being around people with a different set of values—who care about one another and not just about money—made a huge difference to my life."

"I bet."

He wanted to ask her what had drawn her back to tech, but she turned away as one of Grace's puppies came galloping up to her.

"Hey, little buddy." She picked up the puppy. "Are you ready to go back inside? Where's your momma?"

Jackson made sure all the stalls were secure and the horses were okay before helping Daisy gather up Grace's family and take them into the kitchen. Once they'd settled the dogs, he washed up, took her hand, and walked her down the hallway to his bedroom.

"Do you want to use the bathroom?" Jackson murmured, aware that Cauy's door was at the end of the hallway.

"Sure."

He went inside and slowly took off his clothes, placing them neatly on the chair. One of the things Cauy had done since taking over the ranch was replace the heating system, and Jackson was really grateful for that. He lay on his bed, his gaze fixed on the door until Daisy came in and locked it behind her.

Holding his gaze, she stepped out of her clothes and joined him on the bed, her long hair tickling his skin as she crawled all over him.

"I missed you," Jackson murmured.

"When I was in the bathroom?" She gently nibbled his nose. "Or just generally?"

"And you say I'm the one who asks silly questions." He sat up against the headboard as she straddled his lap. "I think about you a lot." He cupped her breast. "I wish—"

He stopped talking before he said something that would make her skittish. Just because she'd confided in him didn't mean the rules of their relationship had changed.

"You wish what?" Daisy placed her hands on his shoulders, bringing her nipples right up against his chest. He forgot how to pronounce words, which was probably a good thing.

He curved a hand over her hip, making her tremble, and cupped her mound. "Kiss me?"

She obliged, rocking into his touch as she opened to his questing fingers like a sultry flower. He was a very visual guy and he liked being underneath Daisy in all her naked beauty. She breathed his name against his lips, and he blindly reached into the drawer beside his bed for protection.

She was here, she was still talking to him, and they were about to have fantastic sex. If he were a clever man, he'd shut his mouth and enjoy it.

Brimming with sexual satisfaction, Daisy tiptoed into the kitchen at home, only to discover Adam sitting at the table, watching the door. As he was sitting in total darkness, she almost didn't see him until it was too late.

"Oh my gawd!" She pressed a hand to her chest. "I wasn't expecting a welcome-home party."

He didn't smile, and she walked over to him.

"Is something wrong?" He shook his head as she studied him. "Are you okay?"

"Will you sit down a moment?" Adam gestured at the seat opposite him.

Daisy sat. "If this is about me and Jackson—"

"It's not." He shoved a hand through his dark, cropped hair. "I just wanted to ask you something."

A thousand guilty thoughts immediately clouded her brain, and she tried to look innocent. Had he found out about her new job? Was he going to call her out on it?

Adam looked down at the table, spreading his fingers wide over the knotted pine surface. "Do you have the money to buy out the Cortez ranch?"

His question was so unexpected, she gaped at him. "*What*?"

"You were in tech. You created a successful business. I wondered if you could somehow lend me the money to buy the ranch. I'd pay you back as soon as I could make it profitable. With interest of course," Adam said.

"Hang on." Daisy frantically tried to gather her thoughts. "Number one, how would Dad manage if you left this ranch to take over the Cortez place?"

"He has five sons, Daisy. He'd be fine, you know he would."

"But you *love* this place."

He shrugged. "Moving down the road wouldn't stop me loving it or the people inside it."

"So they really are planning on selling?" Daisy asked.

"Yeah. I went and asked them. Don't tell anyone else. They don't want to deal with all the bad vibes."

"I think most people are going to work it out soon," Daisy said. "There aren't that many ranches in this valley."

"They said they'd sell it to me right now if I could find the money," Adam said. "They'd rather it was kept in the family."

"They could leave it to you in their will," Daisy suggested.

"They already have, but Carlos has cancer and they need the money now." Adam grimaced. "It's treatable, but they want to move somewhere close to a big hospital so he can get the best treatment possible. That's way more important than me inheriting the place."

"Oh God. I'm so sorry." Daisy reached out and covered his hand with her own. "Poor Carlos."

"So is there any way you can help me out here, sis?" Adam asked gently, curling his fingers around hers.

Daisy stared blindly down at their joined hands. All the money she'd salvaged from the first fiasco had gone into financing the new start-up. . . . Guilt hit her hard.

"I don't have that kind of money right now, Adam." She forced herself to meet his gaze. "If I did, I'd give it to you in a heartbeat."

"It's okay." A shudder ran through him, but he nodded and attempted a smile. "I just hope you don't hold it against me that I asked."

"How could I possibly do that?" she whispered, her eyes filling with tears. "You're my *brother*."

"And you're my little sister." He brought up their joined hands and kissed her knuckles. "It's all good." He released her and got to his feet. "Night, sis. Sleep tight."

She remained at the table as he left the kitchen, his broad shoulders bowed like an old man's. There was a lot she wanted to say to him, but she felt too guilty to attempt it right now. Could she get a loan against her current income? But if she did that, she'd have to tell her family she'd been deceiving them for months, and explain where her savings had really gone.

If the new start-up paid off, she might be in a position to help him enormously and would have no hesitation in doing so, but that wasn't happening right now. By the time she accumulated some excess income, the Cortez ranch might be covered in houses, and Adam would've lost his last link with his wife's family.

Chapter Ten

So you can come out on the Wednesday?

Ian typed the question while Daisy mentally cursed. With all the worry about the Cortez ranch, she'd forgotten all about her promise to go to Silicon Valley and meet with the venture capitalists.

I'll get back to you about that in an hour, okay? Daisy responded, grabbing her purse and setting off at a run toward Yvonne's before Ian could reply. She had a feeling her vague answer wouldn't fill him with confidence.

Nancy was waiting for her in the coffee shop and waved from the table she'd already occupied.

"Hey." Daisy smiled at her. "Did you order already?"

"Nope, I waited for you." Nancy's hair was green today, with yellow stripes. "You're only five minutes late."

Lizzie came up with her notepad at the ready and looked expectantly at them. "Hey, ladies. What are you having?"

"Iced tea and something fattening, please," Daisy answered.

"Care to be more specific?" Lizzie waited, her pencil poised over the pad.

"Cheese," Daisy said. "Melting everywhere."

"I can get you a tuna melt and fries, or grilled cheese, or—"

"Tuna melt," Daisy agreed. "That sounds awesome."

"I'll have the same," Nancy said. "Including the iced tea."

"Got it." Lizzie half-turned away and then paused. "Is it true the Cortez family are selling their ranch?"

Daisy tried to look noncommittal as Nancy answered Lizzie. "I've no idea, but if it is them, I suppose it would make sense."

Lizzie grimaced. "Is Adam okay about it, Daisy?"

Surprised by her friend's concern for her brother, Daisy attempted an answer. "I don't think he'd be pleased if it was true."

"He wouldn't be." Lizzie sighed. "I can't imagine the Cortez family not being around anymore. They've been so kind to me and Roman."

She nodded and headed off toward the kitchen as Nancy set her cell phone on the table. "Jay said he might need some help if the delivery arrives early, so I promised to keep an eye on my messages."

"No wonder you win employee of the year every time." Daisy grinned at her friend.

"Yeah, that's me. An asset to any business." Nancy paused. "Or is that just an ass? I can never remember which one makes me prouder." She checked her texts. "So how's it going with lover boy?"

"Good. I think," Daisy said.

"You think?" Nancy frowned at her. "Girl, I turned him down for you. I hope you're getting value for money out of him."

"You would never have gone out with him in the first place," Daisy protested, laughing. "He's not your type."

"I don't have a type," Nancy said. "That would require

me making an effort to get to know a guy well enough to work out what I didn't like."

"True," Daisy acknowledged. "But you don't pick guys who intend to hang around in Morgantown, do you?"

"Because I'm not interested in settling down yet," Nancy said firmly. "I'm enjoying my life far too much."

As Nancy had started life after high school delving into drugs, Daisy wasn't going to argue with her optimistic outlook now. She knew how hard it had been for her friend to get her life back together and was immensely proud of her.

"Anyway, is Jackson treating you right?" Nancy winked at Daisy. "In all departments?"

"Yes, he is." Daisy knew she was blushing. "He's very . . . competent."

"And nice and upfront."

"He certainly likes to speak his mind," Daisy agreed. "Sometimes *too* much, but I'm used to dealing with nerds, so I know all about lack of social skills."

Lizzie brought their drinks. Daisy stuck a straw in her glass, and stirred in some sugar and a slice of lemon.

"Nancy, if I asked you to keep a secret for me, would you do it?"

Her friend blinked at the sudden change of subject but nodded anyway. "Sure. What's up?"

"I've been doing some IT work in Silicon Valley. I need someone to cover my shop for me for a few days next week while I go out there."

Nancy studied her. "I don't know if you've noticed, but you do have quite a few brothers who could possibly step in for you."

"I want them to know as little as possible about this whole trip," Daisy said firmly. "Because if I start involving them, they'll have questions."

"Why's that?"

"Because they *don't* know I'm still working in the field where I ended up with massive burnout and came home in pieces. I promised them I'd never go back."

"Ah, I hear you." Nancy frowned. "I don't have a lot of free time, but I'm sure between me, Sonali, and Bella, we could keep the doors of the florist's open."

"I'm going to ask Dell because he actually knows how to arrange flowers, but he can't do everything. It will only be for four days, and I can deal with the online orders. Dell only has to make up the flowers," Daisy reassured her friend. "The shop is closed on Sunday."

"How are you going to explain your absence to your family if you aren't going to tell them the truth?"

"I'll tell them I have to go to a craft convention or speak to my suppliers."

"Do you think they'll buy it?" Nancy looked skeptical.

"I'm not sure," Daisy confessed. "I'm not a good liar, and I hate having to do it."

"That's why I asked." Nancy paused as Lizzie delivered their food. "Why don't you get Jackson to take you on a romantic weekend away? Then you could fit your meetings in around that."

Daisy considered that notion. "I don't want to give Jackson ideas, though."

"Ideas about what?"

"That our relationship is the real thing."

Nancy rolled her eyes. "Are you still in that mode? I thought you would've gotten over yourself by now."

"I don't want to raise unrealistic expectations," Daisy repeated.

"Why not, Daiz?" Nancy held her gaze. "I know there was that thing with Brody when you were in college, but you can't let it hold you back forever."

"That *is* the thing, though," Daisy said. "What I had was

so perfect, I want that *again*, and I'm not prepared to settle for anything less."

"I don't think the world works like that, Daisy," Nancy said gently. "And you aren't the same person."

"I get that." Daisy smiled at her friend. "But I'm not going to fake anything with Jackson."

Not that he'd let her. He'd call her out in a second. But asking him to go with her to San Francisco and telling him why she needed his help wasn't a bad idea at all . . .

"Hey." Jackson walked over to where Blue Morgan had parked his truck in front of the house. It was another bright, clear morning, when the air was so cold it almost hurt to breathe. "What brings you out here, BB?"

"I came to do a final check on our horses before we work out how to get them back to our new barn." Blue got out his phone. "If that's okay with you."

"Cauy's in town, but I don't think he'd have a problem with it." Jackson walked with Blue over to the barn. "We'll miss having your horses here."

"But you'll be able to get some more of your own," Blue quipped back. "I bet you're short now that you've gotten the ranch back on its feet."

"We've got to get some more cattle in first." Jackson grinned. "Nothing for the hands to chase otherwise."

"Talk to Roy. He knows all the best places to find good stock," Blue advised as he took a count and then a more detailed note about each horse.

Jackson followed along behind, answering BB's rapid-fire questions. He'd gotten to know all the horses over the past few months, and he really would miss them.

When BB finished up, Jackson politely asked him in for some coffee, and was surprised when BB agreed. The retired marine wasn't known for his sociability, but for his ability to get things done in the most efficient manner possible.

"Nice place," BB said as he walked into the kitchen and bent to pat Grace. "Takes me right back to the eighties."

"Yeah. It definitely needs a bit of work." Jackson re-filled the coffeepot and set the filter working. Cauy pre-ferred the fancy one-cup machine, but Jackson liked to go back for a refill without all the fussing around.

BB sat at the table, his back to the wall and his sharp gaze taking in every detail. Having been around military personnel for ten years and knowing them intimately, Jackson didn't take his guest's steely alertness personally.

"Are you busy this evening?" BB asked as he sipped his coffee. He took it black, just like Jackson did.

"I don't think I've got anything planned; why?" Jackson sat opposite him.

"I'd like to talk to you and Jay Williams about an idea of mine."

"You can't tell me right now?"

"I could, but then I'd just have to repeat myself to Jay. I'd rather do it over a beer, if that's okay with you." BB held his gaze.

"Sure. What time?"

"Eight?"

"Sounds good." Jackson sipped his coffee. "Now, tell me when you plan to ship the horses out, because I'll need to make sure we have all hands on deck."

"Dad . . ." Daisy turned to her father, who was still mut-tering away to himself. "Dr. Tio didn't tell you to give up everything, just to moderate your drinking and watch your cholesterol."

"Young whippersnapper."

She'd taken her dad to the new doctor for his yearly physical because his old physician had retired, and he wasn't too happy. He was rarely happy, so Daisy wasn't too concerned.

"Is that the new pizza place Kaiden was talking about?"

Daisy stopped again and walked back to where her father had come to a complete standstill.

"*Pizza*? Dad, did you listen to anything Dr. Tio just said?"

"I listened. I just don't happen to agree with him. The way I see it, these fools keep changing their minds about what's good for you, so I'm going to carry on eating what I like." Her dad nodded. "You're going to die of something, Daisy. You might as well enjoy it while you can."

She sighed, but the siren smells of pizza sauce and bubbling cheese were calling to her as well, and she had just put in a very trying morning with her father . . .

"Okay, we'll have lunch here if you like. Do you want to sit outside? It's such a nice day."

"Sure." He handed over his wallet. "I'm buying."

Daisy grinned at him. "I could run off now and leave you destitute."

"Be my guest. Wouldn't be the first time that's happened to me. There's twenty bucks in there. You won't get far on that." He perused the menu and then looked up at her. "A slice with everything on it and a bottle of water, which will make your Dr. Tio happy."

Daisy went inside, placed their order, and came out to join her father in the sunshine. The new medical center building was at the far end of Main Street, near Ted Baker's gas station and garage. It had a nice view back toward the historic buildings in town, the new fountain celebrating the founders of the town, and the open countryside.

Her dad pointed at the distant fields. "If the Cortez ranch sells to those developers, you won't see anything but houses over there."

"I know." Daisy grimaced. "Adam is really cut up about it."

He snorted. "That boy needs to get over himself. He can't fix what's already been broken."

"That's a bit harsh, Dad," Daisy said. "He can't help how he feels, can he?"

"Time for him to move on. I didn't sit around complaining when your mother up and left, did I?"

"I don't remember much about it," Daisy confessed. "I was only five at the time. I just cried myself to sleep every night worrying about where she was."

Actually, she remembered the first morning very vividly. Waking up late and wandering into the kitchen to find her father in a rage, smashing plates and mugs. She'd hidden under the table until Adam found her. He'd helped her get dressed and had taken her to school. When she'd returned home, her mother still wasn't there. When she'd asked about her, Adam told her she'd gone away. Daisy hadn't believed she'd be gone forever.

"I'm sorry." Her father reached out and patted her hand. He'd always been way less hard on her than he was on her brothers. "Leanne shouldn't have left you kids, but she couldn't stand me anymore, and I can't say I blamed her."

Daisy blinked at him. "You can't?"

"I was a bad husband, Daisy. I left her to deal with six kids while I was working the land, drinking at the Red Dragon, or going out to compete in rodeos." His smile was sad. "Sure, at the time I was mad as hell that she left me, but that was over twenty years ago, and I thought I had cause. These days I can see her point of view far more clearly."

Daisy nodded, aware that she'd never really talked to him about her mother because she'd assumed he was still sore about it. She'd eventually stopped asking when her mother would come back because he would get angry, and she'd been afraid he'd leave her as well. He'd always held his grudges close to his chest and rarely apologized for his behavior to anyone. If he could reflect on the past and finally admit fault, it was a lesson for her that people really could change.

"You did a great job bringing us up," Daisy reminded him.

"Didn't have much choice, did I?" He chuckled. "There you all were, wanting to be fed and cared for just like all kids. I was lucky your Auntie Rae came and helped me out until you all got bigger."

"Auntie Rae is awesome," Daisy agreed. "She's coming for Christmas, right?"

"Not sure where else she'd be going."

Daisy stood and pressed her dad's shoulder. "I'll go check on the pizza. I'll be right back."

When she returned, bringing their drinks and napkins, Jackson was sitting at the table chatting to her dad like they were old friends. He wore a navy-blue shirt that did wonders for his eyes, his usual jeans, and cowboy boots.

She smiled at him. "What are you doing here?"

"I came to pick up some lumber for Cauy." He nodded over at her dad, his blue eyes crinkling at the corners. "Mr. Miller was giving me his thoughts about Dr. Tio."

"Oh." Daisy sat down. "He's certainly got a few opinions."

"So I hear."

"Hey, Daisy!" Dell Turner expertly skidded to a halt, upended his skateboard, and came over to the table. "I just wanted you to know I'm good for that long weekend of yours. Nancy says she'll be helping out as well, so there's nothing to worry about."

He grinned at her and then moved off, leaving her exposed to the full glare of her father's unwanted interest.

"You didn't mention you were going anywhere, Daisy."

"I was just about to tell you over lunch," Daisy hedged. "I'm going to San Francisco for a few days."

"To do what?"

"Well—" Daisy glanced desperately over at Jackson. "There's a floral convention on new designs for weddings I've signed up for, and—"

"And the rest of the time she's spending with me." Jackson reached over, took her hand, and smiled at her father. "I swear I'll take good care of her."

"You'd better," her dad said. "And don't let her get involved with any of that tech stuff while you're there. It isn't good for her."

Daisy had a crazy visual of her running up to the Google offices and banging on the glass while Jackson implored her to stop and wasn't sure whether she wanted to laugh or cry.

She spotted Gina coming out of the shop with the pizza and leaped to her feet, making her dad spill his drink. "I'll get it."

She almost wrestled the tray out of Gina's hands and brought it back to the table. "Do you want to share my piece, Jackson?"

With food around, at least her father's attention would be diverted from her love life.

"No, I'd better be on my way." Jackson hesitated as he got to his feet. "Are you up for dinner with me at the Red Dragon after you finish work?"

Seeing as he'd just saved her bacon, she wasn't about to be difficult now.

"Sure! I'd love to do that."

"Great. I'll come pick you up at six." He bent down to kiss her cheek and then tipped his hat to her father. "Have a good day, Mr. Miller."

Daisy kept her head down and munched her pizza, all too aware that her father was still staring at her.

"Things heating up between you and Jackson, then?" he finally asked.

"He's a nice guy, Dad."

"I know that, or else I wouldn't be happy about you going out with him, but that's not what I asked."

"We're taking it slow."

"By going away together?"

Daisy put down her napkin. "The thing is, Dad, in this town there are too many people interrupting us at every moment. By going away, we can get to know each other better and have some *privacy*."

Her pointed attempt to shame him into getting off the subject failed miserably and he kept talking.

"You trust him, then?"

"Of course I do!" Daisy finally met her father's gaze. "He's not going to murder me on a romantic weekend when all my family and half the town know where we're going."

"True." He nodded and returned his attention to his pizza. "He'd probably do it a lot more quietly."

Daisy didn't bother to reply to that. He was her father, and his concern for her was completely natural, as was his plain way of speaking. Not going home directly after finishing work and hanging out with Jackson meant she'd avoid further questioning from all five of her brothers, who would have heard the news from her father. The thought of getting away from Morgantown without *all* her relatives hanging around was becoming more and more enticing . . .

"You owe me one." Jackson looked down at Daisy as they walked along Main Street to the Red Dragon. The sky had turned a reddish brown as the sun dropped down over the backdrop of the Sierra Nevadas.

"I am well aware of that." She smiled at him. "You rocked."

"Thanks." He winked at her. "Now, maybe before we get to the bar, you could tell me what's really going on."

She slowed down outside Yvonne's and turned to face him. She'd gathered her hair up in a messy bun on top of her head. All Jackson could think about was plunging his hands into her hair and kissing the life out of her.

"I need to take care of some business in Palo Alto."

"And you don't mean for your flower shop, correct?"

She bit her lip. "I have to go. I don't want to, but if I don't, the whole project will be in jeopardy."

"Okay. So will you have any time to spend with me over the long weekend?"

"Yes, I will."

"Then we're good." He leaned in and kissed her nose.

"I really don't deserve you, you know," Daisy murmured.

"Yeah, you do." He angled his mouth and kissed her properly. She smelled like the sweet roses she sold in her shop.

"Okay, maybe I do." She smiled at him, and his whole body woke up. "Do we *have* to go to the bar?"

"Yeah." He sighed with regret. "I agreed to meet Blue Morgan and Jay over there for a drink."

"Is that why you asked me to come with you?" She grinned up at him. "You needed a bodyguard?"

"I asked because I thought you might have some explaining to do." He mock-frowned at her.

"I was going to call you this evening and ask for your help," Daisy said. "I just wasn't expecting everything to come out over lunch."

He chuckled and she kissed him, which led to more kissing, until Daisy stepped back, her cheeks flushed and her hair now falling down over her shoulders.

"We really have to stop doing this." Daisy fussed with her hair.

"Why?" Jackson asked. "I like it."

"Because we're in public?"

"I didn't even notice." He smiled at her. "One taste of you and I'm a goner."

Her expression changed and she cupped his cheek. "Don't say things like that."

"Why not?"

"Because we agreed to keep this casual," Daisy reminded him.

"That was casual," Jackson argued back. "I didn't use the L word or anything."

"There is that." Daisy grabbed his hand, and they set off again for the bar. "What does BB Morgan want with you?"

"I have no idea. He went all mysterious on me when I asked and refused to say anything until I met him in the bar with Jay." Jackson reminded himself not to care about the relief on her face when he'd stepped back off the dangerous ledge of romantic commitment. "I'm meeting him at eight, so there's plenty of time for us to get dinner."

He held the door open for her and nodded at Jay Williams, the owner, who was alone behind the bar.

"Evening, Jay. We're going through to eat, okay?"

"Sure. I'll come find you when BB arrives." Jay nodded. "Can I get you something to drink to go with the food?"

"Two beers," Daisy spoke up. "Thanks, Jay."

Jackson took his seat and spent a while studying the menu. He was more attracted to Daisy than ever, but she wanted things to stay casual. How could she even say that when they were already way beyond that? What wasn't he bringing to the table? He hated not being good enough.

"Are you okay?" Daisy asked.

"Yeah, I'm good, thanks." He briefly met her gaze and then looked down at the menu again. "I'm thinking of trying the crab cakes. Have you had them?"

Daisy reached across the table and took his hand. "Are you mad at me?"

"Nope. I'm just wondering what BB wants to talk to me about." Jackson wasn't going to get into a stupid fight he'd already lost when he'd agreed to the terms of their relationship. Maybe when they were away together, he'd get a chance to have that conversation again. Jeez . . . He almost wanted to smack himself. Why couldn't he stop wanting things he could never have? Did he think he was somehow magically going to become acceptable or something?

"Jackson . . ."

He put down the menu. "I'm definitely going to try the crab. How about you?"

Daisy held his gaze, but he didn't let his smile waver, and she eventually looked away. She didn't want to have the discussion any more than he did because he *was* helping her out in a difficult situation after all.

As if she'd been reading his thoughts, she started speaking again. "You don't have to come with me to San Francisco."

"If I don't, your dad will want to know why, and I don't want to have to lie to him," Jackson countered evenly.

"I've got a couple of friends in the Bay Area. I can look them up while you're busy working."

Jay appeared with their beers and took the food order, giving Jackson a welcome break from the awkwardness of keeping his mouth shut. He had no right to feel aggrieved. He'd signed up for this, so he'd better stick it out or give it up.

"I don't like lying to my family," Daisy said quietly after Jay departed. "In fact, I hate it."

"Then why don't you just tell them the truth and get it over with?" Jackson wasn't in the mood for laughing the whole thing off yet.

"Because in a few months' time the project will be completed and I'll be able to move on."

"Move on to what? Something else?"

"No." She held his gaze. "If this works, I'll never have to go back there again."

"I believe you said that before—in fact, you promised your family you wouldn't go back."

"I *know* I did, but this . . ." She hesitated. "Means *everything* to me."

"More than deceiving your family?" *More than any potential relationship with me?* His heart bleated, but at least he didn't say it out loud.

"*Yes.*"

"Why?" Jackson was way beyond being polite and respectful of her boundaries now. "I don't get it."

She took so long to answer, he thought she might up and leave him stranded again.

"It's a very personal project for me, but I believe it will make life better for a lot of people."

"In what way?"

"Medically." She swallowed hard. "If someone I cared a

lot about had access to this kind of technology, he probably wouldn't have died."

"He?"

Daisy huffed out a breath. "Trust you to zoom in on that part. I warn you, Jackson, if you start questioning me *right now*, I'm going to burst into tears and embarrass myself."

"Will you talk to me about it when we're in San Francisco?" Jackson asked.

"Yes." She didn't shy away from his direct question or his gaze. "I promise you."

He sat back and picked up his beer. "Then let's enjoy our dinner and talk about something else."

The trouble was, he still wasn't over it when they joined BB and Jay in the bar. Daisy excused herself to talk to Nancy, and Jay sat down with the two guys at a corner table, where both of his companions could keep their backs to the wall. If BB was a hard man, Jay Williams was even worse. A retired Navy SEAL who had been invalided out after an explosion in Afghanistan, he took no prisoners and never had any trouble in his bar.

"Okay." BB sat forward. "I've been talking to Sam about this as well. She thinks it's a great idea, but she's not interested in camping out under the stars right now."

Sam was engaged to BB's brother HW and had served in the army. She'd met Jay in the rehab hospital after they'd both been injured, and they'd remained good friends.

"Makes sense." Jay nodded. "She's still dealing with a lot of flashbacks and PTSD."

"Aren't we all?" BB muttered as he took a swig of beer.

"Could you explain what you're planning?" Jackson asked. "Because at the moment, I still have no idea what you're talking about."

"I want to add a survival camp kind of thing to the ranch programs," BB said.

"Like boot camp?" Jackson frowned.

"I wish, but no, more taking them out, showing them how to start a fire, build a shelter, that kind of thing—survival skills for after the zombie apocalypse."

"It sounds great, but there's no way I'm crawling around Morgan Ranch with my bad leg," Jay spoke up. "I'm happy to advise and talk it through with you, but I wouldn't be able to actively participate."

"That's pretty much all I'd need from you, Jay." BB nodded. "What about you, Jackson?"

"I was in the air force."

"So?" BB raised an eyebrow. "You must have been through basic training."

"Sure, but—"

"Could you at least help me out until I can get the thing up and running?"

"If you really need me, yeah, of course." Jackson nodded. "I'd love to."

"Great. I'm thinking that if this thing works out, I'll be able to employ some retired military guys to run it for me."

"Nice." Jay finished his beer in one swallow.

"And there's one other thing I think you could help out with, Jackson." BB obviously wasn't done with him yet. "Guided trips."

Jackson perked up. "Like hunting trips?"

"Possibly, but I was also thinking about historical ones, like up to the ghost town, with a campout overnight. Or what January calls environmental trips to see the fauna and flora." He rolled his eyes. "Whatever that means."

"I'd definitely be interested in helping out with those," Jackson said. "I'd have to square it with Cauy, though, because at the moment he needs me on the ranch, but I'm up for that."

"Good." BB nodded, his bright blue eyes gleaming. "I'll even pay you."

Jay snorted. "I should damn well hope so. You guys must be raking it in up at the ranch."

"Most of it goes right back into the old place to stop it falling down, but we're doing okay." BB grinned. "Better than we expected, so I can't complain." He drank his beer and rose to his feet. "I'll be in touch."

Jay gathered up the empty bottles. "Do you want another one, Jackson?"

"No, thanks, I've got to drive home." Jackson looked around to see where Daisy was, and offered Jay some beer money, which was waved away.

Jay took the bottles out to the back, and Jackson went up to the bar. The place was almost full of regulars watching sports on TV or playing pool, but he couldn't see Daisy.

"Hey, Nancy, is Daisy around?"

Nancy finished helping another customer and came over to him. "She got a call and had to run. She said you could either catch her back at the flower shop or she'd speak to you tomorrow, and she was very sorry."

Jackson considered what to do. If he went back to the flower shop, he might end up arguing with her again, and he was pretty much done for the night.

"You two lovebirds fighting again?" Nancy loaded up the dishwasher under the bar counter with dirty glasses.

"Is that what Daisy said?"

"She didn't need to say anything. I could see the pair of you facing off in the restaurant."

"She's not very happy with me right now, that's for sure." Jackson sighed. "I suggested she tell the truth about something, and she said she couldn't do that yet." He offered her a hopeful smile. "I'm not sure what to do."

Nancy shut the dishwasher and faced him. "I hope you're not trying to sweet-talk me into telling you stuff about one of my best friends?"

"I wouldn't dare." Jackson considered her. "I'm just . . . trying to understand what's going on with her. She mentioned some guy who died, and—"

"Daisy told you about Brody?" Nancy gawped at him.

"Only a little bit." Jackson hoped he wasn't blushing. "I got the impression he was very important to her."

"Yes, he was." Nancy sighed. "You should get her to talk about him. It would do her good."

"I'll certainly try." Jackson tipped his hat to her. "Good night, Nancy."

He walked out into the rapidly cooling air. The temperature in Morgan Valley could change from boiling hot to freezing cold, depending on what was going on with the Sierras, the seasons, and the snow packet. There were no lights on in the front of the flower shop, but that didn't mean Daisy wasn't working in the back, dealing with whatever crisis had come up in her secret job.

Jackson shoved his hands in his pockets and walked over to where he'd left his truck. Nancy had given him the name of the guy Daisy was still hung up on, but it didn't make things any better. How could he compete with a dead man? More importantly, what was wrong with him that he immediately saw everything as a win-or-lose scenario?

Jackson grimaced. Maybe he'd spent too many years of his life weighing up the risks of combat and making life-or-death decisions. As a child, he'd learned to gauge the risks of when to step in and prevent his father raging on his mom and siblings. In the air force, he'd expanded that skill set into the avenue of modern-day warfare.

He reached his truck and climbed inside, wishing Daisy was right beside him. They might argue a lot, but it didn't stop him from liking and respecting her. He admired the way she dealt with his endless questions and refused to accept his bullshit. He appreciated the fact that she got his weird sense of humor and liked having sex with him.

He turned the engine on and settled into his seat. There was no getting away from it. He liked her a lot more than she liked him . . .

"Fool," Jackson growled to himself as he backed out of the parking space and made sure his lights were on. "She told you not to grow too fond of her, and she meant it, so this is *totally* on you."

Jackson turned onto the street and set off back home to the ranch. Dating Daisy, agreeing to her terms, had been a test for him, and he was failing it miserably.

He should just stop trying to make things go his way. Hadn't he learned that the things he wanted the most were always the most elusive? Hadn't his whole *life* taught him that?

Unable to find any answers that satisfied him, Jackson switched on the radio and tuned out.

Chapter Eleven

"Let me get that for you." Jackson picked up Daisy's suitcase as if it weighed nothing and put it in the overhead bin. The Sierra passes were still snowed in, so they'd decided to fly from the local airport to San Francisco.

"Thanks so much." She waited to see if he wanted the window seat, but as he was still hanging back, and the line behind them was growing restless, she slid into the row.

"Do you want to sit here?" She pointed at the window.

"God no." Jackson shuddered.

She studied him carefully. "Are you okay?"

"I'm not a great flier."

"You were in the *air force*!"

"Yeah." He offered her an awkward smile. "I'd feel a lot safer if I was up front."

"Nearly all commercial pilots were trained by the military, so they're pretty competent." Daisy patted his clenched fist. "You'll be fine."

"It's easier if you don't know all the things that can go wrong, I suppose," Jackson muttered.

"Now you're freaking me out. Stop it." She smiled at him. "There's nothing wrong with blissful ignorance. And just think, if something *does* go wrong, you can be the hero who saves the day."

He gave her a skeptical look but did slightly relax his death grip on the armrest. He'd swapped out his Stetson for a baseball cap but retained his jeans and cowboy boots and looked no different from most of the other passengers in the smallish plane. It wasn't a long flight, so she could only hope he'd hang in there and make it through.

"It might take a while to get from the airport to the hotel." Daisy decided to keep chatting about normal things to take his mind off the plane thing.

"That's if we make it over the Sierras," Jackson murmured. "Remember what happened to the Donner party?"

"*Stop.*" She patted his hand. "Visualize arriving in San Francisco and all being well."

The lone flight attendant walked through the cabin shutting the bins and smiling at the passengers. Within seconds, the door to the flight deck was sealed and they were on their way. Daisy kept hold of Jackson's clenched fist as the plane increased speed and took off, leaving the runway far behind. She glanced at his face and discovered he had his eyes shut and appeared to be praying.

Not wishing to make him feel even worse, she returned her attention to the scenery, and the swathe of endless blue sky around the plane. Even from this height, the Sierras looked formidably black, with patches of snow still clinging to the rocky caverns and pathways.

She tried to take her own advice and focus on what was to come in San Francisco. Venture capitalists weren't known for their sweet dispositions. They preferred to invest money in companies that would definitely succeed and pay back their investments a thousandfold. Having successfully brought one company through an IPO, she and the team at least had a proven reputation. This time, she and Ian would be way more careful about who they entrusted their fate to . . .

Daisy glanced over at Jackson. He still had his eyes closed, so she could study him at length. His eyelashes were longer than hers, and he had the best cheekbones. She wished it was easier to stay detached from him, but it was proving harder than she'd thought. Every time she wavered, she reminded herself of Brody and what he'd meant to her, but somehow, despite all her efforts, his image seemed to be fading.

Sharing time with a vibrant, argumentative man like Jackson would make most men pale by comparison, but she didn't want to lose Brody again. It would be yet another betrayal of everything he'd meant to her. But how could she stop herself from responding to Jackson? He was impossible to ignore, and he made her feel . . . so alive again.

And she'd promised to have a proper discussion with Jackson when they were in the city. She sensed he was growing frustrated, and she could understand why. Maybe telling him the truth and trusting him to make the right decision for himself would be fairer in the long run. If he decided to bail, she hoped they could remain friends.

Jackson hoisted Daisy's case onto the bed and went over to the window to study the view. He'd been to the Bay Area many times and always enjoyed his visits. It was way too crowded for him to want to live there, but he appreciated the upbeat vibe of the place.

Daisy came in from the bathroom. She'd brushed her hair and it flowed down her back, which made Jackson think of wrapping his hand in it and drawing her close.

"Don't tell me you're scared of heights as well?"

He grinned at her. "Nope. I'm good as long as it isn't *too* high. This is a nice place. I can watch the planes coming in at SFO. Do you always stay here?"

"It's close to where I need to be and not too expensive." Daisy came to stand beside him and took his hand. "Are you feeling okay now?"

"I was fine the second I stepped onto the ground," Jackson said. "Thanks for sticking by me."

"Like I had anywhere to go except out the window," Daisy joked. "Thank goodness it was only an hour flight."

"What's the plan for the rest of the day?" Jackson asked.

"I need to call Ian, my business partner, to tell him I'm here, and I'll probably need to go meet the team for dinner." She hesitated. "Will you be okay by yourself for a while?"

So he wasn't invited. "Sure. What time do you think you'll get back?"

"Probably about nine. None of the team is big on socializing." She wrinkled her nose. "In fact, most of them could be called people averse."

"I can meet you in the bar when you come back."

"Sounds good." She went up on tiptoe and kissed him. "Thanks for being so understanding."

"This is a business trip and I'm your decoy. What's to understand?" Jackson said, determined not to be that guy who complained all the time.

"We will get to spend the night together," Daisy reminded him.

"Yeah." He kissed her back. "I'm looking forward to it."

Ian insisted on walking Daisy back to her hotel, which gave them more time to discuss their future strategy in front of the VCs without scaring the more delicate members of their team. She was really pleased at the overall progress of the product and convinced they now had something tangible and, more importantly, sellable to present to the market.

"Thanks for coming back on board." Ian smiled down at her. "We couldn't get it together without you."

"You were doing great, but seeing as I got you all involved in the first place, the least I could do was help bring it home." Daisy hesitated. "Not to sound crude, but how much longer do you think it's going to take to make some money out of this thing?"

"Do you need money?" Ian paused outside the entrance to the hotel. "Because I was thinking we'd need at least another two rounds of funding, and about two or three more years' work before we can retire as bazillionaires."

"I know that, but I was hoping someone else would step up." Daisy let out a breath. "I'm not sure I can commit to that."

"Why not?" Ian asked the question without a hint of stress or aggression, which Daisy appreciated.

"Because I haven't told my family I'm involved in another start-up."

"I'd really appreciate it if you can hang in there." Ian held her gaze. "I'd hate to sell out early and lose control again."

"I get it." Daisy winced. "I sound really selfish, don't I?"

"Nope. Despite what most people think, it's not easy risking everything for something that might never come to fruition."

"But I really believe in this product," Daisy said.

"I know you do," Ian agreed. "So we're just going to find a way to make it work and keep everyone happy, okay?"

She touched his arm. "I really appreciate you not shouting at me right now."

He grinned. "Dude, I don't do that, you know me. I want this to work. We all deserve it—you more than anyone. We're a team. If there's an opportunity to sell earlier, and we're all okay about it, we'll definitely consider it."

"Thank you."

Ian held the door into the hotel open and gave her a look. "You might also consider coming clean to your family."

"You're not the first person to suggest that," Daisy said. "Perhaps it's time I started to listen."

Even without his cowboy hat, she spotted Jackson sitting in the bar and momentarily hesitated, Ian still at her heels. She'd told him she'd be truthful, so why shouldn't she start now, and introduce him to the other part of her life?

"Hey," she called out, and he turned his head and rose to his feet.

"Hey, beautiful lady." His smile was so warm, she couldn't look away.

"Jackson, this is my coworker, Ian Chung. We went to college together."

After a startled glance at Daisy, Ian stuck out his hand. "Nice to meet you, Jackson."

"Same here." Jackson nodded. "Are you a floral guy or a tech guy?"

For a second, Ian looked perplexed, and then a slow smile spread over his face. "Good one. I'm a techie." He glanced over at Daisy. "She sure does live a complicated life."

"Can't argue with you on that. Would either of you like a drink?" Jackson gestured at the bar.

"I would," Daisy said fervently. Three hours of talking tech had made her brain hurt. "Ian?"

"I've got to get home." Ian smiled at her. "Seth will be wondering where I've gotten to."

"Give him my love." Daisy hugged Ian. "And I'll see you tomorrow at one, okay?"

"I can't wait." Ian shuddered. "Back into the lion's den we go. Nice to meet you, Jackson."

"You too." Jackson nodded and put a casual arm around Daisy's shoulders. "Safe journey home."

Ian left the hotel, and Jackson kissed Daisy's cheek. "Sit down and I'll get you something to drink. What would you like?"

"A glass of white wine. I don't care what kind as long as it's Chardonnay."

"Got it. Sit tight and I'll be right back."

It wasn't that busy at the bar, and he returned relatively quickly with a glass of wine, a bottle of beer, and a bowl of mixed nuts.

"How did it go?" Jackson settled beside her on the couch.

"Good, I think." She looked cautiously around the bar and lowered her voice. "We're going to pitch to some VCs tomorrow afternoon."

"Okay. Whatever that means."

"Venture capitalists. The guys with all the money who invest it in start-ups like mine."

"Oh right. Got it." Jackson nodded.

"And this time, hopefully, we won't get screwed."

"I like the way you think." Jackson clinked his bottle against her glass. "Sometimes the hardest lessons teach us the best new strategies."

"Like you not getting to be a fighter pilot?"

"Exactly." His smile was wry. "I learned how to fly several different types of aircraft instead and ended up doing something I loved."

"And then you left."

"Yeah." His smile died.

Before Daisy could follow up, his cell buzzed. He picked it up with alacrity and frowned at the screen.

"Damn."

"What's up?" Daisy asked.

"I told one of my old air force buddies I'd be in town, and as he's leaving tomorrow, he wants to pop in right now and say hi."

"That's fine by me," Daisy quickly assured him. He'd been more than generous with his time for her, so she wasn't going to be a pain. "Unless you want me to go?"

"No, please stay. He's only got time for a quick drink." Jackson was texting as he spoke. "He'll be here in five."

Daisy sipped her wine and nibbled at the nuts. She'd had pizza with the team, but they'd all been so busy talking, she'd only eaten a single piece and she was still peckish.

A tall black guy in uniform appeared at the entrance of the bar and scanned the seats before breaking out into a big smile.

"Five! How are you, dude?"

"Pez." Jackson stood, and the two men engaged in that back-slapping, hugging, testing thing that in Daisy's experience males liked to do.

Jackson grabbed Daisy's hand. "Daisy, meet Pez, I mean Patrick. We entered the United States Air Force Academy together, and we've been friends ever since."

"How did you end up being called Pez?" Daisy asked as Jackson went off to get his friend a beer.

"It's an air force thing." He shrugged. "Everyone gets a nickname. My name is Patrick, so at first, everyone called me Peppermint Patty. When we were in Germany, someone found out that peppermint in German was *pfefferminz*, which is the first, middle, and last letter of PEZ, so they called me that, and it stuck."

Daisy blinked at him. "That's very specific."

"Sometimes we had a lot of time on our hands." He grinned. "Jackson went from Mikey, to Joe, to Five, which was much simpler."

"Oh! The Jackson Five." Daisy nodded. "That's a lot easier."

"But much less fun." Jackson returned to the table and handed his friend a beer. "It's good to see you."

"You too, my friend." Patrick clinked his bottle against Jackson's. "We all thought you'd disappeared off the face of the earth after you left last year."

"I had a lot of stuff to work out with my family. I guess I got busy."

Daisy noticed that Jackson's easy smile wasn't as natural as usual, and that he was fidgeting with his beer.

"Yeah, sorry about your dad. That must've been hard," Pez said.

Jackson nodded and sipped his beer. "Where are you stationed now?"

"Same old place. I've had two weeks leave, but I'm due back out in Qatar. That's why I took a hotel close to the airport, seeing as I'm flying commercial." He grimaced.

"Don't you like flying either?" Daisy asked.

"I love flying. I just don't like being flown," Patrick said. "Five's the same, right?"

Jackson nudged Daisy. "See? I told you it wasn't just me."

"Captain Barnes says your replacement is crap, by the way." Patrick eyed Jackson. "And he's still pissed you left for no reason. If I tell him I saw you, he'll be bugging me about why I didn't persuade you to sign back up again."

"Then don't tell him," Jackson countered lightly. "Why ruin his day?"

"It's a damn shame you left." Patrick sighed. "With you, Tide, and Hopper gone? I don't know who to hang out with anymore."

It was only because Daisy was superfocused on Jackson's face that she saw the flicker of grief in his eyes.

"Yeah . . ." Jackson blew out a breath. "What time is your flight tomorrow?"

Patrick held his gaze for a moment before he answered. "Seven, so I should get to bed and try to sleep as I'm fairly sure I'm not getting an upgrade to first class."

"You never know." Jackson finished his beer. "A decorated war hero like you."

Patrick patted the service medal bar above his pocket. "My fruit salad? I've done my share. Same as you." He rose to his feet. "It was nice to meet you, Daisy."

"You too, Patrick. Take care." Daisy gave him a hug, and he turned to Jackson, lowering his voice.

"Five. You know where I am if you need anything. Don't ever think you're alone out there. We all understand what you went through." After another brisk hug, Patrick walked away, leaving Jackson and Daisy still standing.

"Do you want to go up to bed?" Daisy asked, aware that Jackson was staring after his friend.

"Yeah, if you're ready."

Daisy hastily downed the rest of her wine and set the glass back down. "I'm good to go."

He took her hand as they walked back to the elevators and rode up to the fifth floor, where their room was situated. The drapes were still open. They had a fine view of both the San Mateo Bridge, spanning the bay, and the lights of San Francisco in the distance. Jackson walked over to stare out into the darkness.

"Patrick was nice," Daisy said tentatively, aware that he wasn't his normal chatty self.

"So was Ian."

"Which means we both have great taste in friends."

Daisy yawned hard and covered her mouth. "Excuse me. It's been a really long day."

"Yeah." He didn't turn around. "Do you want to use the bathroom first?"

"Sure."

Jackson waited until the bathroom door clicked shut and the water started running before he let out a long exhale. Seeing Pez again, realizing everything he'd given up had shaken him far more than he'd anticipated. At least Pez hadn't pressed him on anything. His friend wasn't stupid, and knew everyone who served had to come to terms with what they'd seen and dealt with in their own good time.

Except Pez obviously thought Jackson hadn't dealt with it and had chosen to run away instead, which was kind of the truth. At least Pez had offered his support.

Jackson sank into the nearest chair and rubbed his hands over his face and stubbled chin. He needed to get a grip before Daisy came out of the bathroom. She wasn't stupid, and she wasn't averse to asking a few loaded questions of her own. He stripped off his clothes, folding them neatly onto the chair. He'd had a shower just before he'd gone down to the bar and only needed to brush his teeth to be ready for bed.

She appeared in the bathroom door, illuminated from behind by the bright light. He went toward her, swept her off her feet, and deposited her on the bed right underneath him where he needed her to be.

"Jackson?"

He kissed her, tempted her to kiss him back, his hands roaming under her long T-shirt until she attempted to shrug it off, and he helped her throw it to the floor. With a groan, he buried his face in her neck, inhaling the mint of her toothpaste and the slight hint of wine lingering on her breath. This was where he wanted to be. Right here with Daisy, where he could forget everything but his need to be inside her and make her come as many times as she wanted.

He cupped her rounded ass, bringing her against the hardness of his need, and sighed into her mouth as she undulated against him. Changing position, he slid down to tease and play with her breasts, and then even lower to feast on her most sensitive flesh. It was so easy to lose himself in the taste of her, in the sharp scrape of her nails against his scalp and her stifled cries of pleasure.

When he couldn't hold out any longer, he reached for the protection he'd left beside the bed, covered his cock, and drove into her with one long thrust that made her scream his name. Her bare feet climbed the outsides of his thighs until they were firmly planted on his rocking hips and she was coming again.

He drove on, slowing his pace until she begged him to give her more, and then taking everything until he forgot his name, his sense of self, and drowned in the wonderful physicality of making love to Daisy Miller. Eventually, he had to come and let go, crashing down over her, his breathing so ragged, it sounded loud in the air-conditioned stillness of the room.

It took him a long while to roll off her onto his back, where he stared up at the ceiling and struggled to get himself back together.

He blinked as Daisy snapped on the bedside lamp and came up on one elbow to look down at him, her hair sliding over his shoulder and chest.

"Are you okay?"

"Why are you asking?"

"Because of what we just did." Daisy gestured at the disordered bed.

"I'm not sure what you're getting at," Jackson said warily.

"You just . . . took over everything." She wasn't backing down. "You didn't say a word, you just *went* for it."

He eased himself up to sit against the headboard as she moved away from him. "You didn't enjoy it?"

"That's not the point."

"So you did enjoy it, but for some reason you're mad at me." Jackson met her gaze. "Got it."

"Don't get all flippant with me." She pushed her hair behind her ear. "If you don't want to talk to me about something, don't, but don't overwhelm me with sex."

"*Overwhelm* you?" He felt his own temper rise to match hers. "You came at least six times and I only got one."

"That's basic biology and don't you dare start with that!" She scrambled off the bed and found her T-shirt.

"Start what?"

She disappeared into the bathroom, leaving him alone, and the shower went back on. His anger died as swiftly as it had risen, and he got out of bed and followed her into the bathroom.

"Daisy, I'm—"

"Go away, Jackson."

She came out of the shower, grabbed a towel, and pushed past him, slamming the door in his face.

"Daisy, will you just let me *talk* to you?"

She swung around to face him, gripping the towel she'd wrapped high over her breasts. Everything was so confusing—the high of the lovemaking mixed in with the realization that he wasn't being open with her, and that it hurt. But he didn't have to tell her anything, did he? She was the one who'd insisted they weren't in a real relationship.

"You want to talk to me *now*?" Daisy asked.

He came slowly into the room. "Look. I obviously screwed up here and I'm really, really sorry."

"No, you didn't." Daisy found a smile somewhere. "You have a perfect right not to tell me anything, remember? Do you want to shower, because I'm done in the bathroom and I'm ready to go to sleep."

She was offering him a way out. Would he take it?

"Sometimes I find it easier to do something rather than talk about it." He sat down in the nearest chair and studied the carpet with great attention. "I was . . . unsettled by seeing Pez."

"So you decided to sweep me off my feet and make love to me before I could ask you any awkward questions?"

"Yeah." He still wasn't looking at her. "And that's not okay. I realize that now." He shoved a hand through his hair. "I just knew that as soon as I touched you, everything would be better."

She walked over, perched on the arm of his chair, and looked down at his bent head, admiring his honesty even as it made her want to cry. "Did it work?"

"No, because here we are, and now you're mad at me, and I thoroughly deserve it." A sigh shuddered through him. "I'm not making any excuses for myself, Daisy. If you want to tell me to get out, I'll go."

"You just stopped talking," Daisy reminded him. "I'm not used to that from you." She hesitated. "You do know you can tell me anything, right?"

"No, I can't." He slowly looked up at her, his smile making her heart hurt. "You don't want that kind of relationship with me."

"I'd still like to be your friend." Daisy couldn't seem to let it go. "I'll listen."

"That's really nice of you." He stood up and dropped a gentle kiss on her nose. "But I think you've had to put up with quite enough of me for one night, don't you? I'll go brush my teeth."

Daisy waited until he closed the bathroom door before she let out her breath and climbed into bed. So much for them getting on better away from their respective families . . . But hadn't she gotten what she'd wanted? Fantastic sex with no emotional commitment? If so, why did she feel like crying?

Chapter Twelve

"Thank you for your time."

Daisy closed her laptop and tucked it under her arm before following Ian out of the VC's office. She accepted his lame attempt at a high five.

"You were awesome!" Ian whispered.

"Do you really think it went well?" Daisy walked out into the central lobby where the elevators were. They were currently on Sand Hill Road near Palo Alto, where all the venture capitalists tended to have their offices. "It's hard to tell with these guys."

"I saw definite interest." Ian was an eternal optimist. "We're going down to the lobby now, and in ten minutes we have another meeting on the second floor."

"Same building?"

"Yeah, it's like VC central here." Ian dug into the pocket of his pants. "Do you want something from the machine?"

"Just water, if they have it."

She went off to use the bathroom and make sure she still looked presentable in her navy pantsuit, tied-back hair, and lipstick, which was about as far as she was willing to go to impress anybody. She'd left Jackson finishing his breakfast before he went to the hotel gym. He'd been contemplating a ten-mile run or something equally horrific, so she hadn't stayed too long in case he asked her to join him.

He'd been fine with her over breakfast: respectful, funny, and very much his usual happy self, which made her wonder how much of the real Jackson Lymond he was still actually concealing from her. And that wasn't on him, it was definitely on her. She'd wanted him to confide in her, but he'd politely turned her down, reminding her that she didn't have the right to ask him anything.

Which served her right.

She left the bathroom, checking her phone and only looked up when someone called her name.

"Daisy Miller?"

She froze in place as Clive Cassler, one of her least favorite people in the universe, came sauntering—make that slithering—toward her.

"You're back in town?" He stuck his hand in the pocket of his bespoke suit and leaned against the wall, barring her way. "New project?"

"I'm just here to support a friend of mine," Daisy lied.

"That's not what I heard. Word on the street is that you've come up with something amazing again."

She raised her chin. "Like I'd tell you if I had."

"Are you still whining about that?" His smile was smug. "You lost, little girl. Get used to it."

"My team 'lost' because you preyed upon our goodwill until you were able to stick the knife in and take us down," Daisy retorted.

"There's no need to be so dramatic." Clive chuckled. "That's business, my dear. Don't take it personally."

"Good, then don't take *this* personally, but you'll totally understand why I don't ever want to do business with you again." She shoved past him and marched back down to the lobby, her whole body shaking.

Of all the people to run into at this moment, Clive had to be the worst. Now he'd be nosing around, trying to work out how he could get involved in funding the new venture, and screwing them over on that one as well.

"What's up?" Ian handed her the bottle of water.

"I just bumped into Clive." Daisy unscrewed the lid and took a sip of water.

"Our Clive?"

"I don't think there are many people named Clive who happen to be venture capitalists in Palo Alto, do you?"

"Probably not." Ian grimaced. "What did he want?"

"He was nosing around, trying to find out what we were doing here." Daisy snorted. "Like I'd tell him anything after what he did to us last time."

"The problem is that this is a very small world, and venture capitalists do like to gossip," Ian reminded her. "If Clive wants to find out what's up, he probably will."

"It doesn't mean we have to make it easy for him," Daisy retorted. "I'm going to ask all the VCs we speak to for a confidentiality clause."

"We can certainly try, but it's probably too late for that now. Clive's lot have their tentacles in all kinds of shit." Ian checked his cell. "Hey, we're due at the next meeting. Are you okay to go through with it?"

"Okay? I'm super-fired up to make sure Clive doesn't get his paws on our work ever again." Daisy screwed the cap on her water bottle.

"That's the Daisy I know and love." Ian grinned at her. "Now, these guys are more angel investors than straight VCs, and they were very interested in the humanitarian aspects of our product."

"Got it. They sound like our kind of people."

Ian held open the door into the offices so Daisy could

go on through. She smiled at the young receptionist behind the desk.

"Hi, we're here for a meeting with Jake Magnusson?"

"Hi, you must be Daisy and Ian, right? Come on through to Jake's office. He's been looking forward to meeting you all day."

Daisy couldn't help but respond to such positivity after colliding with the black hole of Clive. She was still smiling as she entered the office and saw two guys, one sitting behind the desk and the other perched on the corner of it.

"Daisy?"

For the second time in an hour, Daisy found herself staring at someone who really shouldn't be there. She wished she'd taken the time to look at the notes Ian had offered her about the makeup of each investment firm. She'd been in too much of a rush and trusted Ian's judgment 100 percent.

"Hi, Chase!" She grinned weakly at Chase Morgan, who looked weird without his Stetson. "Fancy seeing you here!"

Ian came forward and shook Chase's and Jake's hands as Daisy's feet were still locked in fight-or-flight mode. How could she have forgotten that Chase spent half his life away from Morgan Valley tending to his tech business? Seeing him was almost as bad as seeing Clive, but in a much more personal way.

"You two know each other?" Jake looked from her to Chase.

"Daisy's family have a ranch in Morgan Valley," Chase said. "I didn't realize you were still involved in the tech industry, Daisy."

Daisy tried to smile. "I've been . . . helping Ian out with this particular project."

"And when she says helping, she means that without her

skill set, we would never have gotten it off the ground." Ian patted her shoulder. "She's the most amazing software designer I've ever met."

Jake gestured at the circle of chairs beside the white-board. "Why don't we sit down, and you can run through the specifics of the project again?" He stood with some difficulty and used a cane to walk the few steps to the chairs. "I assume you're staying, Chase?"

"Unfortunately, I have to run." Chase sighed. "I'm counting on you to fill me in later, Jake, okay?" He smiled at Daisy and Ian. "Nice to see you guys."

"Are you going home tonight, Chase?" Daisy blurted out before he reached the door.

"No, I'm here for a couple of days," Chase said, his blue eyes fixed on her inquiringly.

"Any chance you could meet me for a drink at some point?" Daisy asked.

"Sure." Chase handed her his phone. "Put your number in here, text me the address of your hotel, and I'd be happy to speak to you."

Daisy almost sighed in relief as he went out. Now at least she'd have the opportunity to talk to him and ask him . . . Ask him what? To *lie* to her family for her? Wow, once you practiced to deceive, things really did get bigger and bigger, just like her Auntie Rae had warned her. If she weren't careful, she'd have to pay off the whole darned valley.

Aware that she might be getting a little ahead of herself, Daisy settled down, opened her laptop, and prepared to give Jake her spiel.

Jackson was enjoying a quiet nap when the door opened and Daisy blew in like a miniature storm. She took off her shoes and threw her jacket toward one of the chairs, missing it completely.

"Oh *bother!* I can't get anything right today." She kicked one of her shoes so hard, it hit the wastepaper basket with an earsplitting clang.

"Hey, I'm trying to sleep here," Jackson complained.

She spun around, one hand pressed to her cheek. "I'm so sorry, Jackson. I didn't think you were here!"

He slowly sat up and studied her. "What's up?"

She sighed. "I don't even know where to start."

He patted the bed, and she climbed up onto the mattress and knelt in front of him, giving him an excellent view of her cleavage.

"Did your presentation suck?" Remembering to stick firmly in friend mode, Jackson tried not to let his gaze drop and maintained eye contact.

"No, they all went really well." She frowned and undid the button and zipper of her pants. "Geez, these things are uncomfortable."

"Don't let me stop you taking them off," Jackson suggested. "You might as well get comfortable."

She wiggled out of her pants, making everything male in him sit up and take notice. But he was on his best behavior. Any sexual invitations were going to have to come from her.

He held out an arm and she joined him, her shoulder against his, her back to the headboard.

"So what's going on?"

"Do you want to hear about the bad thing or the *really* bad thing?" Daisy asked.

"Start with the bad thing," Jackson suggested. "Then maybe the other one won't seem so awful."

"Okay, so you know I was involved in a previous start-up?" Daisy turned to look at him.

"You did mention something about that," Jackson said cautiously.

"The guy who screwed us over just *happened* to be hanging around the offices we went to on Sand Hill Road today."

"That isn't good." Jackson considered what to say next. "Does he know what you're doing?"

"Not at the moment, but I don't think it will take him long to find out." Daisy sighed. "He's not a good person, Jackson."

"Is there any way you can stop him getting his hands on what you're currently doing?"

"We can certainly try to keep him out, but he might create other entities or secretly join other VC funding groups to get around us."

Jackson was so out of his depth, he didn't dare comment on the business side of things. He focused on the personal. "Do you think he'll bother?"

"Yes, because he hates me for calling him out publicly, so the thought of financially screwing me again probably makes his evil soul glow."

"Does it now?" Jackson muttered. "He sounds like a real peach."

"He's certainly rotten to the core." Daisy groaned. "That's the worst joke I've ever made."

Jackson pretended to frown. "I'm pretty sure it isn't."

She tickled his side until he had to fend her off.

"He actually *tried* to screw me once, and I kicked him so hard in the shins, he cried," Daisy confessed. "That's probably the main reason he doesn't like me."

"Good for you." Jackson lovingly imagined teaching the guy a lesson by tearing him limb from limb. "Next time, kick higher and do the whole world a favor."

She rubbed her cheek against his T-shirt. "I'm so glad I took those self-defense classes."

"So am I," Jackson fervently agreed.

"I think if we're extravigilant we can keep Clive out."

"Clive? What kind of name is that?" Jackson demanded.

Daisy refused to be distracted. "Any VC we deal with will have to disclose every single one of their partners and funding sources, or we just won't work with them."

"Sounds like a plan." Jackson nodded. "So what's the *really* bad news?"

"Chase Morgan," Daisy said glumly.

"What about him?"

"He was there today."

"With the Clive guy?"

"No, of course not." Daisy gave him an exasperated look "We arranged to meet this guy, Jake Magnusson, and when we went in, guess who was sitting on his desk?"

"Chase Morgan." Jackson paused. "Didn't you know he worked here?"

"Well, yes, I did, in an *abstract* way, but we've never come across each other before, and I assumed we never would. It's not like Morgan Valley, Jackson; there are hundreds of thousands of people here. Chase has made his money. He doesn't need to grub around seeking funding like a start-up."

"He lends money out. That's his thing."

"I know that *now*," Daisy said. "For some reason, I hadn't really thought about what he did to keep his millions turning over. I didn't read the intel Ian had about the firm before I went in, which is *totally* on me."

"What happened with Chase?" Jackson attempted to get her back on topic. "Was he surprised to see you?"

"Yes, but he wasn't unpleasant or anything," Daisy

continued. "In fact, he agreed to come to the hotel, and have a drink with us at some point."

"With us? Why did he want to do that?" Jackson asked, his curiosity piqued.

"Because I asked him to come." Daisy picked at a thread on his T-shirt, avoiding his gaze. "I thought I could ask him not to mention he'd seen me in his office when he gets back home."

"From what I recall, Chase isn't good at . . ." Jackson paused delicately.

"Lying?" Daisy offered the word Jackson had avoided. "I know that's what I'm asking him to do."

"In fact, he's a terrible liar," Jackson concluded. "Almost as bad as me."

For a moment, they both were silent.

"I have to try," Daisy said. "It will be quite a while before I can hand this project over and go back to being just a florist in Morgantown. I hate all this lying. I really *hate* it."

Jackson wondered whether he should say his piece again about maybe it being time to come clean with everyone, but he was still gun-shy from the previous night, when he'd been the one unwilling to ask for advice or to listen. If Daisy wanted casual, that was what she was going to get.

"I'm sure everything will turn out okay." Jackson settled for a platitude.

"Do you really think so?"

Jackson shrugged. "I don't see why not."

"I do." Daisy made a face. "Things rarely work out the way I want them to. If it hadn't been for Clive, I would've made enough money from the first start-up not to ever have to go back to Silicon Valley again."

"But that's not quite true, is it?" Jackson opened his mouth before he thought about it. "You told me this particular project was too important for you to ignore."

She stared at him for so long, he wished, not for the first time, he had the ability to go back in time and shut the hell up. So much for staying in the friend zone and keeping things light.

"You're right," Daisy finally answered him.

Jackson waited her out as she lapsed into silence again, her gaze settling somewhere he couldn't follow.

"This thing we're developing could save lives."

"Okay, that's good." Jackson nodded encouragingly.

Daisy moved away from her position beside him and faced him, her legs crossed and her hands on her knees.

"Just imagine if you were wounded on a battlefield. The first hour is critical to your survival, so what if the software we're developing *improved* your chance of survival by at least fifty percent?"

"That would be great," Jackson agreed. "How do you do that?"

"By allowing the medical team working on you access to a vast amount of data on how to treat battlefield casualties in real time."

"Which would improve the outcome?"

"Yes. Think about it, Jackson." Daisy leaned forward, her eyes shining. "If the team leader could punch in a few data points, such as type of injury, the trajectory of the bullet, or what kind of weapon had been used, the software could instantly search through the database and offer the best way of dealing with the problem. Or even superimpose an image of where the injury and blood loss might be, and the best way to fix it right onto the patient."

"It sounds great, but how do you get all that data to the medical personnel?" Jackson asked.

"Through a handheld device or special glasses offering augmented reality, or something we haven't even come up with yet." Daisy shrugged. "There are several delivery options. The important thing is, the ability to access the most up-to-date response to each specific injury based on previously accumulated knowledge."

"Why is this so important to you personally?" Jackson asked gently.

"Don't you think it's important anyway?" Daisy challenged him.

"Of course I do. I'm former military, but why did this particular project call you back to Silicon Valley?"

Daisy's gaze fell to her hands. "Because a friend of mine died in combat in Afghanistan before he could receive the proper treatment."

"Brody?" Jackson took a wild guess.

She raised her head. "Who told you about him?"

"I worked it out." He refused to look away from the anguish in her eyes and let his next question roll off his tongue. "Did you love him?"

"Yes."

He nodded, the simplicity of her response like a blow to his heart. He swung his legs over the side of the bed. "I need to wash up."

He was almost through the bathroom door before she spoke again. "Are you mad at me?"

"*No.*" He slowly turned to face her and found a smile from somewhere. "How could I be mad? What you're doing is *awesome.*"

He shut the door and locked it before she got any ideas about following him into the bathroom. Sitting on the toilet seat, he buried his face in his hands. He'd always liked a challenge, and getting Daisy to love him had been his number one priority. But now? How could he compete with a dead man? A hero who had inspired Daisy into creating an amazing lifesaving thing?

He wasn't Brody, the All-American Hero, and he never would be. In fact, he was the complete opposite. Jackson slowly raised his head and stared blankly at the shower. Maybe it was time to accept that, and really be what Daisy had asked him to be in the first place—her temporary boyfriend.

Chapter Thirteen

Jackson dropped Daisy at the ranch with a quick kiss on the cheek and a hug. He didn't come in; he said he had to get back for Cauy. He'd been nice as pie since her big disclosure about what she was doing with the start-up, but something had changed, and Daisy wasn't sure whether it was a good thing or not. The fact that she'd shared her secrets was pretty frightening, but she'd wanted him to know, had instinctively felt it was time to tell him the truth amid so many lies.

And she'd believed him when he said how amazing her work was. As a vet, his good opinion meant a lot. Even as he'd accepted her confidences, something had altered, and she still wasn't sure what it was—what she'd lost—but there was definitely a change. On the last night of their stay, he'd made love to her with such fierce, protective tenderness, she'd cried with pleasure.

And yet . . . she looked back down the road where a small cloud of dust from Jackson's truck still danced on the air. Had he been saying goodbye?

She'd spoken briefly to Chase, and he'd assured her he'd

not only keep her secrets but would only be involved in the decision-making at board level, leaving the initial assessment to Jake.

"You coming in, sis, or are you intending to camp out in the yard tonight?"

She swung around to see Adam standing at the open door watching her, his expression inscrutable.

"Sorry, I was just thinking." She picked up her bag and went toward him. "Did you miss me?"

"Always." Adam studied her upturned face. "Are you okay? You look sad."

"I'm fine." She patted his sleeve as he wrestled her case away from her, brought it inside, and set it at the bottom of the staircase. "I'm just tired."

"Did you have a good time?" Adam took her firmly by the elbow and steered her into the kitchen, giving her no chance to bolt up the stairs. "I assume Jackson behaved himself."

"He was great," Daisy hastened to say, knowing the slightest hint of uncertainty would set Adam off in pursuit of her lover. "We had a really lovely time."

And they had—if one discounted the arguing and the sometimes-painful bursts of honesty and evasion from both of them. She'd never met anyone who unsettled and provoked her quite like Jackson Lymond.

Adam went to get her some iced tea and poured himself some coffee. "Dad and the guys are watching a baseball game if you want to pop in and say hi."

"And be told off for interrupting them?" Daisy attempted to sound cheerful. "They'll work out that I'm home when they notice the laundry pile has gone down."

"Ha ha, like you even know where that room is. Talk to me." Adam sat at the table and patted the seat beside him. "Auntie Rae called yesterday. She's coming to see us tomorrow."

"What about?" Daisy wrinkled her nose.

"She wouldn't say over the phone." Adam shrugged. "You know how she likes a bit of drama."

Daisy studied him carefully. "Have you any idea what she wants?"

"I really don't." Adam sighed. "I didn't call or ask her to lend me any money to buy the Cortez Ranch, if that's what you're thinking."

Daisy tried not to blush and hurriedly drank all her iced tea. After helping to bring up her brother's kids, Auntie Rae had married a wealthy man and left cattle country for good to set up house in Sacramento. She had no children, which she said was a good thing, seeing as she'd already raised six who felt like her own. As the youngest, Daisy was particularly close to her aunt and truly thought of her as Mom.

She'd been a rock for Daisy, scooping her up into her loving arms and holding her close when the tears over-whelmed her. She'd patiently answered all Daisy's anguished questions about when her mom was coming back without ever getting angry or asking her to stop. When Daisy had prayed to God to send her mommy home, Rae had prayed alongside her until Daisy had given up in despair.

"Is something up with Uncle Rick?" Daisy asked.

"Not that I know of, but she really didn't give away any-thing on the phone, which is most unlike her."

"I'll make sure the guest room is aired out tomorrow. Is she driving?"

"I think so." Adam grimaced. "I'd better put out a traffic warning for the whole of Morgan Valley and hope Nate Turner's not around when she drives into town."

"How many tickets did she get when she lived here?" Daisy asked. "She'd just park wherever she liked."

"I remember. The first day I got my driver's permit, I offered to park for her, and things got better after that," Adam said. "I passed first time thanks to all the practice."

They grinned at each other, and Daisy felt a wave of love for her quiet, dependable brother.

"Well, whatever she wants, we'll handle it." Daisy got up. "Do you want some hot chocolate? I'm going to make some the proper way."

"Just like Auntie Rae taught you?" Adam turned in his seat to watch her get the milk out of the refrigerator. "She really stepped up after Mom left, didn't she?"

"Yes. I'm not sure I would take on six kids who weren't my own." Daisy shuddered as she got out the cocoa powder and sugar.

"Would you like kids one day, Daisy?" Adam asked.

"I suppose so." Daisy considered his question, her mind immediately conjuring up babies with Jackson's dark hair and great smile. "Not six, though. How about you?"

His smile died. "I don't think so."

"That would be a shame. You'd be a great father and a good role model."

"Yeah, but I wanted that with Louisa." He stood and came toward her. "I can't imagine doing it without her." He ruffled her hair. "Sleep well, little sis, and brace yourself for the whirlwind we call Auntie Rae tomorrow."

"Will do." She went on tiptoe to kiss his cheek and quickly returned her attention to the rapidly boiling milk.

Adam needed to move on.

The thought crystallized as she took the milk off the heat and stirred in the sugar and cocoa before replacing it on the range.

But who the heck was she to be all judgy? She was just

the same, wasn't she? Believing that Brody was her one true love, and that no one else would ever replace him. Perhaps the Miller family stubborn streak was becoming a real problem after all . . .

Jackson went into the kitchen to find Cauy eating his supper one-handed as he texted with the other. From the goofy smile on his face, Jackson guessed he was talking to Rachel, who was currently in Sacramento.

"Hey." Cauy looked up at him. "Did you have a good time?"

Jackson dumped his backpack on the floor and sat opposite his brother. "It was interesting."

"What does that mean?"

Jackson sighed. "It means I'm falling hard for Daisy Miller and she doesn't feel the same about me."

Cauy finally put down both his cell and his fork. "But didn't you go into this knowing that?"

"Rachel told you, huh?"

"Not all of it, but enough to make me worry you were going to get hurt along the way."

"Daisy's done nothing wrong."

Cauy raised an eyebrow. "I didn't say she had. Why are you being so defensive?"

"Because you're right." Jackson shoved a hand through his hair. "I did go into this knowing how she felt, and yet I still thought I'd change her mind—convince her I was really the one for her."

"You can't make people love you, Jackson." Cauy's smile was wry. "I tried for years with Dad, and it got me nowhere."

"But I'm *good* at this shit. You know that." Jackson held Cauy's gaze. "I'm not used to . . . not winning."

"Well, maybe for a start, you should stop thinking of Daisy as a prize to be won and think of her as a person."

"I know what she is." Jackson scowled at his brother. "Don't try that therapy crap on me."

"Sure." Cauy shrugged. "Maybe it's time you figured it out yourself. Life isn't all about winning."

"Says the man who made a small fortune on the oil fields," Jackson reminded his brother.

"And who would still rather have had a father who loved him and a place to call home where he knew he was wanted." Cauy kept talking, which wasn't like him at all. "Coming back here and meeting Rachel has given me everything I ever wanted."

"Then how about you give me all your money and I'll spend it for you?" Jackson tried to lighten the atmosphere.

"Don't try to turn this into a joke, Jackson. Why do you always do that when things get serious?"

Jackson stopped smiling. "Because sometimes that was the only way we all survived around here. Don't you remember that, Cauy? How I tried my hardest to get in between you and Dad? How many times I gave you the chance to get away by acting the fool?"

Cauy stared up at him in silence for far too long for Jackson's comfort until he finally stirred.

"Jackson . . ."

"Do you have any idea how it was around here after you left? Dad didn't stop. He just took his rage out on easier targets, and there was only me left to get in his way." Jackson shook his head. "Sometimes I envied you—that you'd gotten away—and sometimes I hated you for leaving me."

Cauy slowly rose, his face ashen, and held out his hand. "Jackson, I had no idea, I—"

"Can we just forget I said that?" Jackson shot to his feet. "I'm tired, and my mouth is working way harder than my brain. I'll see you in the morning."

He picked up his backpack and went down the hallway to his bedroom. He *was* tired out, having spent most of the previous night either making love to Daisy or staring out over the city. Why was everyone getting at him for being the person who smoothed things over, who never got offended or angry when everyone around him was raging? Why was he suddenly the bad guy?

For once, he didn't immediately unpack his belongings but stripped off and lay down in his bed. He missed being beside Daisy, hearing her little snores and snuffles—the way she turned toward him and held him like he was important to her.

But he wasn't important to her, was he? Daisy loved Brody, and his mom had loved Cauy best. She'd shown it in every caress, every loving word, and had never been the same after he left. Intellectually, Jackson knew there was nothing he could do about either of those situations. He shifted one arm until his hand cupped the back of his head on the pillow. Was that why he chased the other prizes? That he had to win at something? That he couldn't deal with being second best? Even the thought of that made him uneasy.

Cauy was right; people weren't trophies, they were living, breathing, feeling entities, and none of them owed him a damn thing.

When Jackson went into the kitchen the next morning, Cauy was already up and cooking breakfast.

"Hey," Jackson said awkwardly. "I just want to apologize again for—"

Cauy turned toward him, the spatula in his hand. "Don't, okay? I'm the one who should be apologizing. Just because my life is going great doesn't mean I get to lecture you about yours."

He tipped the scrambled eggs onto the plates that already contained strips of bacon and sausages and brought them over to the table, where a stack of pancakes stood waiting.

"You're apologizing to me?" Jackson glared at his brother. "How about you shut it as well? I don't begrudge you your happiness and maybe, just maybe, you said some things that made me think."

"Whoop-de-doo." Cauy sat down and speared a pancake on his fork. "You were right about coming between me and Dad. I'd blocked it out. I didn't think about how it was for you after I left. I was just so damned desperate to get away."

"And you were right that I shouldn't be chasing Daisy like she's a prize."

Jackson locked gazes with Cauy for a long, tense minute before he couldn't prevent his face from cracking into a smile.

"So maybe we should both shut up?"

Cauy ate a slice of bacon. "Works for me."

For a long while, they ate in silence before Jackson got up to get some more coffee.

"What needs doing today?" Jackson asked, glad to be back to noncontroversial subjects.

"The Morgan horses are finally going tomorrow, so we need to make sure all their gear is accounted for, check over the horses one last time, and work out an evacuation plan for loading them up into the trailers."

Jackson grimaced. "Not much, then."

"Shouldn't take too long." Cauy cleared his plate and set it in the sink to rinse. "We should be thinking about getting some more horses."

"Yeah?" Jackson looked over at his brother. "Maybe some more cows, too? You know, like a real ranch?"

"I was talking to Roy about that the other day. He said we can come out with him next time he goes to the county auction."

"Sounds good." Jackson continued eating as Cauy cleared the table around him and opened the dishwasher.

"I've been invited to dinner at the Gardins," Cauy said.

Jackson put down his fork and stared at the back of his brother's head, but Cauy didn't turn around.

"Are you going?"

Cauy shrugged. "Yeah. Tonight, actually."

"Do you want me to come with you?" Jackson offered.

"I think I'd rather handle this one myself." Cauy finally looked over his shoulder. "It's going to be damned awkward enough without—"

"Me putting my foot in it," Jackson completed his brother's sentence. "It's okay, I get it. Did they say what they wanted to talk about?"

"Shep didn't mention anything specific. I think they just want the chance to get to know me."

Seeing as they'd missed out on the last thirty years of Cauy's life because Mark had made that a condition of their mother marrying him, Jackson could totally understand their need to get to know their only grandson.

"Great, then I'll get my own dinner." Jackson nodded.

"Or go see Daisy?" Cauy finished loading the dishwasher. "Maybe it's time to have an honest conversation with her, dude. If you really don't think she's into you, maybe it's time to break free for your own sanity."

"Yeah, there is that." Jackson paused. "Although her reasons for hanging out with me are a lot more complicated than you might think."

"That's on her." Cauy met his gaze head-on. "It's not your job to sacrifice yourself to make her life easier."

"Walking out on her right now would feel wrong," Jackson confessed.

"Are you sure about that, or are you just hanging on in case you can change her mind?"

Jackson raised an eyebrow. "Isn't it my job to ask the stupid questions?"

"Not always." Cauy's rare smile emerged. "I'm just looking out for your interests, bro."

"Great," Jackson muttered. "Complicate everything, why don't you?" His cell buzzed and he removed it from his pocket to check the incoming text. "BB Morgan wants me to come over to his place this afternoon."

"As long as we get the Morgan horse stuff sorted out this morning, you can do what you like this afternoon." Cauy filled his flask with the remains of the coffee.

"Thanks, boss," Jackson retorted, and texted BB a thumbs-up. He wanted to check in with Daisy, but something was holding him back "Then I'd better get a move on."

Roy, the foreman of Morgan Ranch, didn't hold much with computers and liked everything done the old-fashioned way, with paper and ink. Each Morgan Ranch horse had a set of paperwork detailing nutritional needs, veterinary encounters, health, daily exercise, and what kind of temperament the horse had so it could be paired with the right kind of ranch guest rider. Chase had backed everything up on digital spreadsheets, but Roy pretended not to know about that.

Being a numbers-and-information guy himself, the paperwork didn't faze Jackson. He was more than willing to spend his morning reading through each bible and working out which horses would load best together in each trailer. He also checked out their gear, halters, lead ropes, blankets, fly masks, and all the other stuff the horses had accumulated during their long stay at Lymond Ranch.

Cauy did the actual physical checking of each horse and updated Jackson's record keeping as he went. The barn would look empty when the horses were rehoused. Jackson would miss them, as would the remaining Lymond horses, who only numbered five.

Cauy turned the last horse out into the meadow and came back to the barn, swinging the lead rope like a lasso in his hand.

"They're all good to go."

"Great." Jackson checked the rope Cauy handed him and hung it back on its correct peg in the tack room. He liked to keep everything tidy in there. "I'm going to miss these guys."

"Me too." Cauy leaned against the open doorframe. "I wasn't so sure when Chase originally asked to borrow our barn, but the Morgan ranch hands were awesome at helping out around here and saved us months of extra work."

"Yeah, something our dad never bought into—the concept of sharing the load with the other ranchers in this valley," Jackson said. "When I'm at the Morgan Ranch later today, I'll remind Roy about taking us to the next auction."

"Yeah, seeing as we claim to be a ranch, we really should get some more cattle." Cauy nodded. "And maybe some ranch hands, now that we have all the newly renovated accommodation."

"All hat, no cattle?" Jackson grinned. "Ranch hands might be harder to get than the cows. There aren't many guys around who want to bunk together without their families anymore."

"Which is why we need more housing." Cauy turned toward the house. "Did you hear that the Cortez Ranch is for sale?"

"Nope." Jackson reviewed what he knew of the old ranching family. "Didn't the daughter marry Adam Miller?"

"Yeah, she did, but she died really young, and she was the Cortezes' only child."

"That sucks." Jackson grimaced. "Is that one of the ranches Chase was talking about that might end up being sold to a housing developer?"

"I'd guess so. It's pretty close to town." Cauy led the way into the mudroom, where both he and Jackson removed their boots and heavy jackets and washed up. "It would be perfect for new housing."

"Except that it sticks right out into ranching country and would affect the three other ranches around it, including the Gardins."

"Yeah, I know." Cauy paused at the kitchen door. "I'm going to try to find out how much the Cortez family want for the ranch."

"Why?" Jackson followed him through and received an enthusiastic reception from the rapidly growing puppies. "It doesn't affect us."

"I just want to get some idea what it's worth, and it does border our ranch right at the southern end." Cauy went over to the refrigerator and opened it wide. "Do you want some of those sausages I cooked last night? We might as well eat them up."

"Daisy might know," Jackson said slowly. "I bet Adam talked to the Cortez family about it."

"He might have." Cauy didn't sound particularly interested. "But I'd rather talk to them myself, so don't use it as an excuse to go talk to Daisy."

Jackson scowled at his brother. For someone who didn't

talk much, his brother sometimes saw through him way too quickly.

"I'll leave it up to you, then." Jackson tried to sound as unconcerned as Cauy, but he didn't even fool himself. "Let me know what they say."

Chapter Fourteen

"Daisy!" Auntie Rae dropped her overnight bag on the ground and opened her arms wide. "How are you, my *darling* girl?"

Daisy ran straight into the hug and breathed in the well-remembered scent of lavender that always made her feel safe. For an absurd second, she wanted to snuggle into Rae's shoulder and bawl like her five-year-old self. She recovered enough to pull back and grin at her aunt.

"Auntie Rae. It's *so* good to see you!"

Her aunt had short hair dyed an improbable shade of yellow and wore bright scarlet lipstick. She tended toward pantsuits, frilly blouses, and lots of gold jewelry. She'd looked that way even when living on the ranch caring for six kids. She had *style*, and having none of her own, Daisy had always admired her. Rae had given up trying to get Daisy interested in fashion and let her find her own way. At the age of forty, she'd surprised everyone and gone off to marry a guy she'd met at a protest march in Sacramento.

Daisy had visited Rae's house and developed a great relationship with Rick, her new uncle, who did something in politics in the state capital that Rae never bothered to fully explain or understand. Daisy had been away from

Morgan Valley last Christmas and hadn't seen her beloved aunt for quite some time.

Ben picked up Rae's discarded bag and called out to her as she went into the house with Daisy. "Do you have the keys to the trunk, Auntie? I'll get the rest of your things."

"Thanks, Ben. The keys are still in the car." Rae paused, her finger in the air. "I think I left the engine running, so you might want to fix that."

Both Rae and her brother were terrible drivers and had been useless at teaching the kids. Adam had paid for his own lessons, and once he'd learned, he'd been the one to teach everyone else.

"Is that you, Rae?" Daisy's dad came to meet his sister when she walked into the house and gave her a big hug. "You do know it isn't Christmas yet?"

Rae patted his cheek. "I'm not going doolally, you silly old fool. Of *course* I know it's not Christmas. There's no snow, for one thing."

"And the tree's not up," Adam muttered, making Daisy want to laugh.

"So what brings you here then?" her father asked, leading her through into the kitchen.

"Give me a chance to get my breath, Jeff, and catch up with the kids, and I'll tell you." Rae patted his shoulder.

"I've got to get back to work." Daisy's father wasn't one for frivolous conversation. "Can it wait until this evening?"

"Sure it can." Not bothered by his gruffness, Rae waved him away. "Now off you guys go so I can spend some quality girl time with Daisy."

Daisy would rather Rae spilled the beans right away, but she knew her aunt well enough to understand she wouldn't get a peep out of her until the social niceties had been observed. That meant Rae would expect a detailed history of all the families in Morgan Valley since her last visit and at least a summary of the most recent gossip and goings-on in town. Daisy was aware she had been a major disappointment to her aunt in the gathering of gossip but resolved to make up for it now.

The lovely thing about Rae was that five minutes after arriving, she'd already slipped seamlessly into the routine of the household, as if she'd never left. She helped Daisy start dinner, made pastry for pie, and started a shopping list for the following week. She also kept up a constant stream of conversation about her life in Sacramento interspersed with questions about her old friends in town.

"So the Cortez family is selling up?" Rae sipped her coffee and looked over at Daisy, who was just shutting the refrigerator door.

"Yes, Adam said Carlos has some kind of cancer, and they want to move closer to a specialty hospital." Daisy joined her aunt at the table and added cream to her own cup of coffee. "I don't think it's generally known that the Cortez family are leaving town, though, so keep it to yourself."

"Will do." Rae sipped her coffee. "How's Adam taking it?"

"He's not happy." Daisy grimaced. "They offered to sell him the ranch, but he obviously can't afford it."

"Good." Rae nodded, making her earrings jangle. "The last thing Adam needs is the opportunity to create another shrine to Louisa."

Daisy blinked at her aunt. "You think he's still too hung up on her?"

"You know he is, Daisy, and taking on the Cortez place would make things worse. He needs a fresh start, not another attempt to stay stuck in the past."

"He asked me if I'd lend him the money," Daisy confessed.

"I hope you said no."

"I don't have the money to lend him."

Rae sat back. "What happened to those savings accounts I helped you set up?"

"Um . . ." Daisy gulped in air. She'd forgotten Rae had been privy to her financial decisions all those years ago. "Oh, that's all tied up for *years*."

"No, it isn't," Rae retorted. "I know what you signed."

"How do you know I haven't changed things up a little?" Daisy desperately hedged, aware that everything she'd liberated from the accounts had gone into seed money for the new start-up.

"Because I know you, my love. I had to drag you kicking and screaming to set up the first lot of accounts. I doubt you went back voluntarily for more."

Daisy stared at her aunt, wishing she had Jackson's talent for babbling on about nothing,

Rae opened her eyes wide, her voice like honey, and sat forward.

"You're looking really guilty about *something*, Daisy Leanne Miller, so why don't you just tell your Auntie Rae what the problem is?"

Her aunt had always won using guile rather than demanding stuff up-front like her dad.

"I have a boyfriend!" Daisy blurted out the only thing that might divert her aunt from her financial inquisition.

"You *do*?" Rae smiled. "So you've finally gotten over your first love? Maybe you could teach Adam a thing or two."

"What first love?" Daisy demanded.

"Oh for goodness' sake, Daisy, I saw the change in you when you came back from college that first year. I heard you talking on the phone at all hours of the night and I saw your *face*." Rae sighed. "You were . . . *glowing*. And then something went wrong, and you closed yourself up and didn't come home for almost two years. I had to come out to see you at Stanford."

"You never said anything to me." Daisy folded her arms over her chest.

"I tried, but you didn't want to listen." Rae grimaced. "It was the first time you'd ever shut me out. I didn't know how to get through to you. I just hoped and prayed that time would heal you." She hesitated. "What happened?"

"My boyfriend, Brody, had a huge fight with his family, dropped out of college, and went into the army. Six months later, he died in Afghanistan. He'd just turned twenty."

Rae reached across the table and grabbed Daisy's hand, her eyes filling with tears. "The poor boy . . . why didn't you tell me?"

"It didn't seem *right*." Daisy tried to remember why it had seemed so vital to keep her despair to herself at the time. "You'd just met Rick and were finally free of bringing up six kids. Dad wasn't very interested in hearing about my boyfriends. I wanted you to be happy about your new life and not focused on me."

"That was very sweet of you, dear, but I'm a Miller *and* a woman. I can multitask right up there with the best of them."

"It seems stupid now," Daisy confessed. "But at the time, the shock was so all-encompassing, I wasn't functioning properly." She met her aunt's compassionate gaze. "I don't think I'd keep it to myself now."

For a moment, they simply held hands and sat in silence until Rae stirred.

"Tell me about your new boyfriend."

"His name is Jackson Lymond, and—"

"Wait." Rae interrupted her. "I do hope he has nothing to do with that awful drunkard *Mark* Lymond."

"Jackson's his son."

"Poor boy." Rae shook her head. "I remember Mark's wife Anita; she was lovely. I have some recollection of them having two boys because they were of an age with some of your brothers."

"Mark died a couple of years ago, leaving the ranch in a terrible state. His older son, Cauy, came back to take it over." Daisy decided to give Rae the whole rundown.

"Cauy was the quiet one," Rae said. "Mark never had a good word to say about the boy."

Knowing how much her aunt loved gossip, Daisy prepared to unload. "Well, funny you should say that because *apparently*, Cauy wasn't actually Mark's son. Anita was pregnant when she married him."

Rae's mouth made a perfect O. "*Really*? That makes all kinds of sense."

"Cauy left when he was sixteen to get away from Mark. Anita stayed until Jackson went into the United States Air Force Academy and Amy went off to college. Then Anita divorced Mark, stayed with her parents for a while, and went to live in Florida."

"Good for her," Rae interjected.

"For some reason, Mark left the ranch to Cauy, and when Jackson came out of the air force last year, he came home to help his brother restore the place."

"So this Jackson was in the air force and he's now a rancher?"

"Yes." Daisy sat back. "He has Mark's looks, but he's nothing like him at all."

"I guessed that or you wouldn't have agreed to go out with him." Rae pulled the shopping list toward her. "When can he come over for dinner? I can't wait to meet him."

"He's pretty busy right now with . . . ranch things, but I can certainly ask if he wants to come over to meet you," Daisy agreed. "How long are you planning on being here?"

"Rick's off playing golf with his buddies, so I'll be here for at least a couple of weeks." Rae scribbled herself a note and then got to her feet. "The pastry needs folding again. Do you want to help me with the peach filling before we head off into town?"

"Sure."

She'd spend a couple of hours at the shop while Rae got through with her visiting and meet her aunt for a late lunch at Yvonne's. Desperate to direct Rae away from the troubled waters of her current finances, Daisy would've jumped into a vat of boiling oil if necessary. Skinning and chopping a few peaches was a small price to pay for breathing space. She could always claim Jackson was too busy to meet Rae.

She stared down at her folded hands. She was doing it again—expecting Jackson to pull her out of a hole. At some point, whatever he said, he was probably going to get tired of saving her. *And* she'd have another load of explaining to do. After their San Francisco trip, she wasn't sure where they stood anymore . . . She'd reminded him not to get serious, and he'd backed off from sharing his worries with her, which was what she'd wanted. Except now perhaps it wasn't.

"Are you okay, Daisy?" Rae looked back at her from the sink.

"Just peachy," Daisy said.

"Hey." Jackson used the front entrance to access the flower shop. Daisy was behind the counter talking to Bella from the Red Dragon Bar while she made up a bouquet.

"Hi, Jackson!" Daisy smiled at him, which was reassuring, and so did Bella Williams. "Did you want flowers or did you just come to see me?"

"You of course, but I'm not in a rush. I'll wait."

Bella handed over her credit card. "We're almost done.

It's my daughter-in-law's birthday today, so I'm taking her some flowers."

"I'm sure she'll love them," Jackson responded. "Daisy's really creative." He thought about adding, *in many ways*, but that might make her blush and turn his thoughts to sex, which was never good in public.

He still wanted her, but where did he draw the line? And, more importantly, where did Daisy see the line being drawn? Was it time to hash the whole thing out again, or was he too scared to mention it in case she told him to get lost?

Bella departed, the bouquet held carefully in her hand, and Daisy came around the counter to see her out the door. She wore her usual jeans and flower shop T-shirt and Jackson just wanted to grab her and hold her close.

"Hi." She came over and went up on tiptoe to kiss his cheek. "Mmm, you smell nice."

"I borrowed Cauy's shaving gel this morning and used it all up," Jackson confessed. "Don't tell him. That's one of the reasons I came into town today."

"What was the other?"

"To see you of course." He cupped her chin. "I was wondering whether you'd heard anything back from those Silicon Valley guys?"

"Not yet." She made a face. "They have to go back, talk to their board of investors, and secure permission to fund each venture."

"Okay, but Chase doesn't have to do that, does he?"

"Chase isn't the one making the initial decision because Jake's handling it. At some point Jake will talk to his two partners, but yes, they'll probably get back to us more quickly," Daisy agreed. "I hate all this waiting."

"Couldn't you just sell the idea to another company and be done sooner?" Jackson asked.

"It's possible, but the closer we are to offering a complete product and potentially even gaining a client or two, the more attractive we become to buyers." She sighed. "Which means more commitment, more funding rounds, and the potential to lose control of the whole thing along the way."

"Which is what happened before, right?"

"Yes. We diluted our equity too much, got sold for one hundred million dollars, and only got three fourths of a percent out of that between the five of us."

Jackson tried to work out the math in his head and failed miserably. "That sounds bad."

"We got *something*, but most of us had college debt to pay off, credit card debt, and all the stuff we'd lived off for the four years we'd been developing the product." Daisy stuck her hand in her pocket. "It's not quite like the movies. Most start-ups run on a dime. For companies like ours, with high growth expectations and huge market opportunity, if we don't get proper investment, which means offering up some equity in the company, we won't succeed."

"Maybe Chase and his buddies will come through for you?" Jackson asked. "At least you know they're honest."

"You *never* know," Daisy said gloomily. "I'm not even sure I'd trust my mother—no, strike that—I'd never trust her, but you get my point."

He bent to kiss her nose, and she didn't back away, so he kissed her mouth. "Have you got time for lunch today?"

Her brow crinkled. "I *think* that will work if it's later. I was planning on going to Yvonne's around two."

"Works for me. I've got to get some stuff from the store and pick up the mail first."

"Then I'll meet you there." Her smile took his breath away. Jeez . . . he was so screwed.

"Are you okay, Jackson?" Daisy asked.

He took a hasty step away from her, aware he'd been staring. "Yeah, I'm good. I'll see you at Yvonne's."

As he walked down the street, he gave himself a stern lecture about abiding by Daisy's rules, but it didn't help much.

"Yo! Jackson!"

He looked up to see BB Morgan standing beside his truck by the post office.

"Hey, what's up?" Jackson said.

"You free tomorrow night?"

"Yeah, I think so; why?"

"Because I've got a couple of military friends coming in, and I'd like your input on this survival course thing."

"Sure." Jackson was happy to agree. He was really interested in the idea and glad BB had thought to include him again. "Where and what time?"

He continued into the one and only store in Morgantown that was all tourist at the front and all local stuff in the back. He needed new jeans, having ripped his favorite pair on a coil of wire while he was mending the boundary fence.

An unknown woman checking out the racks of Western shirts looked up as he went past, and he tipped his hat to her.

"Ma'am."

"Are you Jackson?"

"Yes, I am." He raised an eyebrow. "Um, should I know you?"

"You probably won't remember me, dear, but you do have a look of your father, and Daisy said you resembled him, although he never smiled, so I guessed it might be you." She beamed at him. "My, what a handsome man you turned into!"

"You know Daisy?" Jackson asked cautiously

"I'm her Auntie Rae." She stuck out her hand, making

her bracelets jangle. "It's so nice to meet you again. I'm just getting some shopping in for the ranch, and I stopped to talk to Maureen because we've known each other for years, and ended up in here spending too much money." She pointed to a pile of bags next to the door.

"Can I help you take your bags to the car?" Jackson offered.

"That would be lovely of you, dear. I parked behind the store so it isn't far, and then I'm supposed to be meeting Daisy at the café for lunch."

"What a coincidence, so am I," Jackson said.

He set his jeans to the side and just about managed to pick up all the bags and stagger out into the parking lot. He hadn't known Maureen sold solid lead bricks, but he didn't want to drop anything and look like a wuss.

"Oh."

He carefully put the bags on the ground and regarded Daisy's aunt, who was staring at the rental car she'd somehow managed to park sideways at an angle over three spaces.

"Is everything okay, ma'am?"

"Please call me Rae. It's much nicer than 'ma'am,' which makes me feel like my grandmother." She frowned. "I don't know what I did with my keys."

"Did you put them in your purse or your pocket?" Jackson asked. His mom never remembered where she put her keys, so he was used to helping out.

She upended her purse on the hood of the car. Jackson rushed to corral half her possessions from either rolling off the car or blowing away in the wind.

"Ah! Here they are!" She unearthed the keys from a mound of tissues. "I'm not used to driving this car and I keep forgetting what the darned key thing looks like." She looked back toward the store. "And I haven't said goodbye to Maureen yet."

Jackson stepped up. "How about I pack the bags in the trunk, lock up the car, and meet you back in the store? Then we can walk down to Yvonne's together?"

Rae smiled and patted his cheek. "You're such a nice man. I can see why Daisy picked you for her boyfriend. I'll go inside and wait for you there."

After loading the bags, Jackson took the opportunity to back the car into a single space. It got busy behind the store, and he didn't want Daisy's aunt getting a ticket from Nate Turner.

He went back in and found Rae talking away to Maureen. While she chatted, he reclaimed his jeans, got the food supplies on his list, and paid for everything. When Rae finally ran out of breath, she took his arm and walked with him along Main Street toward the pink and black awnings of the coffee shop.

Jackson held the door open for Rae and followed her inside to find Daisy sitting at a table near the back. She jumped to her feet when she saw them, a guilty look on her face that didn't surprise Jackson one bit.

"Daisy! Look who I bumped into at the store," Rae called out to her niece. "Your lovely boyfriend! And isn't he just the sweetest thing?"

Rae sat down, placing her purse on the table, leaving Jackson eye to eye with Daisy. He held up his bags.

"I'm just going to put these in the truck and be right back. Can you order me some lemonade?"

When he went back inside, his lemonade was waiting for him. He gulped it down gratefully before turning his attention to charming Daisy's Auntie Rae, which wasn't difficult because she was a complete badass. She questioned him intently about his mother, his brother and sister, and what exactly had been up with his father before his death, but he took it all in good part.

Daisy didn't say a lot, her gaze going between him and her aunt as she managed to slip in the odd word. Eventually, Rae got up to go to the bathroom, leaving him alone with Daisy for the first time.

"I meant to tell you that Rae might be joining me," Daisy said.

"It's all good," Jackson replied, keeping his tone light.

"Sometimes she gets to chatting and forgets the time, so I wasn't sure she'd actually turn up." Daisy still sounded a little tense.

"Your auntie Rae is awesome," Jackson said. "I don't really remember her from before because it was usually your dad or Adam who came to all our games."

"After my mom left, Dad asked her for help, and she dropped everything and came to live with us. I'll never forget that," Daisy said. "She's my hero."

"So did you tell her the truth about our relationship, or does she really think you chose to go out with me? I want to make sure I don't put my foot in it or anything."

"I told her you were my boyfriend." Daisy met his gaze levelly. "She'll take that at face value."

"Great." Jackson finished off his second glass of lemonade. "I'll have to get going soon. I'm meeting Roy up at Morgan Ranch to talk cattle."

"Okay." Daisy messed around with her silverware. "I feel like you're still annoyed with me."

Jackson stood and pushed in his chair. "I don't have the right, remember? We're just friends."

She raised her chin. "I know I'm asking a lot."

"Yeah, you are." For some reason, Jackson couldn't

find a way to laugh it off. "But hey, my bad. I knew what I signed up for."

Daisy sighed. "Can we sit down and talk about this properly, Jackson?"

"Not right now. I've really got to go," Jackson prevaricated.

"Can you meet me after the shop closes tomorrow night?"

"I'm meeting BB tomorrow."

"Then the night after?"

"Sure." He tipped his hat to her. "I'll call you if I can't make it. Say my goodbyes to your auntie Rae for me, okay?"

"Will do." Daisy looked down at her plate, her long hair covering her expression. "Thanks, Jackson."

After paying the bill, he left the shop and went back to his truck. He should've known that with him and Daisy, a collision of some kind was inevitable. They lived to butt heads and their next conversation might well be their last. Jackson considered that as he started the engine. Usually, he was the one who kept things light in his relationships, but something had changed. Daisy brought out all his protective instincts and he didn't want to let her go.

He backed out of the space. Did he want to be that guy? The one who was hopelessly in love with someone who would never feel the same way?

Hell no.

Maybe it was time to have it out and go their separate ways before he lost his heart for good.

Daisy drove home with Rae following merrily along behind in her rental. They'd spent a couple of hours at the flower shop, where her aunt had proven to be an excellent salesperson. Daisy had forgotten that Rae had helped out

Great-Aunt Florrie, who had originally opened the shop back in the sixties.

Rae had also gone on and on about how nice Jackson was until Daisy had felt so guilty, she'd almost blurted out the truth. Jackson hadn't been happy with her either, and she had a sense their upcoming discussion might mean a parting of the ways. Even as she admitted it, her stomach clenched in denial. She didn't want to lose him. Was it time to admit he'd become way more than a stand-in boyfriend?

He was kind, he was loyal to a fault, and he'd been a rock over the past few weeks, shielding her from discovery and encouraging her to do her thing. And that wasn't even considering the closeness between them and the phenomenal sex . . .

When she got home, she would text Nancy and Yvonne and ask them to meet her tomorrow night, when she knew Jackson was occupied. Maybe her friends could help her unravel the tangle she'd gotten herself into with some good, honest, plain-speaking advice.

By the time they entered the kitchen at the ranch, the rich smell of the casserole Rae had put in the slow cooker before they'd left filled the house and several of Daisy's brothers were milling around waiting to be fed. Of course Rae had to hug each brother, interrogate them about their lives, and give them lots of advice before they could finally sit down as a family to eat.

It was toward the end of the meal that Daisy's father, who never ate dessert, poured himself a cup of coffee and turned to Rae.

"So while we're all present, tell me why you came to visit?"

Rae rolled her eyes. "Really, Jeff, you want me just to blurt it out in front of all the kids?"

"Don't see any kids sitting here, Rae." Her father looked

around the table. "They're all old enough to hear whatever you have to say, so spit it out."

Rae dabbed at her mouth with her napkin and put it down. "I had a letter from Leanne."

Daisy sat up straighter and shared a surprised glance with Kaiden, who was sitting opposite her.

"My Leanne?" Daisy's dad asked.

"Yes." Rae sighed. "She wants to come visit the ranch."

"*Why?*"

"She said it's important and that she needed closure."

"What the heck does that mean?" Daisy's dad snorted. "She's the one who walked out twenty-odd years ago. No one was pushing her."

"I know that," Rae said patiently. "I haven't replied to her yet. I wanted to ask you what you want me to do."

There was silence around the table, as if everyone was gathering their thoughts. Adam was the first to stir.

"I don't need to see her, but it's up to Dad. It's his ranch."

Kaiden cleared his throat. "I'd be okay with it, actually— as long as Dad is."

"Me too," Ben said, and Danny and Evan nodded in agreement.

Rae looked over at Daisy. "What about you, sweetheart?"

Daisy crossed her arms over her chest. "I agree with Adam. I don't need to see her."

They all turned to look at their father, who sat at the head of the table staring off into space.

"Jeff?" Rae asked. "What do you think?"

He shrugged. "If she wants to come, I'm not going to stop her."

Daisy's mouth fell open. "Dad, you've never had a kind

word to say about her since she up and left us all. Why would you let her come here now?"

"As I told you the other day, I wasn't blameless." Her dad paused. "Perhaps Leanne isn't the only one in this family who needs closure."

Chapter Fifteen

"Did you find out how much the Cortez family want for their ranch?" Jackson asked Cauy.

They'd been working with the Morgans, moving the horses out all morning, and had finally retired for a late lunch after the last trailer load disappeared down the road. The ranch already felt empty, and Jackson missed the row of friendly faces in the barn.

"What?" Cauy looked up from his contemplation of the hastily reheated burrito on his plate.

It occurred to Jackson that Cauy had been even quieter than usual all morning.

"You said you were going to find out how much the Cortez Ranch was going for," Jackson reminded him.

"Oh, yeah, that." Cauy grabbed a piece of kitchen roll and wrapped it around the leaking burrito. "I didn't bother in the end."

"Okay." Jackson took a bite and hastily breathed out. "Jeez, that's hot." He chugged half his water. "Not spicy, just damn overheated." He chewed his food and then contemplated his brother again.

"Is everything okay, Cauy?"

"Yeah."

Despite the positive response, Cauy didn't sound very sure as he ate, his distant gaze directed out the window.

"Did you speak to that coin guy yet?" Cauy suddenly asked.

"No, I forgot. Why are you asking?" Jackson eyed his brother curiously at the abrupt change of subject. "I did leave him a message a couple of weeks ago, but he hasn't returned my call."

"I wonder where he lives?" Cauy mused. "Maybe it would be better to just take the coins over and pay him a surprise visit."

"What's the sudden rush?" Jackson asked. "Don't you have enough money?"

"You can never have enough money, bro." Cauy gave up on his burrito.

"Says the man who was telling me last week that he could live on love alone," Jackson muttered.

"I could, but luckily I don't have to." Cauy finally smiled at him. "What are you going to do for the rest of the day?"

"I thought I'd muck out the empty stalls and give them a hosing down."

"Great idea." Cauy nodded. "I've got to go into town."

"I'm meeting BB at the Red Dragon this evening." Jackson took another more cautious bite of the burrito. "I don't think I'll be that late back."

"You're not going to see Daisy?"

"I don't see her every day, bro." Jackson eyed his brother. "We're not like you and Rachel."

"Rachel's been away all week in Sacramento," Cauy pointed out. "She's coming back this weekend."

"If that's a hint, I'll try to keep out of the house over the weekend." Jackson winked at his brother. "I wouldn't want to embarrass Rachel."

He rose from the table and tossed the rapidly congealing

remnants of his burrito in the trash. "If you can find out where the coin guy lives, I'm happy to go see him with you."

"I'll ask January Morgan. She's the one who put me on to him." Cauy gave up on his own meal. He handed over his plate to Jackson, who dumped the food and put the plate in the dishwasher.

"How did it go with the Gardins?" Jackson was fairly sure something was still bothering his brother, but he wasn't sure what angle to take. Cauy could never be described as chatty.

"Good." Cauy nodded. "They're a really nice couple. It's a shame Mark wouldn't let Mom and me visit with them when I was growing up."

"Sounds just like him." Jackson shrugged. "He never wanted anyone to be happy." He rinsed his hands. "I'd better get a move on or I'll never get the barn cleaned out."

Daisy looked cautiously around the Red Dragon, but there was no sign of Jackson, so she walked through and took the booth at the farthest end of the space, well away from the bar. Nancy had to work and had asked if Daisy and Yvonne could meet her at the bar while she took her break.

It was midweek, and the bar was never as busy then as it was on the weekends. Daisy tried to gather her thoughts as she waited for her friends. What did she actually want to do about Jackson? She liked him. She really liked him. And then there was the other matter of the reappearance of her mother . . .

"Hey!" Yvonne slid into the opposite side of the booth and sat down. She'd tied her long black hair back in a ponytail and wore her favorite navy-striped T-shirt and skinny jeans. Her enormous engagement ring sparkled under the lights. "How's my favorite girl?"

"Don't let Nancy hear you call me that or she'll be jealous." Daisy smiled at her friend.

"I can have more than one favorite, you know." Yvonne checked the menu. "How could I possibly pick one of you? Are we going to eat or just drink?"

"Both, I think," Daisy said. "My Auntie Rae is holding down the fort tonight, so she told me to take as long as I needed."

"I love your Auntie Rae." Yvonne sighed. "She always looks so *chic.*"

"Which coming from you is a huge compliment." Daisy took a look at the menu. "I'm going to have the fried chicken. What about you?"

"A salad. I've been cooking with chocolate all day." Yvonne gathered the menus and stood up. "I'll put the order in at the bar, get our drinks, and see if Nancy is able to join us yet."

Nancy arrived with the food order, and for a while they just ate before Daisy got another round of beers, and they had time to talk.

"So what's up?" Nancy stole one of Daisy's fries. "And why is your Auntie Rae here when it isn't Christmas?"

"Guess what happened?" Daisy asked.

Yvonne and Nancy looked at her expectantly.

"My mom wants to visit the ranch."

Nancy blinked at her. "Your mom? She hasn't been around for over twenty years."

"I know. After she walked out and divorced Dad, we didn't hear a thing from her."

"And she suddenly wants to visit?" Nancy frowned. "What the hell?"

"I didn't even realize your mother was alive, Daisy," Yvonne said. "I've been here for years and this is the first time I've ever heard her mentioned."

"My dad wouldn't talk about her, and we weren't encouraged to mention her name," Daisy said. "It was an acrimonious divorce and we've heard nothing from her since. Not a Christmas card or a birthday card, just complete silence."

She'd been seven when it had finally dawned on her that her mother didn't care about her enough to even send her a birthday card. She'd foolishly hoped there would be something in the mail for her. She'd even seen a big pink letter once, but her father had assured her it wasn't addressed to her. That was when she'd taken the scrapbook she'd made of pictures of her mom and previous birthday cards and thrown it on the fire.

"That's really tough." Yvonne reached over and patted Daisy's hand. "How old were you when she left?"

"About five." Daisy grimaced. "Auntie Rae came to live with us almost immediately, so I never lacked a mother."

"Did your aunt deliver the message from your mother?" Nancy asked.

Daisy nodded. "Apparently, Leanne contacted her and wanted to know if it was possible to visit the ranch and see everyone. Rae wanted to check with Dad before she replied."

"Makes sense." Nancy nodded. "And I assume your dad told her no?"

"That's the weird thing." Daisy paused. "He was okay about it, and so were Kaiden, Danny, Ben, and Evan. Only Adam and I weren't happy about the idea."

"Figures Adam wouldn't go for it. He's very black-and-white about everything," Nancy mused. "But why don't you want to see her?"

"Why would I?" Daisy gazed at her friends. "She walked

out when I was five, never gave a damn about me for over twenty years, and now I'm suddenly supposed to be okay with that?"

"Maybe it would be good for your family to have closure on this?" Yvonne suggested gently.

"That's apparently what Leanne said." Daisy took a slug of beer. "I keep wondering what she means."

"Well, the best way to find out is to see the woman." Nancy put down her fork and wiped her mouth with her napkin. "What's the worst thing that can happen?"

Daisy stared at her friends. They could obviously see she was upset about the idea, but both of them seemed to think a meeting would be beneficial. Was she the one being obstinate about nothing? If so, why did her stomach cramp up at even the thought of seeing the woman who'd given birth to her and then walked out without a care? She'd idolized her mother, had loved every minute she'd spent with her, only to be left behind and forgotten.

"Why does she get to be the one who comes back?" Daisy demanded. "Why can't she just stay put wherever she is and not bother us?"

"I don't know, Daisy." Yvonne held her gaze, her eyes full of sympathy. "And you won't know unless you get the opportunity to see her."

Daisy crossed her arms over her chest. "I don't have to like her or anything, do I?"

"Of course you don't," Nancy agreed. "In fact, you could use it as an opportunity to tell her how you *really* feel."

"I suppose I could. The thing is—I don't know how I feel." Daisy imagined the scene and shuddered. "Or maybe I should just think about my dad. He wants to see her for whatever reason, and I should respect that."

Both her friends nodded and Nancy finished her beer. "When is she coming?"

"I don't know. Rae's going to reach out to her and find a good date." Daisy finished her second beer and decided to slow down. "Can we talk about Jackson now?"

Nancy had already half-risen, but she sank back down again.

"There's *more*?"

"Don't worry if you have to get back." Daisy waved her onward. "It will keep."

"Like I'd walk away when you're dissing on your fake boyfriend," Nancy joked. "Has he fake dumped you?"

"I've been *awful* to him. I think he's getting close to giving up on me," Daisy confessed.

"Which is okay, isn't it?" Nancy reminded her. "You said you didn't want him getting hurt. If he's the one who chooses to end it, he won't feel so bad."

"I'm not sure I want him to end it," Daisy blurted out. "I . . . *like* him a lot."

Aware that both her friends were staring hard at her, she kept her gaze on the table.

"Okay," Yvonne finally spoke. "So tell him to stay."

Daisy rolled her eyes. "You make everything sound so easy."

"Only because it is, and that sometimes you overcomplicate things," Yvonne pointed out.

"I'm . . . scared," Daisy said.

"That he'll reject you?" Yvonne sounded incredibly gentle. "I don't think he will. I've seen the way he looks at you."

"So you think I should just be brave?" Daisy finally raised her gaze to Yvonne's. "And tell him how I feel?"

"Yes, I do." Nancy nodded as well. "Just go for it."

"Okay." Daisy blew out a breath. "Then I'll talk to him."

"I've got to get back to work." Nancy gathered the plates. "Let me know how it goes, and if you need me to kick his ass." She winked at Daisy and turned toward the bar. "And hey, he just walked in with BB Morgan. Talk about perfect timing."

"Jackson did?" Daisy resisted the urge to turn around and take a peek herself. "I can't interrupt him *now*."

"Then why don't you hang out here with Yvonne for a while and catch him on his way out?" Nancy suggested. "I'll let you know when BB leaves."

Jackson went to the bar where Jay Williams was talking to Nancy and ordered a couple of beers for him and BB. He took them back to the table and handed one to his companion.

"Thanks." BB took a long swallow. "Getting all those horses into the new barn was exhausting, and made much worse by my stupid older brother and his algorithms."

"His what?" Jackson placed his beer on the table.

"Chase worked out a specific way to place the horses in the barn and Roy was having none of it. They argued about every damned horse, and I was the one who kept having to move them around." BB finished his beer.

"Can I get you another one?" Jackson offered.

"Nah. I'll let this one settle first. I don't want to be drunk in charge of this meeting." BB grinned at Jackson. "Two of my old marine buddies are passing through town tonight, so I asked them to come along to discuss the survival course idea. They've both worked on something similar on a ranch in Utah."

"Sounds good." Jackson took another sip of beer as Jay Williams joined them. He was way quieter than BB, but twice as dangerous.

"I've been doing some research myself, BB. I think we've got the perfect setup here in Morgan Valley to try out a variety of exercises, depending on the terrain, the weather, and the level of experience of the participants," Jackson said.

"Yeah? Good for you." BB nodded. "I occasionally run a class about basic horsemanship at the marine base near Bridgeport that ties in nicely with the overall theme."

"Why do the marines need that?" Jackson asked.

"For when they go into places like Afghanistan where trucks and tanks won't do the job." BB shrugged. "Riding in can be the only option, and it's much safer if you have the basics before you end up in a situation where you have to get the hell out of Dodge and a mule is your only form of transportation."

"I hear you." Jackson nodded, even though he'd never had to deal with the risks of conflict on the ground.

"Hey, guys." Samantha Kelly, HW Morgan's fiancée, who'd been invalided out of the army after she'd lost her foot in an explosion, came up behind Jay and took him in a headlock. "Getting a bit slow, big guy? Married life deadening those lethal reflexes?"

"Nah." Jay grunted as she squeezed him hard. "I heard you coming a mile up the road."

Sam looked down ruefully at her cowboy boots. "That's the problem with literally having a lead foot."

The bar door opened, and three guys Jackson didn't recognize came in. Jay tensed, his sharp gaze assessing the threat of the obviously military men.

"Are these your friends, BB?" Jay murmured.

"Two of them are. I don't know the third." BB stood and beckoned the guys over. "Hey. It's good of you to come."

Jay and Jackson rose as well. Two of the guys were smiling at BB, but the third was too busy sizing up the bar, his cold eyes everywhere.

"Thanks for stopping by, Pasco and José." BB clapped the two guys on the shoulder. "Who's your friend?"

"This is Mayer," Pasco said without much enthusiasm. "I've been working with him this last month on a security detail."

BB shook hands with the guys, and so did Jay, Sam, and Jackson.

"Good to meet you all," Jackson said as they sat down. "What would you like to drink?"

When he returned from the bar with five frosted bottles of beer in his fingers, BB was already holding forth on his idea. José and Pasco were also chipping in as Jay listened intently.

Mayer glanced at the beer as Jackson set it down. "Hey, would you mind getting me a double whiskey to go with that?"

"Sure." Jackson turned back to the bar.

"Put it on my tab," Jay called out to him.

"Thanks."

Jackson got the double whiskey and delivered it to Mayer, who downed it in one swallow. On closer inspection, Jackson noticed Mayer's hands were shaking, and his flushed skin betrayed the lines of a heavy drinker. Having lived with an alcoholic, Jackson's opinion of Mayer didn't improve. Not that he blamed any retired serviceman for coping with the horrors of war however they could, but Mayer was obviously pushing the limit.

They talked for a while about the different kind of survival courses, what worked in a civilian setting and what didn't. Pasco was very knowledgeable, and so was José, whereas Mayer just liked the sound of his own voice.

"Yeah, lady, but—" Mayer cut in on Sam for the third time, and she leaned in toward him, her hands planted on the table.

"Will you just let me finish a *sentence*, dude?"

Mayer smirked at her. "Well, actually no, seeing as you don't seem to understand the topic."

"I'm retired military police; I sure as hell understand the topic." Sam raised her voice sufficiently to make Jay put a restraining hand on her arm.

"She's right." Jay spoke up for the first time. "Lay off her and listen. You might learn something."

Mayer shrugged and rose to his feet. "If she's going to talk, I'll get another whiskey."

He went off toward the bar, unaware that behind him, Sam had risen from her chair and was being physically held back by Jay.

"Settle down, Sam. He's not worth your time," BB said, and then turned to Pasco. "Where the hell did you find him?"

"He hitched a ride from us." Pasco grimaced. "I don't like him, but I couldn't leave him sitting out in the truck all night in case he got it into his head to take off."

"He'd better keep a civil tongue in his head or I'll let Sam loose on him," Jay warned as she growled.

Sam continued to glare at Mayer, who was drinking way faster than everyone else as they continued their discussion. Jackson talked as much as everyone, and felt his excitement growing. If he could help BB with the course, it would give him an extra purpose in Morgan Valley, and a new stream of income so he could eventually purchase his own ranch.

And if he stayed, maybe once Daisy was free of Silicon Valley, she would come around to seeing him as the right man for her.

A man could dream, right?

Sam and José were getting more drinks at the bar while BB caught up writing notes on his phone. Jackson realized he'd had three beers in quick succession and he'd better stop. Working outside in the heat all day had dehydrated him, making him feel the effects of the alcohol way too quickly.

"So what did you do in the service?"

He turned to Mayer, who had addressed him.

"I was in the air force."

Mayer slapped his palm on the table and towered over Jackson. "I should've known it. You've got the look of a man who never set foot on the damned ground."

"I did my basic training like everyone else." Jackson met the other man's derisive gaze. "I was involved in combat missions."

"From where? Freaking Las Vegas? Where your lily-white ass couldn't get hurt?" Mayer scoffed. "You chair merchants make me sick."

"Hey—" Jay spoke up, but Mayer didn't stop.

"How many men did you send into danger without fricking air cover? How many died because you bunch of traitors ended up bombing your own side?"

Before he even registered he'd moved, Jackson was on his feet. He shoved Mayer hard in the chest, making him stumble backward.

"Oh, pretty boy wants a fight *now*?" Mayer jeered. "Only one he'll ever get into, while everyone else fucking dies."

"Shut the hell up."

"Why? You scared, cupcake?" Mayer asked. "You bunch of traitorous cowards, I—"

Jackson stepped in, grabbed Mayer around the throat, and lifted him off his feet.

There was a confusion of shouts around him, but Jackson didn't take his gaze away from Mayer's rapidly darkening face.

"Let him go," Jay murmured in his ear, his arm wrapped

around Jackson's chest like an iron bar. "Now. He's not worth it."

Jackson reluctantly released his grip and stepped back, breathing hard.

Pasco and José escorted Mayer out of the bar. He protested as he departed, while the other guys loudly apologized over him.

"Promise me you won't go after him if I release you," Jay said.

Jackson nodded, the rage leaving him as fast as it had appeared. He sat down, his whole body shaking with the spike of adrenaline.

"You okay?" Jay squatted in front of Jackson's chair.

Jackson blinked hard and tried to focus on Jay's calm expression. Did anything get under his skin? Did the retired Navy SEAL look like this when he was killing someone?

"Yeah. I'm good." Jackson took a much-needed breath. "Sorry."

"Nothing to be sorry about; the man's a complete jackass." Jay half-smiled. "I was so busy holding Sam back, I didn't pay attention to you. My bad."

"You're not responsible for my behavior," Jackson said. "It's on me." His gaze strayed around the bar, where the majority of the inhabitants were trying to pretend they hadn't noticed a thing. On the dining side of the bar, he focused on one appalled face.

Yeah. Of course Daisy was here to see him getting into a drunken brawl just like his father. It just wasn't his night.

When he abruptly left the bar, Daisy ran after Jackson and followed him into the parking lot behind the building.

"Jackson?" Her breath condensed in the cold air. She

wished she'd remembered her jacket and wasn't puffing from the two-minute run.

Jackson stopped walking, but he didn't turn around.

When she reached him, Daisy placed a tentative hand on his rigid arm. "Are you okay?"

"I'm great. Thanks."

She came around him and looked up into his eyes, shocked by the devastation in his gaze.

"Did that guy hurt you?" Daisy asked.

"No."

"Then why did you go for him?"

"Because he was telling me stuff I didn't want to hear." Jackson slowly exhaled. "Can we just forget it happened?"

"No, because . . ." Daisy tried to think of the right words to convince him to talk to her. "It sounds to me as if you might have unresolved anger issues about your military service, or maybe some PTSD, and . . ."

"Stop right there, okay?" Jackson was glaring at her now. "You're so way off-base you don't have a clue what you're talking about."

"I'm trying to help!" Daisy stamped her booted foot. "Seeing you attack someone? That's not *like* you!"

"How do you know? Maybe I got kicked out of the air force for being violent or something."

"You did not." It was Daisy's turn to glare at him. "Don't lie to me."

He looked away from her, his attention fixed on the distant mountains. "He was right, you know. I never experienced combat on the ground. I did get to sit there and make decisions in the safety of our command center."

"So *what*?" Daisy asked. "You did your part."

"From the safety of *Qatar.*"

She gently shook his shoulder. "You did what you were ordered to do, right?"

"Yeah."

She didn't like the flatness of his tone, or the way he refused to look at her.

"Will you come back inside?" Daisy asked. "I was hoping to talk to you about something . . ."

He stepped away from her and shoved his hand in his pocket. "It's okay. I don't need to come inside to hear you dump me. Let's just take it as a given."

"Hang on . . ." Daisy squared up to him again. "Who said anything about *dumping* you?"

He shrugged. "It's obvious I've made you feel uncomfortable."

"You're right I'm feeling uncomfortable, but that's because I've never seen you lose your temper before, and I'm *worried* about you!"

"Sorry you had to see that." He stared back toward the bar, as if dying to get away from her. "I've got to get my stuff, but I won't get in your way. It was nice knowing you."

"Jackson . . ." Daisy stared up at him. "Why are you doing this?"

"Doing what?"

"Pushing me away."

He blew out a breath. "Because we both know this isn't going anywhere, okay? And maybe you should be congratulating yourself because you just got to see the real Jackson Lymond—the one who has a mean temper just like his father."

"You got mad because that guy suggested you were some kind of coward by doing the job assigned to you," Daisy said. "That's—"

"That's the goddamn *truth*." His voice rang out in the

silence. "I *am* a coward, and hell yeah I didn't have to get my *hands* dirty, but I killed people all right."

He turned away and stalked back into the bar, slamming the door behind him.

Daisy stayed where she was, trying to process exactly what had happened, still unwilling to believe the words that had come out of his mouth. She *knew* him. He wasn't that person, so who had convinced him he was?

She glanced at the lights in the bar, where everything appeared to have settled down again. She'd have to go back inside. Her purse and jacket were still in the booth—at least she hoped they were. Would it be better to wait for Jackson to calm down and speak to him tomorrow, or would he be back to his usual charming, evasive self? If this *was* the real Jackson, maybe it was time for her to get to know him.

Chapter Sixteen

Jackson spent a while in the bar, making sure BB, Sam, and Jay knew he'd calmed down and wouldn't be going after Mayer. He also wanted to make sure BB wouldn't drop him from the project after seeing him get mad. To his relief, none of them said a word about his outburst and instead heaped their disdain on Mayer, who certainly wouldn't be invited back to Morgan Ranch anytime soon.

Jackson was aware that Jay in particular was keeping a close eye on him, but he didn't resent it. Jay owned the bar, and the last thing he needed was for another brawl to break out. He obediently drank three cups of black coffee and some iced water until he was ready to leave with Jay's blessing.

He hadn't seen Daisy come back inside, but he guessed she must have collected her things and gone home. When he'd seen her watching him, he'd felt like he was the one who'd been assaulted. He rarely lost his temper, but it wasn't pretty when he did, and her seeing him like that? No wonder she'd come after him.

"I'd better get home." Jackson stood and fished in his pocket for his wallet. "What do I owe you, Jay?"

"Nothing." Jay waved away his offer and rose to his feet. "I'll walk you to your truck."

Jackson accepted the escort, said his goodbyes to BB and a still fuming Sam, who was annoyed she hadn't gotten in a punch herself. He went back out into the parking lot behind the bar. Jay walked to the right of him, his gaze constantly flicking around the quiet streets and the crosswalk beyond.

"Force of habit." Jay shrugged as he caught Jackson watching him. "Even though I grew up here, my lizard brain still thinks there's a threat hidden around every corner."

"It's okay. BB and Sam are the same." Jackson found his keys and opened the door of his truck. "I'm sorry about what happened earlier."

"Nothing to be sorry about." Jay held his gaze. "Mayer was dead wrong, you know. Just because you're on the ground doesn't mean you can always save lives. I've been on missions when my orders were to observe and not interfere until given the signal to advance. I've seen shit go down that still gives me nightmares when I know I could've done something, but the success of the overall mission depended on me staying in place and 'observing.'" He grimaced. "You did your job. It's not easy. I get that."

"Thanks." Jackson nodded at the retired Navy SEAL. Jay didn't speak much, but when he did, it was wise to listen up. "I appreciate that."

"Good man." Jay clapped him on the shoulder. "Drive safely."

Jackson got into his truck, started the engine, and drove carefully out of town, aware that Nate Turner usually set his speed trap up on the county road just past the town boundary. The last thing he needed to make his night even worse was to get a ticket.

He focused on locating the unlit turnoff onto the Lymond Ranch road and got out to unlock the gate and close it behind him. When he reached the house, there were lights on in the kitchen, but no sign of his brother's truck.

He went into the kitchen, where Grace was already snuggled up with her puppies beside the fire. She wagged her tail at him but didn't come over to be petted. There was a note on the table with his name on it and he picked it up.

> *Rachel's plane delayed for six hours. Have gone to pick her up at the airport. We will probably crash in a hotel and come back tomorrow. Cauy.*

Well, that was good news. Jackson folded the note and tossed it into the trash. At least he didn't have to get past his brother's eagle eye and explain what had gone down at the bar. Cauy would find out soon enough from the local gossip, but at least Jackson would get a good night's sleep.

He drank another gallon of water and took two painkillers in anticipation of the headache he was fairly sure was due in the morning. Grace didn't seem inclined to go out again, so he locked the back door, turned down the lights, went to the bathroom, and then into his bedroom.

"Jeezus!" He clutched his chest like an old-fashioned movie heroine. "What the *hell* are you doing here?"

Daisy sat on the end of his bed. Her arms were folded over her chest and there was a determined expression on her face.

"Did I startle you? Sorry about that. I did ask Cauy if it was okay if I hung around."

Mentally strangling his suddenly forgetful brother, Jackson scrambled to find his composure.

"What do you want?"

Wow, that had come out smoothly, and not at all like a demand . . .

She raised her chin. "I didn't feel like we'd finished our conversation."

"I was okay with it." Jackson stared her down. "Where did you park?"

"On the other side of the barn. I figured you'd turn around and drive away if you realized I was here."

"You're right. I would've done that, which should tell you just how much I don't want to talk to you right now." Jackson walked backward to the door and turned to go. "You're welcome to stay. I'll take Cauy's room."

"Which particular thing that idiot said got to you?" Daisy asked almost conversationally. "Was it when he called you a coward?"

Jackson froze and looked back over his shoulder at her. "Are you trying to suggest that's what I'm being now?"

"Maybe." She shrugged. "It's hard to tell when you keep running away from me."

Jackson leaned against the doorframe and banged his forehead on it three times. With a resigned sigh, he reversed course and took the only chair in his bedroom, which was right opposite where Daisy had chosen to sit.

"You're not going anywhere, are you? What do you want to know?" Jackson mimicked her stance, his arms folded, his feet planted on the floor.

She met his gaze, her brown eyes steady. "Can we clear up a couple of things first?"

"Sure." Jackson glanced down at his watch, as if he had far more important things to do, which was kind of pathetic, and wouldn't fool anyone.

"You weren't let go from the air force for being violent, were you?"

"No." He was tired, he wanted to go to bed, and he had no energy left to fight with her.

She nodded. "Your friend Pez seemed to think if you wanted to go back, you'd be welcomed."

"Pez is a good guy."

"Which doesn't answer my question."

"That wasn't a question; that was a statement of fact," Jackson objected.

"Jeez." Daisy sighed. "I'd forgotten how pedantic you are."

"I just like to keep things straight." Jackson stared at her, but she didn't look away. "I chose not to renew my contract."

"Why?"

"Why does it matter?"

She sat forward, her hands clasped between her knees. "Because it matters to *you*. What happened to make you leave a job you were apparently good at and loved?"

He glanced furtively at the door. Maybe he could make a run for it, but if he wanted to live in Morgan Valley, he wouldn't be able to escape Daisy Miller for long. And hadn't he run away from enough people lately? His job, his mother, his brother . . .

"Okay. I planned a mission over Afghanistan. There was some miscommunication and our information was compromised, which meant that I, we, sent the planes to the wrong drop zone. Several of our own people were killed."

He forced himself to meet her gaze, but she didn't speak, she just looked at him until he felt compelled to continue.

"A couple of my good friends didn't make it back."

"That must have been terrible."

"Yeah. There's not much you can do when you see everything going wrong and you're hundreds of miles away. You can hear them, though—the pilots, the crews, the soldiers being dropped in the zone—you can hear them dying."

"Oh Jackson . . ." Her voice softened and her eyes filled with tears. "I'm so sorry."

He didn't want to look at her. He'd already lost his temper. Now he felt as if he might fall apart completely, and he couldn't allow that to happen.

"Hey, I'm alive." He shrugged. "They aren't. Save your tears for those who deserve them."

She came toward him, and he flinched as she wrapped her arms around him. God, he wanted to drop his head onto her shoulder and stay there forever . . .

Instead, he took her gently by the elbows and set her away from him. "It's getting late. You should go."

"Jackson . . ." She met his gaze. "I—"

He found a smile somewhere. "I don't need pity sex, okay? I've lived with this for a while, and I'm going to have to learn to live with it for the rest of my life. We agreed that last time I tried to use sex to forget my problems, it was a disaster, so let's just leave it at that."

"*Pity* sex?" Daisy repeated, her sympathy for Jackson rapidly becoming infused with way less kindly emotions. "I'm trying to help!"

"Yeah, by offering me sex."

She raised her eyebrows. "I haven't offered you anything yet."

"But you will." Jackson held her gaze. "I know you."

"You think I go around offering sex to anyone I feel *sorry* for?" She raised her chin. "Wow. If that's what you believe, you really don't know me very well at all."

"You're a good person, Daisy."

"I'm currently lying through my teeth to my entire

family and I've used up all my capital on a new start-up so I can't help my brother!" Daisy only realized she might be yelling when Jackson winced. "And let's not forget I've screwed you around horribly as well! I'm hardly a good role model."

"All that shit is solvable, and you damn well know it."

"So we're *comparing* now? That your shit is worse than mine?"

"You damn well *know* it is." He shoved a hand through his dark hair, his gaze frustrated. "And you also know that one fricking honest conversation with your family will sort it all out because they *love* you. So who's the real coward, Daisy?"

She swallowed hard and forced herself to keep looking at him. "Nice deflection, dude, and yes, I am a coward. Thanks for reminding me." She half-turned toward the door. "And I think that's my cue to leave. You can't possibly have anything worse you want to say to me?"

He dropped his gaze to the floor, sending her heart plummeting along with it.

"Daisy, if you need me to keep covering for you with your family, I'm more than willing to do so."

He sounded weary and defeated, and it hurt her to breathe.

"Don't worry. I don't expect you to keep lying for me." She found her jacket and put it on. "I appreciate everything you've done, I really mean that."

She couldn't tell him she'd changed her mind, that she wanted more now. He wouldn't believe her. He'd think she was still feeling sorry for him or trying to regain his cooperation to shield her from her family. And to be honest, she deserved it. She'd messed him around, demanded loyalty, and enjoyed his lovemaking without making him any commitments.

"I'm sorry." She faced him one last time. "I should never have started this because now I've hurt you, and that was the last thing I ever wanted."

He slowly lifted his head to look at her.

"There's nothing to be sorry about. I made a choice, Daisy. I agreed with your terms."

She nodded, her eyes filling with tears. "Okay." She turned to leave but couldn't quite make herself go. "If you need someone to talk to, like *really* talk to, about all this stuff, I'm more than willing to listen. I'd like to think that one day we could be friends." She surreptitiously swiped at her eyes, using her long hair to shield her face. "Just call me, all right?"

She managed to leave then, her tears finally falling as she blundered her way down the hallway and into the kitchen. It took her a while to figure out how to unlock the back door, but she finally managed it and got into her truck. She was crying so hard at this point, she couldn't see out of the windshield. She mopped up her tears and sat there taking deep shuddery breaths until she was capable of driving.

She'd come to the ranch to have it out with Jackson—to tell him she had developed real feelings for him—and she'd completely blown it. He didn't even want her sympathy, so how could she possibly offer him her *love*?

He'd taught her so much about moving on, about finding someone who liked you just the way you were, and she'd screwed it up, discounted his growing feelings and pushed him away. She swallowed hard and turned the engine on. She'd picked herself up and moved on after Brody had died, and she knew in her soul she'd survive

Jackson. The trouble was . . . she wasn't sure she'd ever
feel the same about anyone ever again.

Jackson stayed where he was until he heard the faint
rumble of Daisy's truck heading down the driveway. He'd
stood his ground. And what had that brought him? An
empty bed, and the woman he'd come to love apologizing
for caring about him, taking all the blame on herself, and
still offering to be his friend.

Yeah, he loved her, and it sucked. With a low sound, he
buried his face in his hands and muttered, "You absolute
and complete *fool*."

He'd thought her admitting to messing him around
would've made him feel victorious, as if he'd somehow
won, but instead, he felt even worse, and kind of mean
along with it. He'd gone into the relationship with his eyes
wide open, and the fact that his feelings had changed and
Daisy's hadn't was entirely on him.

Not her.

She'd listened to him spill his guts and not condemned
him. She'd tried to comfort him, so of course he'd had to
open his big mouth and make her pay for that.

He got up from the chair, went into the bathroom, and
washed his hands and face. He'd be having the old familiar
nightmares as soon as his head hit the pillow. Where was
the happy-go-lucky, goofy Jackson Lymond—the persona
he'd cultivated since he was a kid, caught in the middle of
a violent marriage? This tortured stranger with secrets in
his eyes staring back at him was normally well hidden
from everyone.

But Daisy had seen the real him and not flinched until
he'd made it impossible for her to stay. Was he going to end
up like his father? A man who had pushed away affection

and love because he was too caught up in being angry? A man who'd taken his drunken frustrations out on his wife and kids until he'd splintered his own family, dividing them even after his death?

Because that was what Mark had done. Sown seeds of trouble between the two brothers, making one responsible for a ranch where he'd been made to feel unwanted and the other gutted by not being allowed to inherit half of what should've been his by right of birth. And Jackson had played right into it, refusing to allow Cauy to share the ranch with him because of a misguided chip on his shoulder.

He wiped his face with the towel, stripped down to his boxers, and got into bed. The small indentation where Daisy had sat on the end made his heart ache. She'd come to help him, he'd done everything he could to make her mad, and eventually he'd succeeded in running her off because this time he couldn't run away himself. But she hadn't left in a huff. She'd left offering to still be his friend—if he'd let her.

Jackson turned off the lamp beside his bed and lay unblinking in the darkness. Nothing felt right. He tried to convince himself he'd done the best thing for both of them, but it didn't work. It was like he'd ripped off a Band-Aid too fast and was left with a wound that wasn't going to heal and might just scar him for life.

Chapter Seventeen

"Who rattled your cage this morning?" Cauy looked up from his coffee at Jackson. "I leave you alone for two days and you're snapping my head off."

"I'm good." Jackson drank some more coffee. "I'm thinking of taking a road trip to find that Mr. Perkins. Did January get back to you about him?"

"She did." Cauy took out his cell. "I'll forward you her message. Do you want me to come with you?"

"Nah. Rachel just got back." Jackson's cell buzzed as the text came through. "She'd kill me if I took you away from her right now."

"You going to ask Daisy to go with you?" Cauy asked.

Jackson set down his mug. "We broke up."

"Well, that explains your bad mood. I'm sorry, bro. What happened?" Cauy looked genuinely concerned.

"Nothing much. She just got sick of me." Jackson shrugged, like it was no big deal. "She's way too smart to hang around with someone like me."

"She's never struck me as someone who cares about that kind of crap." Cauy kept studying Jackson. "Are you sure this isn't fixable? You guys do like to argue."

"It's not fixable, so can you just shut the hell up?" Jackson poured more coffee.

"Okay, there's no need to get all defensive. If you want to talk things through—"

"I don't." Jackson chugged the coffee in one and got to his feet, wiping his mouth. "I'll check on the horses. Are you okay if I leave this afternoon?"

Cauy leaned back in his chair. "Sure. Don't forget to take the coins with you."

"They're in the bank in town, right?" Jackson asked. "Do I need your permission to get them out of the safe?"

"I'll call the bank manager to make sure everything's good for you to take them," Cauy assured him. "We're named as co-owners of the safety deposit box. Remember, half the value is yours to keep."

"And half is yours, gotcha." Jackson made sure he had the necessary documentation to get into the vault. "Although I have no idea whether it's even worth pursuing. Dad wasn't known for his financial acumen."

"He always collected coins and, hey, if it gets you away for a few days while you're pining over Daisy, I'm all for it."

"Cool, thanks." Jackson nodded at his brother and went toward the mudroom to put on his work boots. "I'll check in with you later."

"You do that."

"Hi, Jackson!" Rachel, who was just coming out of Cauy's bedroom, paused in the hallway to smile at him. She wore one of Cauy's old T-shirts and a pair of his boxers and still managed to look beautiful. "How are things?"

"Great." Jackson smiled back. "I'll see you around."

He knew Cauy would tell Rachel about Daisy, but he hoped to be well clear of the house before she could ask him what was going on. He wasn't ready to talk about it while his head and heart felt like they were being crushed in a vat of misery.

After he finished with the horses, he took a quick shower, put on his going-to-town jeans and boots, and drove out in his truck. The fields were a regimented, sun-dried yellow now, and the creeks were starting to dry up. The endless skies were clear blue until they hazed up over the still snowy Sierras. Jackson took some deep breaths. He loved it out here. It sang to his soul.

He'd checked out the details on Mr. Perkins and found he lived in the Bay Area. His plan was to drive there, taking his time, and call the guy when he was practically on his doorstep. January seemed to think he'd welcome the company, and Jackson hoped she was right. The journey would give him a chance to get his head on straight. If he wanted to stay in Morgan Valley, he'd have to find a way to get along with the Millers.

There was no parking directly behind the bank, so he found a space behind the new health center. Four of the shops hadn't been rented yet, which meant there was always plenty of room. He decided to walk along Main Street to Maureen's general store to stock up for the journey and work his way back to the bank.

It was coming up to lunchtime, and after a morning cleaning out stalls, he was already hungry. He hesitated outside the health center, looking up and down the street. He'd have to get gas for his truck at Ted Baker's. Yvonne had the best food, but she was also a great friend of Daisy's, and he didn't want to bump into her just yet.

But Maureen's was quite close to the flower shop, and Nancy occasionally helped her mother out there. Jackson groaned. Wherever he went in this town, he was toast, so he'd better get used to it.

He set off toward the general store, his Stetson rammed

low over his eyes, and reached the door safely before anyone called out to him. Letting out a relieved breath, he went inside and naturally ran straight into Nancy, Auntie Rae, and Daisy.

"Hey." Jackson tipped his hat and focused on Rae, who was smiling at him. "How's it going?"

"Great, thanks!" Rae stood on tiptoe to kiss his cheek. "I'm just about to take Maureen and Daisy out to lunch while Nancy minds the store. Would you like to come with us?"

"Thanks for the offer, ma'am, but I've got an appointment at the bank in twenty minutes that I can't miss. I just came in to get some supplies."

"Oh, that's a shame, isn't it, Daisy?" Rae exclaimed.

"Yes."

He couldn't even look at Daisy for more than a second, it hurt too much. He turned and grabbed a wire basket. "Nice to see you all. Have a great day."

Maureen appeared, and the three of them went out, leaving him alone with Nancy. For once, he prayed a busload of foreign tourists would suddenly descend on the store and keep her busy.

"You okay, Jackson?" Nancy asked as he brought his provisions up to the counter.

"I'm good, thanks."

"Jay was worried about you after what happened in the bar." Nancy gave him a paper bag, and he placed his purchases in it at top speed.

"Yeah, sorry about that. I don't often lose my temper." Jackson swiped his debit card. Perhaps Daisy hadn't had a chance to rat him out to her best friends yet, because he was fairly certain he'd be hearing about it right now if she had.

Nancy snorted. "That idiot deserved everything he got."

"I still lost it." Jackson dropped the receipt in the bag. "It wasn't cool."

"I dunno." Nancy studied him speculatively. "I kind of felt like it was good to see you stop being so nice to everyone, you know?"

"And turn into an angry drunk like my father?" Jackson managed a smile. "I don't want to be like him. I'll stick with being nice."

"Daisy was worried about you, too."

"She's a very caring person." Jackson hoisted his bag off the counter. "I've got to go put this stuff in the truck before it melts. It was good talking to you."

"Not so fast." Nancy came around the checkout, cutting him off from the door. "Where are you going?"

"I told you, I'm going to the bank."

"And after that?" She pointed at the bag. "I'm a professional, Jackson. I know when someone's buying stuff for a road trip and not making dinner back at the ranch."

Jackson considered his options, but running over his ex-fake-girlfriend's best friend didn't seem right, so he attempted a version of the truth. "I'm going to be out of town for the next day or two."

"Okay." Nancy nodded. "Which explains why Daisy was giving you attitude."

"Yeah, exactly." Jackson agreed with her and almost sang with relief when she stepped out of his way. "Have a great day, Nancy."

Knowing she was watching him from the door, he forced himself not to run toward the parking lot and the bank. She'd probably mention his trip to Daisy, which would cheer Daisy up immensely.

He walked along the wooden boardwalk and imagined how he'd sound if he had his work boots and spurs on. Morgantown still had the look of a town where the local sheriff and his posse could come around the corner, tie up their horses, and swagger into the nearest saloon for an old-fashioned shoot-out.

He loved this place and didn't want to leave. The realization that it was time to stop running hit him anew. But could he make a life for himself here when he'd be falling over Daisy every five minutes knowing he'd lost her—not that he'd ever had her in the first place? For the first time in his life, his heart was being broken in two.

Perhaps after he got a valuation on the coins his dad had collected, he'd have some idea where he stood financially. He wasn't expecting much, but they had to be worth something, and at least it would give him some capital.

Jackson reached the bank and paused for a second before he went inside. If he wanted to stay here, he'd have to speak to Daisy again to make sure they could live with each other. The fact that even the idea of speaking to her brightened his mood was an indicator of how far he had to go to view her as just a friend.

He wished he could drown his stupid hopes, but that wasn't going to happen for a while. Daisy had settled herself in his heart, and he wasn't willing to give up on her yet. Maybe, just maybe, he could find a way out of the terrible mess he'd gotten himself into. With that in mind, Jackson went into the bank and asked to speak to the manager.

"Jackson was very quiet," Rae said as she, Daisy, and Maureen settled into their seats at Yvonne's.

"I think he had a lot on his mind." Daisy considered what the heck she was going to say next, but luckily, Rae carried on talking.

"I was going to ask him to dinner tomorrow night and I completely forgot!"

"I can text him to ask him if you like?" Daisy suggested. He might not choose to reply to her, but that just meant she could make up an excuse that would satisfy her aunt.

"Sure! Why don't you do that? You can let me know what he said when you come home tonight." Rae picked up the menu and studied it.

Daisy already knew what she was going to eat. Being miserable meant something with fries, followed by something with sugar, and she sure was miserable right now.

Seeing Jackson angry, and seeing him afraid hadn't changed her opinion of him. In fact, she liked finding out what lay beneath that great charm, handsome face, and positive attitude. But did he like her knowing that? From his reaction, she guessed not.

Lizzie came up, and they all ordered their food and drinks. Maureen and Rae chatted about their dinner plans with Bella Williams, Jay's mom. Daisy allowed herself to wander off into dream scenarios, where she got a redo on her last conversation with Jackson and everything turned out fine.

"So, I called Leanne," Rae said casually. Daisy sat up and took notice.

"Leanne Miller?" Maureen asked. "Good Lord, we haven't seen her for over twenty years, have we, Rae?"

"She wants to come back to see Jeff and the kids," Rae told Maureen. "She wants 'closure.'" Rae did the bunny ears thing.

Maureen snorted. "Which is a funny way of saying she wants to stir up a wasps' nest of trouble."

"She didn't sound like that was her aim, but you never know," Rae agreed. "Jeff is happy for her to come, so she says she'll book a room at the Hayes Hotel and be here in the fall."

"Why so far out?" Daisy asked. "That means we're going to sit around worrying all summer."

"I wouldn't worry, dear." Rae patted her hand. "I don't think she wishes any harm."

"Then why come back at all?" Daisy grumbled. "She was happy enough to walk away all those years ago and leave us to manage by ourselves."

Maureen and Rae exchanged a long glance that Daisy caught. "*What*?"

"Your dad . . ." Maureen paused. "Didn't make things easy for her, Daisy."

"She's the one who left." Daisy adored her father and wasn't okay with Maureen's tentative suggestion. "Maybe she should've had it out with him and stuck around."

"Jeff is a very stubborn man." Rae sighed. "And Leanne did try. I'm surprised you don't remember all the arguing that went on before she finally left."

"I've probably blocked it out." Daisy sipped her iced tea. "I only remember when you arrived and made everything better."

Rae squeezed her hand. "It was my pleasure."

Lizzie and Yvonne arrived with their food, and they all set to eating. Daisy had time to wonder why Jackson was visiting the bank. He'd looked pretty serious, but that might have been because he hadn't intended to bump into her twelve hours after their fight. Was he looking for a loan to buy land in Morgan Valley, or was he taking his money elsewhere? She knew he loved the place. How hard would it be if he stayed and she had to see him every day, watch him settle in, find a wife, start a family . . .

Too hard.

Maybe she'd be the one who had to move away.

After their meal, Daisy accompanied her aunt back to Maureen's to pick up the bags of shopping Rae had stowed in Maureen's apartment behind the store. Daisy lingered at the cash register while Nancy helped a bunch of Japanese tourists, who seemed impressed by her command of their language.

Eventually, Nancy waved them off with a last immaculate bow and turned to Daisy.

"What's up?"

"Nothing much. You?" Daisy wasn't ready to talk about what had happened with Jackson until she'd sorted it out in her own head.

"I'm good." Nancy signed out of the register as one of her cousins came to take over. "Where's Jackson off to?"

Daisy blinked at her friend. "My Jackson?"

"Yeah. He said he was going on a road trip."

"He . . . *did*?" Daisy leaned back against the wall for support.

"You didn't know?" Nancy came around the counter.

"No."

"Weird." Nancy took a closer look at Daisy. "Are you *sure* everything is okay?"

Daisy shook her head. This was her fault. She'd driven him away from the place he wanted to call home.

"Hey, don't *cry* . . ." Nancy hurriedly handed her a wad of tissues. "I'm useless with tears."

"I'm not crying, I'm just trying to process what . . ." Daisy couldn't even complete the sentence.

"Look." Nancy wrapped an arm around her shoulders. "I'm supposed to go to work, but if you want to hang out with me, I'll call Jay and tell him I'm sick."

"Like he'll believe you." Daisy sniffed.

"He won't, so I'd probably end up telling him the truth, and he'd be okay with that, too."

"I've got to go back to the flower shop anyway," Daisy said.

"Then how about we meet at Yvonne's at six so we can

talk this through?" Nancy kissed her on the forehead. "Can you hang in there that long?"

"Sure I can." Daisy nodded. "Although I'm not sure exactly what I'm going to say. I might just cry."

"It doesn't matter what you do, Yvonne and I will cope." Nancy patted her shoulder. "Now, blow your nose before my mom and Rae come back or they'll never let you out of here before they get an explanation."

Chapter Eighteen

Daisy took a deep breath and went to find her father, who was out in the barn. He smiled as she approached him, his brown eyes crinkling at the corners; his face was tan from a lifetime of living outdoors. He took in her backpack, case, and all-weather jacket. She hadn't slept well, her mind busy thinking about Jackson.

Ian's frantic early morning text had caught her at a good time and she'd made a quick decision.

"You off somewhere, sweetheart?"

"Yes." She smiled at him. "I have to go to San Francisco. I'll be back by the weekend."

He raised an eyebrow. "Have you got someone to mind the shop?"

"Auntie Rae offered. She said she hasn't got much to do."

"She sure hates to be idle." Her father set his broom against the wall. "Have a safe trip, okay? Call me when you get there."

"Will do." Daisy braced herself. "Aren't you going to ask me what I'm up to?"

"Do you want me to?"

"Not really." Daisy hastened to reassure him. "It's just that you usually—"

"Rae told me I was being too hard on you—that I was overprotective," he interrupted her. "And she was right. I never expect the boys to give me a detailed itinerary of all their movements, and you're just as capable, if not more, than any of your brothers."

"At least they've all stuck around to work with you on the ranch, while I've been all over the place," Daisy reminded him.

"Yeah, and I can still barely break even." He grimaced. "If I had to hire in more outside help, we wouldn't survive."

Daisy suppressed another surge of guilt and held his gaze. "I promise I'll tell you all about my trip when I get back, okay?"

"Sure, if you want to." He patted her shoulder. "What do you think your mother will make of this place after twenty-three years away from it?"

Halfway between glad at the change of subject and stymied by the new one, Daisy struggled to find words.

"I expect she'll find it's changed quite a bit."

"Yeah. New barn, new fencing, new breeding program, and a whole lot of work on the house."

Being a typical rancher, her father's achievement scale always started with the livestock and ended with the family home. He carried on talking. "I'm looking forward to seeing her."

Daisy studied her father carefully. Had a pod person replaced him? None of his answers were making sense today.

"Really?" Daisy asked cautiously.

"Yeah. We parted on bad terms."

Daisy wanted to say "duh" but restrained herself, and settled on something less controversial. "It sure will be interesting."

"You look just like her."

"So I've been told."

Daisy hadn't seen a picture of her mother since she'd left the ranch and could only hope the resemblance had faded. The first year after Leanne had left, Daisy had taped together a photo of her mother her father had ripped up and kept it under her pillow. Eventually, after too many years without a single loving word, she'd given up hope of her returning and had thrown it in the trash.

Her father picked up his broom. "You planning on seeing Jackson while you're in Frisco? I heard he was heading out that way as well."

"I don't know." She shrugged, like she didn't have a care in the world. "I'm not sure exactly where's he's going."

"Isn't that what phones are for? You guys are always ragging on me about using mine, so why don't you just call him up and pin him down?"

"Maybe I will." Daisy smiled at her dad.

"He's a keeper, Daisy," he said gruffly. "I never thought I'd say that after seeing the kind of boyfriend you usually bring home, but Jackson's a good man."

"He is that." Daisy nodded, even as her heart clenched.

"Don't tell him I said so. We don't want him thinking I'm getting soft in my old age."

"I swear he'll never know," Daisy said solemnly. She leaned in to kiss his weathered cheek. "I love you, Dad."

"Love you, too, sweetheart. Safe travels."

She picked up her bag and went around the barn to where her truck was parked. She'd decided to fly out and would leave her truck in the long-term parking lot at the airport.

Ian had asked her to come back to Silicon Valley to meet the final group of VCs, and to have second meetings with the first batch. From what he'd said, there was a great deal of buzz about their new product, with several big companies eyeing it as a potential acquisition.

She'd meant what she'd said to her dad. When she got back, she was going to come clean with her family and hope they understood. They did love her, and she could only hope they'd forgive her for not using her money to help them but to finance yet another start-up. Perhaps when she'd got that out in the open, she could tell Jackson he'd been right all along . . .

Daisy sighed and turned on her headlights and windscreen wipers as wisps of fog and swathes of rain drifted across the county road. Like Jackson would even care that she'd finally owned up. He'd left without telling her where he was going, leaving her having to work it out from town gossip. Was he looking for somewhere to set down roots away from Morgan Valley? She couldn't picture him thriving in the Bay Area.

When she reached the small airport, she checked her bag and went through security to find the flight delayed for an hour. She sent Ian a text to let him know she would be late and then sat and stared at the blank screen of her phone.

Should she text Jackson just to make sure he was okay? Despite everything, she still wanted to be his friend.

Wincing at her desperate attempt to delude herself when she wanted so much more, she found his number and sent him a quick text.

Are you okay? Nancy said you'd left town.
I'll be in Palo Alto for the rest of the week if you need anything.

She pressed Send and immediately regretted it. He was going to think she was stalking him.

She didn't realize she'd been holding her breath, waiting for his reply, until she felt slightly dizzy. But the screen remained blank, the cursor blinking, which wasn't really surprising. Her flight was called. She set her phone to airplane mode and boarded with the rest of the passengers.

Jackson glanced over at his phone and read the text from Daisy. He'd stopped to get gas and was contemplating where to stay for the night. He was close to his destination, but he desperately needed to sleep and shave before he presented himself at Mr. Perkins's door the next day.

There was a hotel close to the gas station, and he figured he'd crash there. It gave him way too much time to ponder the meaning of Daisy's unexpected text as he followed the directions on his phone. He wished he'd manned up and told her he was leaving town rather than letting her hear about it from Nancy. Driving over the majestic Sierras had given him plenty of time to calm down and remember what a small speck he was in the big scheme of things.

He hadn't expected to hear from her. The fact that she was going to be in the same part of the world he was currently inhabiting felt like the gods were trying to throw them together—or were having a huge laugh at his expense. He was too tired to work out which one it was and hoped a night's sleep would remedy that.

It didn't take long for him to get a room, park his truck in front of the relevant door, and collapse onto the bed. He wouldn't text her back. He'd say something stupid or reveal something she didn't want to hear. For once in his life, he was determined to keep his mouth shut, focus on the current mission in front of him, and worry about the gorgeous and desirable Daisy Miller after that.

He woke up when his alarm went off at six the next morning, still in his clothes, facedown on the bed, and dragged himself into the shower. Half an hour later, after stuffing his face with the free doughnuts the hotel called breakfast and snagging a gallon of coffee, he was on the road again, heading to a city in the East Bay called Walnut Creek, where Mr. Perkins lived.

He'd stop and get an early lunch, call Mr. Perkins's number, announce his imminent arrival, and hope the old man would see him. He'd had a text from January the night before confirming she'd managed to speak briefly to Mr. Perkins, so he was technically expected. All he had to do now was navigate his way off I580 onto I680 and he'd be almost there.

He checked the coins were still in their locked box and concentrated on his driving. He wasn't used to so much traffic and couldn't imagine living so close to San Francisco. Sure, it had culture and things to do, but he was currently done with too much excitement, and would much prefer having space around him and clear air to breathe.

Would Daisy ever move back to Silicon Valley? If her company became megasuccessful, perhaps she'd have no choice. He tried to imagine Morgantown without her and couldn't even deal with it. It was slowly becoming obvious to him that he couldn't walk away from her. He just wasn't sure how he was going to survive if she really didn't want him.

He wanted to text her to arrange a meeting in the city. He mentally slapped his hand away from his phone. "Focus, Jackson. One step at a time." Okay, he was talking to himself now, which was never good, but he had to try *something*. Get the coins valued, find someplace to stay for the night, and then maybe, if he was still willing to open himself up to more hurt, he'd text her back.

But first, he had to deal with Mr. Perkins. It was a long way to come just to fail, but he'd like to think he had enough charm to get inside the house and finally find out whether his father's hoarded coins had sent him on a fool's errand.

"Daisy? Are you coming?"

She looked up from her one-hundredth surreptitious look at her text messages to find Ian waiting patiently for her by the exit.

"Sorry." She hurried along the corridor. "It's going well, isn't it?"

"Yeah." He grimaced. "It's a little hard to take all the attention after being in stealth mode for all these years."

"Agreed." Daisy put her sunglasses on as the midday sun glared down at them from a cloudless blue sky. "Are we doing lunch?"

"Sure! There's a great place around the corner that does some nice vegetarian options."

"Then let's go there. We can FaceTime with the gang about how the meetings are going."

Ian held the door open over her head and she went into the bustling café, which reminded her a lot of Yvonne's. Cold air blew over her, and she enjoyed the sensation.

The food was organic, healthy, and plentiful, which suited Daisy just fine as long as they also had coffee. She sat on the same side of the table as Ian and they spoke to the other team members about how things were going.

"I heard back from Jake Magnusson," Ian said as he unwrapped his veggie wrap. "He wants to talk to us. I said we were pretty booked up, but he's superkeen."

"Jake is a very focused guy," Daisy said.

"So I gathered." Ian grinned. "Did you know the three of them made their first millions when they were still undergraduates at Stanford?"

"Yes, and more importantly, they managed to hang on to them," Daisy joked.

She ate her salad, her thoughts far away from Silicon Valley as she considered what on earth was going on with Jackson. She'd have to talk to him soon. She couldn't leave things as they were . . .

"Damn."

She looked up to see Ian staring at his phone. "What's up?"

"Seth said the washing machine repair guy is five minutes away from our apartment and he's not there to let him in."

"Then why don't you go? You can walk from here," Daisy suggested. "I'll finish my lunch and meet you back at Sand Hill Road. What time does our next meeting start?"

"Not for an hour." Ian looked conflicted. "Are you sure you'll be okay?"

"I'll be fine." She waved a hand at him. "Hustle."

She drank her second cup of coffee and went over her notes for the next set of meetings, checking her messages as she read. Someone slipped into the seat opposite and she raised her head.

"That was quick—" Her smile died. "What the hell do *you* want?"

"*Someone* could work on their manners." Clive Cassler smirked at her.

"Someone could go away," she countered, putting her cell away in her backpack and stacking her dishes on the tray.

"I just wanted to run something by you."

She eyed him suspiciously. "Whatever it is, I'll save you some breath and just say no."

"You really should hear me out. If you don't, I'll just ask the others in your team to see if they'll go for it instead."

"Go for what?" She sat back and crossed her arms over her chest.

"My offer. And this is a personal offer rather than from my VC company because I like you guys so much."

Daisy tried not to let her disgust show and said nothing.

"I want to buy you out."

"Surprise, surprise," Daisy said. "What's the catch?"

"There is no catch. I'll offer you forty-five million dollars cash for your shares in the company."

"That's way over the current valuation," Daisy objected. "Why would you waste your money?"

Clive sighed. "And this is why you get taken advantage of, Daisy. You're *far* too honest."

"You're offering us a one-time payment just so you can own the intellectual property?"

"Not *quite*. It would be a fifteen million down payment between the five of you as an incentive, and then a commitment to work on the product for the next two years. The remainder of the money would be distributed to you at the end of year one and at the end of year two."

If she agreed, Daisy could buy the Cortez Ranch for Adam *and* help out her dad right now, but she'd no longer have any say in how the company was run.

Clive must have seen her hesitation because he reached over and grabbed her hand.

"Think about it. You'd be shot of me in two years, you'd have nine million dollars in your pocket, and you'd be set for life."

She eased her hand free, and he sat back, his expression gloating.

"I'm going to make the same offer to the rest of your team, so don't think you can keep this to yourself. They deserve to have options as well, don't they?"

Daisy shrugged. "I can't stop you from approaching them."

She had no intention of telling him they'd all agreed

everyone had to go for a deal or it wouldn't happen. The lure of all that money after the lean years of developing the project and company might sway some of her team. But would they be prepared to relinquish control of a project they all believed in so strongly?

Daisy stood and put on her backpack. "Goodbye, Clive."

"No answer for me, sweet cheeks?" He leaned back in his seat and regarded her, his gaze lingering on her breasts. "I'd love to have you under me again. Let me know when you're ready to capitulate, and make it soon because this offer won't last."

Daisy left the café congratulating herself on not dousing Clive in coffee. She made her way back to the offices on Sand Hill Road, her mind struggling with the allure of all that money against the awfulness of having to work with Clive again. She'd be free in two years, which was less than she'd probably have to commit to Ian. She'd be wealthy enough to help her whole family and could probably buy both the ranches that were up for sale in Morgan Valley.

But she'd have to work with Clive . . .

As she pushed open the doors and went into the lobby of the next VC's offices, she hoped someone would come up with a better way for her to avoid Clive Cassler for the rest of her life before she gave in and took his money.

"Mr. Perkins?" Jackson offered his best smile to the elderly man who was regarding him suspiciously through the narrow gap of his front door. "January Morgan told me it would be okay to call on you. I'm Jackson Lymond."

"January did?" Mr. Perkins opened the door a tad wider and looked Jackson up and down. "You have a look of your father. I suppose you'd better come in."

"Thank you, sir." Jackson stepped into a hallway lined with books on either side, leaving a narrow passageway through to the rear of the house. "I appreciate your time."

He ended up walking sideways just in case his broad shoulders took a book out and the whole pile came tumbling down. The kitchen beyond the books was remarkably clutter free, and sun shone through the windows.

"Would you like some coffee, son?"

"Yes, please, sir. That would be nice."

Mr. Perkins indicated that Jackson should sit at the kitchen table, which he did, placing the locked box on the surface in front of him. There was no TV in the space, no laptop, and no sign of a cell phone. The big old-fashioned rotary phone, with its long curly cord, hung beside the refrigerator. It was like stepping back in time to when Jackson was a kid.

Mr. Perkins brought the coffee to the table, along with two mugs, lumps of brown sugar, and cream. "Help yourself."

"Thank you."

While Jackson added sugar to his coffee, Mr. Perkins retrieved a green folder from a pile on the countertop and set it in front of him.

"I sold your father a number of coins over the years, so if you still have those, I have a fair idea of their current value."

"That's awesome." Jackson found the key and opened the small strong box. "I did try to check some of them out online, but to be honest, I wasn't sure whether they were genuine or not." He hesitated. "My dad didn't always make the best business decisions."

Especially when he was drunk, but Mr. Perkins didn't need to know that.

"I can assure you, young man, everything *I* sold your

father was completely verified and has excellent provenance," Mr. Perkins said pointedly.

"I'm sure it was," Jackson rushed to agree with him. He didn't want to be thrown out before he got a full accounting from the man. "I'm just not sure where he got half these coins."

Mr. Perkins put on his glasses, got his magnifier out of his pocket, and bent over the coins Jackson was taking out of the box. Up close, the guy smelled like mothballs and cedarwood, which made Jackson's nose itch.

"Hmm . . ." Mr. Perkins deftly sorted through the coins, consulting his list and separating them into two piles. "This lot are the ones I sold him over the years and are definitely genuine."

"Awesome." Jackson breathed through his mouth.

"I'd place their value now at around seventy-five thousand dollars."

"You're kidding me." Jackson gazed at the small pile of coins. "That's *amazing*."

Knowing his father, he'd been expecting the worst, so that much money was a surprise. "What about the rest?"

"I'll have to go through them individually." Mr. Perkins squinted at one small silver coin through his magnifier. "This one is quite old. Mark told me he first got interested in coins as a boy when he found them at the Morgansville silver mine and down in the creek. Everyone else was looking for gold, but he preferred the coins the miners and townsfolk had left behind."

Jackson tried to imagine his father at a young, carefree age and failed miserably.

"We found the box of coins in an old filing cabinet in the Lymond side of the old silver mine," Jackson said.

"Most of the mine is going to be filled in now, so I'm glad we got them out."

"Indeed." Mr. Perkins turned his attention back to the coins. "Some of these are quite . . . unusual, and will require a little cleaning up before I can date them with any accuracy."

"Take your time." Jackson waved him on. "I've got all day."

Mr. Perkins frowned. "Well, you can't stay here, young man. I'm going out for lunch. If you give me your cellular phone number, I'll call you when I'm done."

"Do you think that might be today?" Jackson asked.

"It depends. I should be able to call you by the latest tomorrow evening."

"Okay." Jackson nodded. "I really appreciate you taking the time to see me, Mr. Perkins." He hesitated. "If I wanted to sell the coins, would you be willing to help me with that?"

"For a small fee." Mr. Perkins finally smiled at him. "And I promise I won't run off with them in the meantime."

"Good thinking, seeing as I know where you live." Jackson winked at the old man and stood up. "If I don't hear from you by tomorrow night at eight, are you okay if I call you?"

"Sure, but I should be finished by then." He glanced back at the table. "Most of these aren't very interesting or valuable, but I'll have a total value for you and we can take it from there."

"Great." Jackson shook his hand. "Thanks so much."

Jackson let himself out and got into his truck. He'd noticed a mall on the way to the house, so he'd go park there, get something to eat, and consider his next move.

Seventy-five thousand dollars was peanuts to Cauy, but half of it was the deposit on something for Jackson.

He considered texting his oil-rich, penny-pinching brother but decided to wait until he had the final total. Cauy would be stoked. Despite his wealth, he'd never say no to extra money.

Jackson parked at the side of the mall and went in to celebrate in solitary style at the sports bar. He still hadn't replied to Daisy, mainly because he didn't know what to say.

He was just about to enter the bar when there was a screech of brakes behind him. He turned just in time to see a big rig truck that was backing out of one of the loading bays, lose traction and slowly sideswipe a whole row of parked vehicles—including his.

"Shit," Jackson breathed.

He ran back the way he came. He wasn't the only person who'd seen what had happened, and everyone was shouting and screeching. On first investigation, it didn't appear that anyone had been hurt. There were a couple of abandoned shopping carts and one empty stroller, but no one lying on the ground or injured.

Sirens wailed in the near distance, and Jackson walked around to take his first proper look at his truck. He'd been in the first slot and the whole left side was caved in from the force of the collision. Under cover of the noise, Jackson let off a whole string of curse words. There was no way his truck was drivable.

He whistled softly and stepped back as the local cops arrived on the scene. After he'd talked to the police, he'd be able to find someone to tow the truck to a local garage. He'd noticed there was a BART station right in the center of town, which meant he could go into the city, take a plane home, or stick around to hear from Mr. Perkins, who still had the coins.

He found his cell and looked for Chase Morgan's number. He could only pray Chase was in town and would be willing to help out a fellow Morgan Valley dude. If not, he'd have to find someplace to stay, rent a new truck, or get a flight home late the next night.

Chapter Nineteen

Daisy's cell phone buzzed, and she took it out of her backpack. After the series of meetings, she'd immediately told Ian what had happened with Clive. He'd agreed they needed to meet up the next day to talk the offer through with the rest of the team. Daisy had hoped he'd instantly repudiate it, but like her, the thought of all that money after years of disappointment and debt was incredibly alluring . . .

Hey, are you okay to come on a rescue mission with me?

Daisy checked who the text was from and wondered what the heck Chase Morgan was on about.
As in . . . ? Daisy texted back.

You're staying at my place tonight, correct? There's a complication. I've got to pick someone up from the BART station and thought you might want to come along rather than me coming back for you later. If that's okay, I'll pick you up in five minutes. I'm parked just behind my office, so meet me there.

Okay, Daisy agreed.

She didn't want Chase going off and forgetting to come back to pick her up at all. She's spent quite enough of her day adulting for VCs as it was. A diversion to the BART station was no big deal, seeing as Chase was offering her accommodation in his spare room for free.

She went out into the hazy evening sunshine, the roar of commuter traffic from the freeway a constant sound that never seemed to dim. Chase was already sitting in his all-electric car, which was about as far away from the Ford F-450 he drove on the ranch as you could get. He also left his cowboy hat at home, which made him look weird.

Daisy waved at him and got into the passenger seat.

"Thanks for this," Chase said as he backed out of his space. "Do you mind if I take a couple of calls while we're driving? Hands-free of course."

"Sure, go ahead. I'm done talking today," Daisy said.

His bright blue eyes narrowed with laughter. "I hear you're very popular in the valley right now, Ms. Miller. All the sharks are circling."

"Tell me about it." Daisy leaned back against the seat and briefly closed her eyes.

Chase's phone buzzed and he was off, talking to someone in Austin about something so complex Daisy gave up listening and just luxuriated in the knowledge that he wasn't going to ask *her* anything. She and Ian might be the most outgoing of their gang of five, but they were still basically introverts who didn't do well in company. That's why she and Jackson got along. She didn't do social chatting and his frankness didn't bother her much.

Chase ended his call and frowned as he circled the BART station. "I hate this place. It makes no sense."

Daisy pointed to the right. "If you pull off here, you can pick passengers up."

"Well spotted." Chase moved over a lane and put on his blinker. "Look out for a guy possibly wearing a cowboy hat."

Daisy squinted at the crowd of people, her gaze immediately going to the tall, dark-haired guy with a backpack and a blue baseball cap on his head.

"We're picking up *Jackson Lymond*?"

"Yeah." Chase grinned at her as he pulled up at the curb. "I thought that would cheer you up."

Chase got out of the car to shake Jackson's hand and put his bag in the trunk, while Jackson got in the back. Daisy slowly turned around to stare at him.

"Hey."

Jackson sighed. "I'm sorry. I don't know why the hell this keeps happening. It's like the harder I try to get away from you, the more the fates laugh their asses off."

"Thanks a bunch," Daisy said. "It's nice to see you, too."

"See? There you go. One second in your company, and I've already ticked you off." He rubbed a hand over his unshaven jaw. "I'll tell Chase to drop me at the nearest hotel, okay? And then you can go back to doing whatever it is you have to do out here."

"There's no need."

Daisy turned back around as Chase got in the car.

"Everyone good?"

Daisy and Jackson both nodded as Chase moved off.

"So what exactly happened to your truck?" Chase asked Jackson.

"Totaled in a mall parking lot," Jackson said. "Luckily, I wasn't in it." He exhaled. "My insurance said they can get me a rental tomorrow. It's really kind of you to help me out, Chase. I appreciate it."

"Not a problem." Chase headed back onto the freeway. "It's always nice to help a friend from Morgan Valley." He glanced over at Daisy. "And further the course of true love, right?"

She smiled, because what else could she do when he was being so nice to both of them? Chase chatted away to Jackson, and Daisy focused on looking out of the window until Chase stopped at a barrier leading into an underground parking lot and punched in his code.

"We're here. Follow me."

The fast elevator opened up onto a landing with only four doors leading off it. Chase unlocked one of them and beckoned them inside.

"Wow . . ." Jackson stopped so abruptly, Daisy cannoned into his back. "That's some view."

The floor-to-ceiling windows on two sides of the corner apartment looked out over the Bay Bridge, the city, and the bay itself. They were jaw-droppingly high. Daisy didn't have a problem with heights, but from the way Jackson was gripping the back of the couch, she remembered he'd confessed to not liking to be *too* high.

"It's awesome, isn't it?" Chase dropped the keys on the counter and went into the kitchen, which was a sea of stainless steel, granite, and high-end appliances. "I bought it during the construction stage. I also own the one next door, and Matt and Jake have the other ones on this floor."

"Nice." Daisy finally remembered to say something as Chase started opening doors.

"There are two bedrooms, both en suite, and a powder room back down the hall. The kitchen is stocked up. If you need anything specific, or want take-out, just call down to the concierge and he can go pick up what you need."

"Thanks." Daisy followed Chase around while Jackson stayed in one spot, pivoting his head and nodding.

"Great." Chase turned to the door. "Then I'll see you both tomorrow morning."

Daisy blinked at him. "You're going?"

"Yeah. As I said, I own the one next door as well." Chase gave her a funny look. "This is our guest suite. I thought you two would be more comfortable here without having to worry about me." He winked at Daisy. "If you need a ride in the morning, let me know. I go in around eight."

"Thanks, Chase," Jackson said.

"You're welcome. I'll take you to the rental place whenever you're ready as well." Chase slapped Jackson on the shoulder as he went past him. "I've left the keys and programmed in all the codes, so if you want to go out to dinner, you'll be able to get back in. If you have any problems, just call me, okay?"

He shut the door, leaving silence behind him as Daisy stared at Jackson. She sank down onto the couch and laughed so hard, she almost peed herself.

Jackson's rigid stance slowly disappeared as he stared down at her. "It is kind of funny, isn't it?"

Still wiping tears from her eyes, Daisy could only nod like a fool.

He walked around the side of the couch and took the seat opposite her, his back to the view.

"I can go explain things to Chase and ask if I can bunk at his place if you'd like," Jackson offered.

"No, it's all good." Daisy finally managed to speak. "There are two bedrooms, and we're perfectly capable of behaving like reasonable human beings." She fought another gurgle of laughter. "Well, I am anyway."

She got up and swiped a piece of paper towel to mop her face. "Why don't you go choose a bedroom while I make some coffee?"

He stood and shouldered his backpack. "Okay, thanks. I'll do that."

"The one at the back has no view at all," she called out to him as she opened the refrigerator and discovered it was stocked with three kinds of milk, including soy and almond, and two types of creamer.

The coffeemaker was the cup kind she was familiar with, so she made them both coffee, added cream to hers, and left Jackson's black. Just the sight of him did something to her heart. She resolved that whatever happened next, she would do her best to make sure he felt welcome in Morgan Valley, and wouldn't feel he had to leave.

He came back in after removing his cap and jacket. He took the mug of coffee and cradled it in his hands. "This is great."

Daisy perched on one of the high stools set against the countertop. "Your truck was totaled?"

"Yeah. I went to meet with this guy in Walnut Creek, parked afterward to get some lunch, and got hit by an out-of-control supermarket big rig." He sighed. "I'm just glad I wasn't in the truck at the time."

"So am I," Daisy agreed fervently. "Was anyone hurt?"

"Not as far as I could tell. Apparently, the driver's brakes failed as he was backing out of the loading bay, and he lost control of the rear of the vehicle."

"Why were you in Walnut Creek?" Daisy decided if she kept asking questions, it would stop her wanting to reach across to hug him, and kiss him, and . . .

"It's a long story—"

"Which of *course* you don't have to share with me!" Daisy interrupted him way too brightly.

He gave her a look. "I'm quite happy to tell it to you. I just didn't want to bore you."

"Okay, then, I'll leave it up to you. Would you like more coffee?" Daisy asked. "I'm going to have another cup, and then we can decide what we want to do about dinner.

There's loads of stuff in the refrigerator and freezer, or we can get take-out?"

"Daisy."

"What?" She looked back at him over her shoulder as she set the coffee machine going again.

"Are you going to keep this up all night?"

"I'm not sure what you mean. I'm just trying to be pleasant." She opened the refrigerator, hoping the cold air might cool her flushed cheeks. "I don't want you to think you have to leave Morgan Valley just to avoid me when we really can still be friends."

He didn't say anything, which made her want to stare into the refrigerator forever rather than turn around.

"I don't want you to think you have to leave Morgan Valley either," Jackson said quietly.

Daisy let out a breath she hadn't even realized she was holding. "That's good because I'm not going anywhere." It suddenly occurred to her he hadn't actually said he was going to stay.

"Are you looking at property out here, then?" She forced herself to face him.

"No." He met her gaze squarely. "I'd rather be in Morgan Valley."

"Okay." She smiled goofily at him. Maybe one day, in about a million years, when he'd settled down and forgiven her, she could ask him out on a date or something. "So what do you want to do about dinner?"

Jackson finished his beer and half of the pizza he'd shared with Daisy. She was being really nice to him, and it was awful.

Not that she was awful; it just felt that way when all he wanted to do was sit her on his knee and kiss her until she kissed him back. But this was what civilized people did, right? Stayed friends even when things hadn't worked out the way they'd wanted?

Maybe it was time for him to grow up and not be the impulsive bigmouthed fool Daisy had come to know and love. He corrected himself. Not love, tolerate. The only fool babbling about love was him, and even he didn't have the nerve to serve that up to her right now.

"So how's it going with the start-up?" Jackson wiped his mouth with his napkin and sat back.

"Good, I think."

"You don't sound very sure."

She leaned back against the couch. They'd ended up sitting on the floor with their pizza, which suited him just fine, seeing as he didn't want to look out the window.

"Well, you know how I told you that I wanted out?"

"Out of me, or out of Silicon Valley?" Jackson asked.

She gave him a patient look. "How about we focus on the Silicon Valley end of things right now?"

"Sure, go ahead." He gestured with his empty bottle before tossing it toward the trash. It bounced off the side and he winced as it hit the carpet. "Sorry about that." He retrieved the bottle and put it in the recycling bin.

"Someone made me an offer to buy the business today."

"The whole thing?"

"Yes." She nodded, her hair falling over her face. "A good offer."

"And?"

"Do you remember me telling you about that Clive guy?"

"The dickhead?" Jackson got up to get them both another beer. "He wants to buy the company?" He turned back to her, the frosted bottles in his hand. "I hope you told him what to do with his offer."

Her silence as he resumed his position opposite her went on way too long.

"You didn't say yes, did you?"

"Of course not, but . . ." Her voice trailed off. "It would mean I'd be free and clear in a maximum of two years, with loads of money in the bank."

"Two years working for the dickhead?" Jackson asked incredulously.

"That's the part that's sticking in my craw," Daisy said. "I really don't—"

"Then don't," Jackson spoke over her. "If you let him win again, he'll make your life miserable."

"I know." She tried to smile. "The thing is—we all agreed to talk over every offer, and I can't guarantee that the others won't leap at the chance to get out of debt. Ian has a huge mortgage, Casey has a sick kid who has long-term medical needs, and I wouldn't say no to a chunk of money myself right now."

"For what?" Jackson asked.

She blinked at his directness. "Family stuff."

"You want to buy the Cortez Ranch, don't you?"

"I want to buy it for Adam's sake, *and* for our whole community. I *want* to help my dad, who's perpetually short of money and shouldn't have to be." She leaned forward, her hands clasped together between her knees. "Don't you think it would be a great thing to do?"

"Not if it meant I had to put up with being humiliated by an asshole for two years." He folded his arms over his chest. "What happened to you last time you stayed too long in Silicon Valley?"

"I got burned out." She met his gaze. "But I was much younger then. I'd deal with it better now."

"Didn't you tell me all five of you have to agree to any proposal regarding the business?" Jackson asked.

"That's right, but if the other four all wanted to go ahead, I'd feel awful being the only holdout, especially when it was my pet project to begin with. I dragged them all into it and then walked away for almost three years. I owe them."

Jackson tried to consider her argument, which was hard when he didn't give a rat's ass for the other four dudes in the company. But he didn't have the right to argue her case now, did he?

"Okay, so are you going to talk it through with the others?"

"Yes. I'm seeing them all for breakfast tomorrow."

"Then, great." He nodded. "Do that." If she could make an effort to be pleasant, he damn well could as well. "I hope it all works out for you."

"Thank you." She was eyeing him like he was a stranger. "I'm fairly certain they won't want to go ahead, but it's always best to be prepared for the worst to happen, isn't it?"

"Sure." Jackson agreed and finished his second beer way too fast. "Let me know how it goes, okay?" He rushed to clarify as he got to his feet, the pizza box in his hand. This being-friends stuff was hard work. "If you want to, that is."

"I will." She stayed on the carpet, her gaze drifting out over the fantastic view of the city lights. "Thanks for listening."

He fussed around in the kitchen, cleaning the counters, loading the dishwasher, and stashed the remains of the pizza in the refrigerator. He should go to bed. He was exhausted, but he didn't want to walk away from her.

"Would you think badly of me if I caved and went along with what everyone else wanted?" Daisy asked.

Jackson went still. "It's not my place to tell you what to do, Daisy."

"I know, but would you think I was betraying Brody if

I didn't stick with what I'd promised myself I'd do? How would I feel if I handed the company over to someone, and they didn't complete the project or misused the technology, and people like Brody didn't get help?"

Jackson abandoned his cleaning and came around to sit on the chair opposite her.

"That's between you and your conscience."

She sighed and pushed her hair behind her ear. "I know you're trying to be all neutral, but for once, I'd *really* appreciate knowing what you think."

"I think Brody would be very proud of the woman you've become," Jackson said gently.

"That's not an answer."

He smiled at her. "It's the only one I've got for you right now, sweetheart." He rose to his feet and headed for the bathroom. "I'm going to bed. Will I see you in the morning? Chase is going to drive me to the car rental place."

"Jackson . . ."

He paused at the door, stupid hope rising in his chest. "Yeah?"

"I really am a coward, aren't I?"

He looked back over his shoulder. "I'm hardly the best person to ask about that, am I?"

Tears glinted in her eyes, and he kept on talking. "You're a good person, Daisy, trying to do good things for the people you love. There's nothing wrong with that."

"But I can't make everyone happy, can I?"

"No, you can't." He held her gaze. "So maybe this time, Daisy, you should think about yourself for a change. What do you want?"

"I wish I knew." Her laugh was a little wobbly and made his heart clench. "Thanks for everything, Jackson."

"It's all good. Night, Daisy."

He didn't dare kiss her good night because he'd be

kneeling at her feet begging her to take him back, and she didn't need that right now. She had enough shit to deal with. For the first time in his life, he was holding back and being an adult. He hurt, *everything* hurt, and he hated every second of it, but this time he needed to give Daisy the space to make her own decisions.

"You okay?" Chase glanced over at Jackson as they sat in traffic on the freeway. Jackson hadn't slept well, knowing Daisy was five feet away from him and probably snoring away, oblivious to the world and his pathetic yearnings.

"Yeah, I'm good." Jackson drummed his fingers on the window. "Can I ask you something?"

"Sure, what's up?"

"You know what Daisy's company is developing, right?"

"Yeah. It's an amazing concept, and what's more important, they have the technical ability to execute their vision and make the product a huge success."

"So if you were Daisy, you wouldn't sell out now?"

"Hell no." Chase squeezed into a gap in the next lane and then braked again. "I'd hang in there until the bitter end."

"Will you tell her that if she asks you for advice?"

Chase smiled. "She's looking for funding. She's probably not going to be asking for advice from me. Her current job is to sell me on the huge potential of the company so I'll invest in it."

"Okay, but if she *asks* . . ."

"I promise I'll tell her." Chase gave him a half glance. "What brought this on?"

"Just something we were talking about last night," Jackson said. "But don't tell her I said anything."

"I'll do my best. We're meeting at the office today to

decide on our future investments, so I might have news for her soon."

"Awesome," Jackson said. "And I won't tell her you told me that."

Chase chuckled. "If you can't get the truck issue sorted out and you need a ride home, call me, and you can come on my company jet."

"You have a *jet*?" Jackson sat up straight. "How did I not know that?"

Chase shrugged. "It makes life easier."

"Can I fly it sometime?"

Chase turned to look at him. "I don't know. *Can* you?"

"Probably." Jackson shrugged.

"Good to know if I ever have pilot problems in Morgan Valley." Chase was finally able to get up some speed, only to start indicating he was coming off the freeway again. "I mean that. Sometimes when the weather gets bad, no one can get out to me at the ranch."

"Consider me your backup plan," Jackson said. "And if I need a ride tonight, I'll text you. What time are you planning on leaving?"

"Around nine." Chase stopped at the lights at the bottom of the spiral ramp. "The car place is just over here. Call me if you need anything."

Chapter Twenty

Jackson had only just finished up at the rental place when his phone rang. He checked the number and accepted the call.

"Hey, Mr. Perkins. What's up?"

"What's up? What on earth is a person supposed to say in reply to that, young man?" Mr. Perkins squawked.

Jackson winced. "Sorry, I meant how are you?"

"I'm in excellent health, thank you. I've finished my summary of the coins, and you may come to see me at noon to discuss their value and their future."

"That's great." Jackson checked the time. "I'll be there at twelve."

"You'd better be, because I have a ballroom dancing class at two, and I can't miss that."

"Of course you can't. I'll see you at noon, sir." Jackson ended the call with a grin on his face and considered his options. He could go over to the East Bay, check up on his truck, and arrive at Mr. Perkins's house in good time.

He tapped the name of the place his truck had been towed to into his phone and got into his new vehicle, which was way fancier than his old one. It was a beautiful clear day in northern California, and he was going to do his best to put his misery over Daisy to one side and focus on the positive. He'd spoken to Cauy the night before to tell him about the truck, and had promised to let him know the final verdict on the coins.

Mr. Perkins hadn't sounded terribly excited, so it was possible all the other coins their father had collected were duds. Still, seventy-five thousand dollars wasn't to be sniffed at.

Jackson turned on the radio and hummed along as he headed for the Dumbarton Bridge, which would take him over the bay to the other less-well-known side, where the port of Oakland dominated the skyline, along with the ominous-looking Mount Diablo.

At least he now knew there was room for both him and Daisy in Morgan Valley. They'd been polite to each other and caring, and he'd respected her boundaries even if it had killed him. But he still couldn't let go of hope, and the quiet certainty she was the right woman for him—the *only* woman for him.

Maybe in ten years, or when she returned from her years of servitude to that asshole Clive, she'd be glad to see him again, and let him woo her properly. But even if she didn't, he'd made a friend who would stand by him, and vice versa.

Eventually, he reached Mr. Perkins's house after discovering his truck was indeed a write-off and not only would his insurance cover it, he stood to get a nice sum of money from the supermarket, the haulage company, and the mall for the distress caused him.

"Come in, young man." Mr. Perkins met him at the door. "Coffee?"

"Yes, please." Jackson eased his way through the towering stacks of books into the kitchen and took his previous seat at the table. The coins were neatly laid out in plastic baggies with writing on them, the empty box by the side.

"I did find one interesting coin among the rest of the collection." Mr. Perkins sat opposite him and passed over a small plastic packet. "This is a 1927 D St. Gaudens double eagle."

Jackson peered at the golden coin. "That's not very old."

"It's not the age that counts, it's the rarity, and this one, which has a face value of twenty dollars, doesn't turn up very often." Mr. Perkins took it out of the packet. "I'm fairly certain its genuine, but it's not in good condition, which means the value comes down a bit."

"To what?" Jackson asked.

"About twenty thousand dollars."

Jackson whistled. "That's *crazy!*"

"If it was in mint condition, it could fetch upward of two hundred and seventy thousand dollars."

Jackson just gawped at him. "So how much are we talking about now for the whole of Dad's collection?"

"Around a hundred thousand dollars." Mr. Perkins allowed himself a small congratulatory smile. "Less my commission, obviously, and the vagaries of auctions."

"That's . . . great." Jackson picked up the metal box, which clanged. He opened it up and stared inside. "Did you hear that?"

"It was probably just the clasp." Mr. Perkins put on his glasses, found his folder, and opened it. "Are you happy for me to represent you in this matter?"

"Sure, but it will be for me and my brother. We're co-owners of the coins." Jackson shook the box again, close to his ear. "There's definitely something still in here."

He took the box over to the window to get more light, and searched around the seams. "There's a fingernail opening here." He tried to get in without success. "Do you have a screwdriver or something?"

Mr. Perkins sighed, went into the kitchen, and returned with a small tool. "Try this."

Jackson carefully levered off the bottom of the box and discovered two thick brown paper pouches and the single penny that had been rattling around. He brought them out and handed them over to Mr. Perkins, who opened the first one and went very still.

"Good Lord."

He examined the coin and then stared at Jackson. "If this is genuine—and it looks like it is—you and your brother are very lucky young men indeed."

"What is it?" Jackson asked.

"It's a 1901 Morgan silver dollar," Mr. Perkins said reverentially. "I've only ever seen one other in such good condition."

"Did you say Morgan?" Jackson laughed out loud. "That's probably why my dad hid it for all these years. He would've hated the Morgan name being associated with anything he owned."

It also explained the discrepancy in the accounting books Jackson had discovered if his father had turned his profits into coins.

"And the second coin is an 1889 CC Morgan silver dollar, with a one-dollar face value. If it is genuine, it's ninety percent silver." Mr. Perkins turned the coin over. "They both look like they've never been in circulation, which is quite extraordinary, considering they were minted in Philadelphia and traveled right across the country."

"I have family in Philadelphia," Jackson said. "I wonder if the coins came out with them?"

"I doubt it." Mr. Perkins looked up at Jackson. "I don't

want to get your hopes up, but both these coins might be extremely valuable."

"Even more so than the twenty-thousand-dollar one?"

"Yes." Mr. Perkins was suddenly all business. "I'll need to make some calls, but if they are genuine, you could be looking at a small fortune." He touched the brown-paper envelopes. "You also have provenance here, because these pouches have the name and date of the auction house where your father, or whoever purchased these coins, got them."

"That's good, right?"

"That's excellent." Mr. Perkins made a shooing gesture. "Now go away and let me make some calls."

Jackson stood. "Don't you have a ballroom dancing class at two?"

Mr. Perkins looked at him over the top of his spectacles. "Sometimes in life, young man, one has to prioritize. The rumba can wait. I'll call you when I have some numbers, which will probably be in the next day or so."

"Thanks," Jackson said. "I appreciate this."

"When you see the size of my commission, you might change your mind." Mr. Perkins winked at him, which was quite unnerving. "But I'll treat you fairly, I can promise you that."

"You come with the highest recommendation from January Morgan, so I'll agree with you. Call me when you're done."

Jackson made his way out to his rented truck in something of a daze. If Mr. Perkins was correct, he and Cauy would have at least a hundred thousand dollars to share between them, possibly a lot more. He couldn't quite wrap his brain around that.

After checking the time, he decided to drive back home rather than take Chase up on his offer of a ride. His insurance company had told him to keep the truck until his settlement came through for the write-off. He needed time to think, and the long journey back to Morgan Valley might clear his head and reset his expectations. He sent a text to Chase, telling him he was leaving and wouldn't need a ride, and another to Cauy to expect his return that evening.

He hesitated over Daisy's name in his contacts. He hadn't told her about the coins, but she was still the person he wanted to share his excitement with. He sent her a text anyway.

Heading back to Morgan Valley. Hope all went well with your biz partners. See you soon.

She didn't immediately reply, so he got into his truck and drove to the nearest gas station to fill up his tank. The last thing he needed was to get overconfident and run out of gas halfway across a mountain pass just when his life was getting exciting.

"I bet the Donner party said exactly the same thing," Jackson muttered to himself as he headed down the highway. "Primary mission: get home in one piece."

By the time he parked at the ranch, he was exhausted, hungry, and dying to lay down and get the crick out of his neck. He was also delighted to be home. The kitchen lights were on and he went in to find Cauy sitting at the table waiting for him.

"Hey." Jackson put down his backpack and patted Grace. "What's up?"

"Good to see you all in one piece," Cauy replied. "Do you want some coffee or are you heading for bed?"

"I'll take the coffee. I've got stuff to tell you." Jackson yawned so hard, he cracked his jaw. "I'll just dump my bag. Where's Rachel?"

"She's doing something over at Morgan Ranch with her grandma," Cauy said. "But as it has to do with baking and cookies, I encouraged her to go."

"Smart move, bro."

When Jackson returned, Cauy had set a mug of black coffee on the table opposite him, which Jackson immediately dived into.

"It's good to be home."

"Is it?" Cauy offered him a refill. "How did it go with Mr. Perkins?"

"Well, so far, Dad's secret stash is worth a hundred thousand dollars. It might be worth a lot more when Mr. Perkins gets back to me about the last two coins."

"Really?" Cauy whistled. "That's amazing."

Jackson grinned at his brother. "The best part is that the two coins he thinks are the most valuable are Morgan coins."

"You're kidding me."

"Nope. Can you imagine how much Dad must have hated that?" Jackson said. "I doubt he bought them himself, but I'm surprised he didn't sell them immediately. He must have known they were too valuable to give up, so he hid them away." Jackson paused. "Or he inherited the box from someone in his family and didn't know the coins were there at all."

"So our Morgan family minted coins?" Cauy asked.

"No, these were minted in Philadelphia, but they do have a high percentage of silver in them, so maybe that came from the Morgansville mine."

"I doubt it, but it makes a great story, and I'm good with us getting some money back," Cauy said.

"Like fifty thousand bucks means a lot to you," Jackson joked.

"It's fifty thousand bucks I can put straight back into the ranch to replace all the harm Mark did by taking it out in the first place," Cauy retorted. "And it sure is a nice nest egg for you."

"Yeah." Jackson held his brother's gaze. "It really is." He paused. "I've been thinking about the offer you made me."

"The one about owning half the ranch?"

"Yeah, that one." Jackson spread his fingers wide on the table. "I said no because I was hurt Dad hadn't left anything to me directly in his will."

"Understandable." Cauy nodded.

"But the more I thought about it, the more I realized Dad *wanted* to divide us over the ranch even after he died. He could've just left the place to Mom, but he deliberately made a choice to keep us all on separate sides. It's just the sort of petty, vindictive thing he'd do to load all the debt on you and give me nothing."

"I came to the same conclusion." Cauy set his mug on the table. "Which is why I wanted you to have a stake in this place."

"I can't afford to buy a ranch by myself, and I don't even have the right skill set to run one yet," Jackson confessed. "But I'd love to have some say in managing the place where I was born." He took a deep breath. "I'd be willing to invest my fifty thousand dollars back into the ranch as well."

Cauy sat back, and the silence lengthened until Jackson was shifting in his seat.

"Unless you've changed your mind about the offer, which is totally okay with me as well," Jackson said quickly, even as his heart sank to his boots.

"I haven't changed my mind, but there's a complication," Cauy said slowly.

"As in what?"

"The Gardins asked if they could leave me their place in their will."

"Wow." Jackson blinked at him. "Really? What did you say?"

"I said I'd have to think about it. They really want to move to town, so they'd prefer coming to some arrangement that benefits us all. I'm thinking that I might finance their move to Morgantown and help Shep keep the ranch going. When they die, the place would then come to me."

"So they're the other ranch that might be up for sale to the developers?" Jackson grimaced. "That's sad. They're good people. What are you going to do?"

"I don't know." Cauy sighed. "A lot of it depends on you."

"How come?" Jackson regarded his brother.

"I can't manage two ranches by myself," Cauy said. "The question is, would you be willing to take one of them on?"

Daisy sat back and closed her eyes as Chase's private jet took off and headed for Morgan Valley. She'd had a long intense day, and the thought of not having to deal with anyone from Silicon Valley for a while was a huge relief. She could do the talking and representing for the company, but at heart, she was still a nerdy introvert who liked her quiet space.

There were five VCs really interested in funding them, including a very enthusiastic Jake, and the team was ecstatic. Daisy had spent the morning breakfast meeting going over every detail of each possible partner, trying to decide who they could trust and who would try to screw them. Clive's VC board had presented a formal offer, alongside Clive's personal one. To Daisy's immense relief, none of them had jumped on his offer to buy them out.

It had been hard not to beg them not to listen to Clive, but they'd all shared their disgust and shuddered at the prospect of being beholden to him for two years. Daisy was almost ashamed of having doubted them. Her paranoia reminded her of the deceit and corruption beneath the surface of the entrepreneur community, sometimes poisoned by vast amounts of money. There were good people there like Chase, but there were also a lot of sharks.

She couldn't live there full-time again, but she wasn't sure she could completely give up that tech part of her either.

"Are you okay to talk about your company, Daisy?"

Daisy refocused her attention on Chase. "Officially or unofficially?"

He smiled. "That's up to you."

"How about you run it by me now and then put it in writing, so I can share it with my team?"

"Sounds good." Chase opened his laptop. "I've already set up the term sheet, but here's what we'd like to offer you. We'd prefer to be your lead investor, which means either Jake or I would take a seat on your board—probably Jake, because of our personal connection."

"Okay." Daisy nodded.

"We calculated a price of ten dollars per share and we'd like to take thirty percent of the company, meaning we'd invest thirty million dollars in you."

Daisy slowly closed her mouth. "And?"

"That's it." He shrugged. "And we'd like you guys to keep running it just the way you've been doing it."

"That sounds . . . *great*," Daisy babbled, and then caught herself. "I mean, I'd have to talk to the guys, but—"

"Yeah?" Chase smiled. "Cool. I'll send you the term

sheet so you can present it to your team, and we can take it from there."

He typed away on his keyboard as Daisy tried to make sense of the more-than-generous offer. Sure, they'd dilute the number of their shares by only having 70 percent of the company between the five of them, but the value of each share would significantly increase. They'd keep control of their company and work with an ethical and involved investor who truly seemed to care about the product.

She closed her eyes in a silent prayer. It wasn't as good as the cash offer Clive had made them, and they wouldn't be able to take money out for a few more years, but the future suddenly looked glorious.

Daisy opened her eyes as the truth hit her.

She wanted to be like Chase and have a foot in both worlds. If he could do it, why couldn't she? She wanted a home in Morgan Valley, a family who loved and accepted her just the way she was, and a man who . . .

"How do you do it, Chase?"

At her hasty question, her companion looked up from his laptop.

"Do what?"

"Compartmentalize your life so successfully?" Daisy asked.

"I'm not sure I do." He grimaced. "I hate not being around January and the baby. I *miss* stuff."

"You seem happy in both places," Daisy pointed out.

"That's because I am." He hesitated. "But it's a constantly changing balancing act. I tend to get hyperfocused on certain things. I rely on January to tell me when I'm not getting it right and I'm acting like an ass."

Jackson would do that for her. He'd tell her when she was out of line without any prompting at all.

As if reading her mind, Chase smiled at her. "I suspect Jackson would be great at sharing the hard truths with you, too."

"He would," Daisy had to agree.

She had a hard truth to face herself. If Jackson weren't around, period, everything else wouldn't work. She'd survive, sure, but he made sense of things for her, didn't mind telling her when she was wrong, and yet was always there when she needed him.

"I think I'm in love with him," Daisy blurted out.

"With Jackson?" Chase nodded. "I can totally see that. He's a good guy." He returned his gaze to his laptop, a smile lingering on his lips. "Just a thought: Maybe you should be telling him that, not me."

Chapter Twenty-One

"But I need to talk to you guys," Daisy said plaintively as she followed her father and Adam out into the boot room, where they put on their outside coats. She'd gotten back too late to talk to everyone the night before and then missed them at breakfast because she'd slept in.

"That's great, sweetheart, but we're going to the meeting in town first, so you can tell us anything you like when we get back." Her father patted her shoulder. "I'm sure it can keep. Chase has news."

Daisy resigned herself to another wait. She'd kept the secret for years, so another few hours wouldn't make much difference. She'd decided to tell them what she was up to in Silicon Valley and ask for their support. With Auntie Rae at her side, she hoped things would go as smoothly as possible. They all loved and wanted the best for her. It was time for her to tell *them* what that meant, not allow them to impose their concerns on her.

"I'll come with you." Daisy grabbed her coat.

"Keen to see lover boy, eh?" Adam winked at her. "I hear he's back in town as well."

"Is he?" Daisy prevaricated, although she knew he'd been coming back because he'd sent her a text the previous day.

"Weird how you two always seem to end up in the same town." Kaiden nudged her side. "Almost like it's fated or something."

"You watch way too many soaps," Daisy muttered. "You big romantic dope."

Kaiden laughed and linked arms with her as they all crowded into their dad's big SUV. "The Korean ones are best. So dramatic."

"You don't speak Korean."

"Doesn't matter." He moved along, squishing her up against the door as Ben joined them. "I understand the language of *lurve*."

Adam and her dad were in the front and Auntie Rae was already in town visiting Maureen. She'd be leaving at the end of the week and Daisy was going to miss her dreadfully.

"What's Chase got to say that's so important?" Daisy asked her dad as they drove into town.

"How should I know?"

"Didn't he even give you a hint?" Daisy raised her eyebrows. "You're not usually that keen on dropping everything and going to Morgantown."

"This *is* important," her dad said with great finality. "I know it in my bones."

"Right . . ." Beside her, Kaiden snorted, and Daisy buried her face against his arm and inhaled the scent of fresh wood shavings that always hung around him. Kaiden spent less time at the ranch than Adam and Ben, so she always appreciated spending time with him.

She got out of the truck and went into the community hall, where half the town was already assembled. Whatever Chase had to say, Daisy hoped it was good.

"Hey."

She turned to find Jackson right behind her and felt her

face heat up like a teenager's. He wore a green check shirt over a blue T-shirt and looked good enough to eat.

"Oh! Hey! How are you?"

"I'm good actually." He studied her carefully. "You look a bit flushed. Are you sick or something, because if so, you'd better not stay here and give it to the whole community."

"I'm fine, thanks." She smiled at him. "Did the rest of your trip go okay?"

"Yeah, great actually; in fact—" He pulled himself up short. "How did yours go? Are you going to work for the moron?"

"No, we all decided we didn't want to do that," Daisy explained.

"Awesome." He paused. "What would you have done if they'd all said yes?"

"But they didn't." She blinked at him.

"But what if they had? Would you really have stayed there and worked for Clive for two years?"

"No, I don't think I would've been able to do that." She slowly exhaled. "Sometimes you have to make a stand, right? Just like you said."

"Yeah?" He kept on looking at her, his blue gaze intent as his smile broadened. "You do."

Oh God, was he still interested in her? Was there still hope? She kept talking. "So I won't be based in Palo Alto for two years. I'll be right here. Chase's company made us an awesome offer, which I think we'll probably accept."

His smile intensified, making her sway slightly toward him. "Good to know."

Behind her, someone cleared his throat. "Hey, can you two lovebirds, move it along? Some of us need coffee to get through this meeting."

She turned to find BB Morgan grinning down at her.

"Sorry, was I in your way?" Daisy eased past Jackson,

who put a hand on her arm and drew her close against his side as BB hit the coffee. The heat from his skin and his mere presence made her feel so much better.

"Hey, Jackson, will you come up to see me at the ranch sometime this week?" BB asked. "I've got some formal documentation I want you to look at for the formation of the survival tours company."

"Sure, I'd love to." Jackson nodded.

"I've got Jay, Sam, and my two Marine buddies onboard, and Ben Miller; you know him, right? He's the best trail guide in the valley."

"Sounds awesome." Jackson shook BB's hand. "Thanks for including me."

Daisy looked up at Jackson as he steered her toward a seat near the back of the hall, well away from both their families. "I think you'll be great at the survival thing."

"I'm really interested, and while I lack actual ground experience, I'm fantastic at risk assessment and planning out missions." He took the seat beside her, his expression wry. "I don't think I'll ever get over my guilt about not being in the forefront of every battle, though."

"You did your assigned job, and you probably saved countless lives you aren't even aware of," Daisy reminded him, her hand catching hold of his and squeezing it tight. Despite all the people milling about, she felt like she and Jackson were alone in their own little bubble.

He sighed. "I went to see my friend Tide's wife after he died, and she didn't feel that way. She screamed at me to get out, that it was all my fault."

Daisy cupped his cheek. "She was grief-stricken. She probably didn't even know what she was saying. Have you spoken to her since?"

"Nope." He swallowed hard. "I haven't been able to find the courage."

"You will." She stared into his eyes. "I'll come with you if you like."

Up front, Chase banged on the table and started the meeting by assuring everyone he'd be as quick as he could as they all probably wanted to get back to the baseball game.

Aware Daisy was still holding his hand, and unwilling to draw attention to it, Jackson sat quietly beside her. What was happening? She seemed different—more open to him, more *his*? Whatever it was, he was all for it. He and Cauy had thrashed out a few things between them during the day, but he was hoping to ask Daisy what she thought before he made a final commitment. Somehow, that was the most important thing of all . . .

Chase mentioned the application for the traffic changes was progressing toward Sacramento, and then turned to the piece that was of interest to Jackson.

"I'm pleased to tell you one of the ranches that was in danger of being bought out by developers has decided to sell privately instead."

"Awesome!" BB gave a piercing whistle that made his grandma Ruth, who was sitting beside him, wince and slap his arm. "Which one of you rich guys bought it?"

"Me." Cauy stood up. "The Gardins wanted to keep it in the family."

Jackson braced himself as the whole town turned to look at him and his brother.

"The family?" Daisy's father asked. He obviously hadn't been paying attention when they'd been branding cattle up at the Gardin ranch. "What's the connection?"

Cauy held his ground. "Ben Gardin was my father."

"Well, that makes a lot of sense, seeing as Mark treated

you worse than dirt." Daisy's dad nodded. "Good for you, then, son."

"What about the Cortez place?" Adam stood and addressed Chase. "Why can't your charitable arm buy that?"

"We're still looking into it, Adam," Chase said. "But we certainly don't want to lose it if we don't have to."

Adam sat down, but Jackson saw the frustration on his face. Beside him, Daisy stirred.

"Don't even think about it," Jackson muttered as Chase wrapped up the meeting and everyone got up to mingle and have more coffee.

"What?" She jumped guiltily.

"You know what." He looked down at her. "Adam's a big boy. Let him deal with his own problems."

"Like you let Cauy solve yours?" Daisy asked.

"What's that supposed to mean?" he countered.

"Cauy just bought you a *ranch*."

He raised an eyebrow. "Where did you get that hare-brained idea from?"

"It's the *truth*!"

"No, it isn't."

Daisy took a deep breath and stood up. "Let's not do this, shall we? It's great that Cauy has enough money to throw around on buying extra ranches. I'm very happy for you."

"You don't sound happy," Jackson commented. "And he didn't buy me the ranch, we—"

"I don't care!" Daisy's voice was rising, and several people in their vicinity were turning their heads to listen in. "I just want you to be *happy*!" She stamped her foot.

"I *am* happy, and if you'd just give me the chance to explain, I'd—"

"You don't need to explain anything to me." Daisy sniffed, her nose in the air. "We're friends, that's it! Because I was too stupid to realize I'd fallen in love with you until it was too late and I pushed you away!"

Jackson blinked at her. "Come again?"

"I *love* you!" She flung her arms wide in a very un-Daisy-like way. "I didn't mean to love you, I tried not to, but it was useless. I was *hoping* once the tech company launched, I could buy us a ranch here and you could live on it with *me*."

"What tech company?"

Jackson winced as Jeff Miller called out to Daisy. Way to blow her cover wide open in public.

"The one I've been working with for the past few years and not telling you about!" Daisy said, her gaze now on her father. "The one I sunk seed money into so I couldn't help my own brother and father!"

"Daisy—" Adam stepped forward, but his sister kept talking.

"I'm sorry, Dad. I know I promised you all I wouldn't go back, but this project was very special to me."

Jackson put a hand on her shoulder. Apparently, when Daisy wanted to let everything out, she was something of an unstoppable force.

"How about you talk that through with your family at home later and concentrate on me right now?" Jackson suggested.

Adam cleared his throat. "Great idea. In fact, why don't we go home, Dad, and Jackson can bring Daisy back when she's ready?"

For a moment, Jeff looked like he was going to balk at being told what to do. With one last ferocious glare at Jackson—for no reason whatsoever, because for once he was blameless—Jeff turned and went out, taking his sons and sister with him.

Chase Morgan sauntered over to grin at Daisy. "I know

I told you to tell Jackson how you felt, but I didn't figure on you telling the whole town."

Daisy winced, as if suddenly aware of her surroundings. A wave of love swept over Jackson as he hugged Daisy to his side.

"She can shout it from the rooftops for all I care."

"She might as well have." Chase looked around. "At least she got it over in one shot. The whole town knows where she stands right now, so I suggest you make sure her bravery is reciprocated."

"I will if she'll let me get a word in edgeways." He looked down at Daisy. It was a novel experience for him to be the trouble-free one in a relationship. "Can we go somewhere quiet and talk?"

"Let's go to the shop." Her head was down and her long hair covered her face. "I'm so embarrassed."

"There's no need to be." Jackson took her hand and led her past the remaining townsfolk and Cauy and Rachel, who were giving him a thumbs-up. "As someone who regularly embarrasses himself in public, I can tell you, no one will remember anything about it in a day or so."

"Or until I do something else stupid," Daisy muttered as they walked down the quiet street toward her shop.

"What could be more stupid than telling the entire town you love me?" Jackson asked.

Daisy groaned while in Jackson's heart birds and huge choirs were singing hallelujahs.

"Hey." He drew her to a stop in front of the door. "I kind of liked it."

"I just lost it," she confessed. "I'd been making up all these scenarios in my head about backing off, giving you time to recover from my awfulness, and then apparently you're all set up by your brother with your very own ranch. I was *going* to lure you back."

"*Lure* me back? With a ranch?" He slid his fingers under her chin so she had to look up at him. "Daisy, if you snapped your fingers, I'd come running back to you for nothing. Don't you *know* that?"

"But I told you to stop!"

"And I tried, but I just couldn't stop wanting and loving you." He smoothed her tangled hair away from her face. "I decided that if I hung out here long enough, eventually I'd break you down and you'd come back to me."

"No big gestures?"

"You're the one with all the money, remember?" He kissed her very carefully.

"But I don't *have* any money yet. Going with the Chase offer and not the Clive one means I don't have the money to help *anyone*, just the possibility of it."

"Daisy." Jackson kissed her nose. "Will you get it into your thick head that everyone who truly loves you doesn't care about the money and that includes me? We'll be okay and if, in the future, we get to roll around naked in million-dollar bills because your ship comes in, I'm all for it. But I'd rather have you."

She sighed and leaned against his chest. "I'm glad I remembered money doesn't buy love."

"Good, because I just knew in my soul you'd give me a second chance."

"*Second* chance?" She huffed against his lips. "I think you're on your twentieth at least."

"Which indicates just how much you love me and are willing to put up with from me." He kissed her again. "I know I've got a big mouth and I often stick my foot in it, but you're never going to find a man who loves you more than I do." She gazed into his eyes and he held his breath. "Except Brody of course." Damn, there he went again, undermining his own cause because he just couldn't shut the hell up.

"Brody was very special to me and he always will be, but you . . ." She smiled so sweetly, he caught his breath. "Are the right man for me right now and for the future." She pressed a finger to his lips. "Let's leave it at that, okay?"

"Okay." She kissed him, and he wrapped his arms around her and lifted her against his body, wanting simply to feel all of her.

"Let's go inside." Daisy gently pushed on his chest. "I don't need the whole town to see this!"

He was still laughing as she deactivated the alarm, dragged him over the threshold, and threw herself back into his arms. And then the laughter ignited his pent-up desire and he was stripping her naked and feasting on the sight of her breasts.

With Daisy's encouragement, he raided her purse for some protection and then looked up to find her settled within a nest of their discarded clothes like a wanton summer flower. He fell to his knees in front of her and groaned her name.

"Daisy . . . God, you're so beautiful."

He leaned forward and dropped a kiss on her hipbone and then licked a trail down over her rounded stomach to the delights between her legs. She sighed as he tongued her most intimate flesh, his fingers adding to her pleasure until she was coming all around him.

"Please . . ." She tugged on his hair. "I want you inside me."

He'd never been so happy to do as he was told and was soon sliding inside her, gasping as she wrapped her arms and legs around him, holding him a willing captive.

"I love you, Daisy Miller." Jackson braced himself on his elbows and looked into her brown eyes.

"Good, because I love you right back." She slid her foot up over his hip. "I'm such a dork. I've missed you so much and I've wasted so much time pushing you away from me."

And now he wanted to cry, and that wasn't acceptable, so he'd better set about making love with the most amazing woman in the world.

"Are you okay, Jackson?" Daisy whispered as he buried his face in the curve where her neck met her shoulder.

"Mm-hmm."

He nipped her skin; the soft brush of his stubbled chin against her flesh was both subtle and so powerful, she wanted to gasp. Their bodies were joined together, he was part of her, and she never wanted to let him go.

She slid one hand into his short hair and gently scraped her nails against his scalp, making him pulse inside her. With a muffled groan, he gathered her bottom into one of his big hands and rocked into her, the intensity of his strokes sending her to a new level of passion she'd never experienced before.

She climaxed around him and he held still, letting her clench and release his still-hard cock until she was lost in a sea of pleasure so deep, she never wanted it to end.

"More?" he murmured against her mouth. "Can I take more?"

"I don't know if I have more," Daisy gasped. "This is pretty intense."

"Yeah?" He eased back, and she grabbed onto his broad shoulders as he eased his elbows under her knees, spreading her even wider. "You can give me more, I know it."

He thrust back inside in a driving rhythm that took her higher until each stroke set off a string of sensations that grew until she almost cried with the pleasure of it. She wanted to close her eyes, but he was watching her, and she wanted him to see what he was doing to her.

"Oh . . ." Daisy's fingernails snagged into his skin like a kitten's claws as she climaxed so hard she screamed.

He came, too, his big body pinning hers to the floor, his expression half ecstasy and half pain as he finally let loose.

"Daisy . . ." He fell over her, his chest heaving, and stayed there, driving all the breath from her lungs. But she didn't care if she ever breathed again.

He rolled off her and lay on his back, one hand coming to rest on her stomach.

"I thought I'd never get to do that with you again," he murmured.

"I thought I'd have to wait about ten years to convince you to do it again, and then maybe you wouldn't want me anymore because I'd be so old," Daisy confessed.

"I'll always want you." He turned to kiss her cheek. "I always did from the first moment I saw you in your shop."

"Not quite," she reminded him. "You were buying flowers for Nancy."

He came up on one elbow to look down at her. "True, but I couldn't stop coming back to you."

"Nancy would've made mincemeat out of you anyway." Daisy sniffed.

"Also true." He bent to kiss her. "She's awesome, but not my type. When I came back into your shop and saw you up that ladder, your beautiful ass just about level with my face, I was totally sold."

"It took a while longer to convince *me* you were serious."

"I know." He grinned down at her. "That's because you're the sensible one."

"The sensible one who tells the whole town she loves you?" Daisy groaned. "I'll never live it down."

"You will." Jackson got to his feet. "Let me clean up and I'll be right back."

She grabbed as many pieces of her clothing as she could and waited for him to come out of the small bathroom before scurrying in to fix herself up. Her mirror showed her a very satisfied woman with eyes like stars, making her lean in and kiss her reflection.

When she rejoined Jackson, he'd put on his T-shirt and jeans and was making them both coffee. She paused at the door to admire his tall frame and to try to accept he really, truly was totally into her.

"You know I said I love you in public?" Daisy fingered the doorframe.

"Yeah?" He turned toward her. "What about it?"

She kept her gaze on the woodwork. "You don't have to feel obliged to say it back to me just because I made a fool of myself."

He didn't say anything, and after a long while, she risked a glance at him. He was leaning against the counter, arms folded over his chest, his amused gaze just waiting for hers to find him.

"Daisy, this is me, Jackson Lymond, your very own adorable bigmouthed truth-telling fool. If I hadn't agreed with you, don't you think I would've mentioned it by now?"

She held his gaze and saw nothing but kindness and truth in it. He wasn't going to lie to her, or leave her. If he had something to say? She'd hear about it.

"I love you, Daisy, so get used to it. Now, do you want your coffee, or shall I drink it for you?"

She released her breath and walked over to him. "I'll take the coffee and the love, please."

* * *

Jackson glanced over at Daisy as he drove home. She'd spoken to Rae on the phone and agreed she'd come back the next morning and sit down with her family to tell them about her secret work project. Rae had assured her no one was mad at her, which had cheered Daisy up considerably.

To keep his hands off her on the journey back, he'd regaled her with the story of the coins his father had collected, and what had happened on his trip to Walnut Creek. She'd been fascinated and thrilled that he finally had some capital to invest in the ranch he loved.

When they walked into the kitchen, there was no sign of Cauy or Rachel, which was nice of them. Cauy had written him a note all in caps and left it on the table, so while Daisy used the bathroom, Jackson read it.

"Holy cow!" he whispered, clutching the sheet of paper to his chest, and then raised his voice. "Cauy? Are you still up?"

The door to his brother's room opened, and both he and Rachel came into the kitchen grinning like fools.

"Is this right?" Jackson's hand was trembling so hard, the paper was shaking. "Am I misreading the zeroes?"

Cauy took the paper from him and checked the figures as Daisy reappeared from the bathroom.

"What's going on?" she inquired as Jackson drew her close. "Did someone win the lottery?"

"Pretty damn much." Jackson swallowed hard. "Those last two coins I told you about? The mint condition Morgan ones? Mr. Perkins reckons between the two of them, we might make half a million bucks." He stared at his brother.

"That's just . . . unbelievable."

"Yeah, I know." Cauy nodded. "And it gives you choices,

too. You could buy me out of this place and make it your own."

Jackson focused on his brother's face. It was always difficult to read Cauy, and this time it was impossible.

"I don't want to do that." He hesitated. "I was thinking maybe I could work at both ranches for a while? I could help Shep Gardin, and when he wants to retire completely, we could talk about this again?"

"Fine by me." As usual, Cauy sounded way too calm, but Jackson knew his laconic brother well enough now to understand he was pleased by Jackson's decision. "We can work out a financial settlement that will allow the Gardins to retire whenever they want to and take it from there."

Jackson grabbed hold of his brother and hugged him hard. After a second, Cauy hugged him back and murmured, "Welcome home, Jackson. Welcome home."

A second later, Rachel and Daisy piled onto the hug, and then there might have been crying, but Jackson wasn't going to tell tales.

Eventually, he was alone with Daisy in his bedroom with the door locked, and everything was right with his world.

He climbed into bed next to her and slid an arm under her shoulders. "How would you feel about living on a ranch when we're married?"

"Well, firstly, I've lived on a ranch my whole life, so it's not exactly a problem as long as you don't expect me to be much help. And secondly, you haven't asked me to marry you."

Jackson came up on one elbow and looked down at her. "And you say I'm the pedantic one."

She wrinkled her nose at him. "But you *haven't* asked me."

"I was going to do it properly. Take you out to dinner, get down on one knee and all that romantic stuff," Jackson objected. "I haven't even bought you a ring yet."

"Oh." Daisy considered him. "That sounds rather nice actually."

"Then how about you leave the details up to me?" Jackson said firmly. "Although it would be good to know what kind of ring you'd like."

"Ask Nancy, Lizzie, and Yvonne." Daisy yawned and closed her eyes. "They know all about my dream boyfriend/ engagement/wedding scenarios."

"How come?"

"We used to get drunk on Saturday nights, watch romantic movies, and share our dreams."

"That's kind of cool."

"Don't men do that?"

"Hell no." Jackson shuddered. "I'll definitely talk to them. Would you like a big wedding or a small one, and what about venue? Do you have a preference on that? Because I'm sure the Morgans would give us a great rate."

"Jackson." Daisy spoke without opening her eyes. "I love you, but if you keep this up, I *am* going to kill you."

"Okay. I love you, too." He kissed her nose and lay down again, his thoughts buzzing. There was a lot of planning to do. Perhaps he'd talk to Avery Hayes, the wedding planner up at Morgan Ranch. He opened his mouth again.

"How soon do you want to get married?"

A gentle snore was his answer, and he turned to see that Daisy was asleep. He'd probably worn her out with his lovemaking and his worrying. The thought of her being his wife, of them sharing their lives together, was amazing. He buried his face against her shoulder and breathed her in.

Between Cauy and Daisy, he'd learned more about family and love than he'd anticipated and found everything he ever needed right here in the valley he'd grown up in. His father's bitter legacy would be forgotten. The ranch would flourish with new money, new ideas, and a positive attitude his father had *never* had. The scars from his service would fade, and he'd make sure he kept in touch with everyone who had been important to him during his military career.

Jackson sighed into the stillness. For a man who had learned to rely on his second chances, he really had come home for good.

Jackson's Roasted Vegetable Lasagna
(Kate's own recipe)

9 sheets of oven-ready plain or spinach lasagna
   sheets/noodles
2 large onions
2–4 zucchini, depending on size
1 large red pepper
4 large portobello mushrooms
Olive oil
Salt and pepper
Fresh basil leaves
3 cloves fresh garlic
2 oz. butter
2 oz. plain flour
36 fl. oz. milk
6 oz. strong cheese
Parmesan cheese
1 can diced tomatoes or fresh tomatoes, which you
   can roast with the other vegetables (any other
   roast-worthy vegetables you wish to add)

Set oven temperature to highest available.

Chop all vegetables into big chunks and put in a bowl or bag. Add 2–3 tbs. of olive oil, salt and pepper, and torn basil leaves, and mix well. Add crushed garlic and place on a baking tray at the top of the oven for 30 to 40 minutes until vegetables are just browning up.

While the vegetables are roasting, make the cheese sauce by melting the butter, adding the flour, and then gradually whisking in the milk. Bring to a boil until thickened and add the cheese.

Add a thin layer of canned tomatoes to the bottom of a lasagna dish (or mix the tomatoes gently in with the roasted vegetables), top with roasted vegetables, cheese sauce, and 3 sheets of lasagna (noodle). Repeat twice more, ending with a layer of cheese sauce and a covering of Parmesan.

Cover with foil and place in the oven at 350 degrees for 45 minutes. Check to see if pasta is softened enough, uncover top, and cook until cheese is browning and bubbling, about 10–15 minutes.

Connect with U(s)

Visit us online at
KensingtonBooks.com
to read more from your favorite authors, see books
by series, view reading group guides, and more.

for sneak peeks, chances to win books and prize packs,
and to share your thoughts with other readers.

facebook.com/kensingtonpublishing
twitter.com/kensingtonbooks

Tell us what you think!

To share your thoughts, submit a review,
or sign up for our eNewsletters, please visit:
KensingtonBooks.com/TellUs.

More from Bestselling Author
JANET DAILEY

Calder Storm	0-8217-7543-X	$7.99US/$10.99CAN
Close to You	1-4201-1714-9	$5.99US/$6.99CAN
Crazy in Love	1-4201-0303-2	$4.99US/$5.99CAN
Dance With Me	1-4201-2213-4	$5.99US/$6.99CAN
Everything	1-4201-2214-2	$5.99US/$6.99CAN
Forever	1-4201-2215-0	$5.99US/$6.99CAN
Green Calder Grass	0-8217-7222-8	$7.99US/$10.99CAN
Heiress	1-4201-0002-5	$6.99US/$7.99CAN
Lone Calder Star	0-8217-7542-1	$7.99US/$10.99CAN
Lover Man	1-4201-0666-X	$4.99US/$5.99CAN
Masquerade	1-4201-0005-X	$6.99US/$8.99CAN
Mistletoe and Molly	1-4201-0041-6	$6.99US/$9.99CAN
Rivals	1-4201-0003-3	$6.99US/$7.99CAN
Santa in a Stetson	1-4201-0664-3	$6.99US/$9.99CAN
Santa in Montana	1-4201-1474-3	$7.99US/$9.99CAN
Searching for Santa	1-4201-0306-7	$6.99US/$9.99CAN
Something More	0-8217-7544-8	$7.99US/$9.99CAN
Stealing Kisses	1-4201-0304-0	$4.99US/$5.99CAN
Tangled Vines	1-4201-0004-1	$6.99US/$8.99CAN
Texas Kiss	1-4201-0665-1	$4.99US/$5.99CAN
That Loving Feeling	1-4201-1713-0	$5.99US/$6.99CAN
To Santa With Love	1-4201-2073-5	$6.99US/$7.99CAN
When You Kiss Me	1-4201-0667-8	$4.99US/$5.99CAN
Yes, I Do	1-4201-0305-9	$4.99US/$5.99CAN

Available Wherever Books Are Sold!

Check out our website at **www.kensingtonbooks.com**.